I0612702

C. R. SOLOMON

Rings of Fire: Book One

Self-published
JAMAICA

First published in 2015
Copyright © June 2015 Cheryl R. Solomon

National Library of Jamaica
12 East Street
Kingston
Jamaica

ISBN: 978-976-95823-0-9

Contents

About the Author

I grew up in the inner city in the 80s and 90s in Kingston, Jamaica. From my younger days, I always believed that education is the instrument that can be used as a tool to elevate you out of poverty. With this desire in mind I began reading, as my knowledge increased I found it a pleasure to share with my peers. The greatest gift you can give to mankind is knowledge. Giving this your achievement can be infinite. As I fell in love with reading I knew I wanted to write stories. But not just any story, those that accentuate on the life journey of man. While my dream to become a writer became more passionate, life gave me a blow when I was twelve years old. I was diagnosed with Retinitis Pigmentosa, a chronic hereditary eye disease characterized by black pigmentation and gradual degeneration of the retina, which transformed me into a severe state of depression. My world was uprooted with one diagnosis because I knew my education would have to be adjusted drastically. I was recommended to leave my school and attend a special one for the blind. My rehabilitation was commenced immediately to adjust me to living without sight. Nevertheless, with good encouragement from family and friends I realised that life was not ending it just took me on a different path. Ten years after my diagnosis, I graduated from the University of West Indies with a BSc. in Psychology. I came to realise when you are born with a passion it doesn't decrease over the years. So I went back to my first love, writing and sharing my knowledge. Take it from me, life is like a boxing ring you either take the blow and stay down or fight your way through.

Foreword

When I conceptualized the characters of **Rings of Fire** I wanted role models and heroes for Jamaican teenagers to emulate. Each character is unique. It doesn't matter what their background is; their economic, cultural and social stagnation; they were determined to fight their way through life. They had friends, families and even strangers that fought against them but each of the characters in the stories showed resilience for survival. As they grew from childhood to adulthood, they made an impact not only on the individuals around them but also on the Jamaican society on a whole. The characters were created for teenagers but young adults can assimilate their life journey also. Please enjoy.

Before the Dawn

As the sun rises over Kingston, bringing to life the sleeping city, everyone is out, busily pursuing their respective agendas; vendors selling, hand cart men pushing their heavy loads, and retailers opening their shutters. There is only one thing on the minds of everyone; how much money will be made today.

It has never ceased to amaze me, how Kingston could appear to come to life at a single moment. Vendors claiming their spots for the day in the streets, changing two lane streets into a single lane thoroughfare which drivers are forced to make-do with. Cooks in makeshift kitchens preparing their menus, designed to cater to the varying appetites of potential customers. Offerings ranged from bread and tea to soup, stew chicken and ackee and saltfish. Self-proclaimed 'Police' providing unsolicited services to buyers and sellers, including guided parking, parking security, and security of goods. People waking and folding away their beds of cardboards as noisy shutters of the 'China-man' shop rise with a new sense of business. Old abandoned buildings, packed with families, buzz with new life as music squeaks, the aroma of food escapes, and underpants and other items of delicate cloth flap from makeshift lines.

Locked in my own thoughts, I did not hear the voice. "Move out the way, pickney gal!" I heard a voice shout from behind. I jumped from the sidewalk as a three-hundred- pound woman shuffled past me. The hand of the woman was like a broom sweeping me in the path of the oncoming handcart.

"Mine mi run ova yu red dundus". I was just in time to get her foot out of the way as the hand-cart man zipped past. I was only ten years old, but I already knew the meaning of hard life. Her Mother, Miss Kitty had eight of them, and I was the last. It was rumoured that my father was a Syrian man who owned a wholesale on Duke Street, but nothing was concrete. My mother was a higgler who sold on the street, and ever since she knew herself, I was by her side selling with her.

I held her goods tightly; mostly 'bag juice' and biscuit, in order for the crowd not to bounce it out of my hand. Hunger was moving through my belly like a storm, but I knew I dared not touch her goods, as I would consume my profit. Using my free hand I wiped away the sweat from my face. The sun was extra hot this morning. It did not help that there had been no rain for a month, and as a result the dust was sticking to my skin like glue.

As I moved through the crowd calling out for sale, I began to feel sick, as the sun's rays penetrated my skin.

"Wey yu a go, Jasmine?" I heard a voice. "Yu nuh see yu a get redder and redder inna di sun? Come, man, come sit beside mi for a few minutes."
Reluctantly, I walked over to her. My feet burned, but I knew I did not have a choice; this life chose me, I did not choose it.

It was the middle of the week. I should have been in school like a normal Jamaican child, but instead I have to be out on the street 'hustling'. As my mother would often say, "If yu nuh work, yu nuh eat."

"So wey yu Madda dey?" I stared at her with a blank look on my face. Holding me by the hand, she drew me down beside her pinching me on the cheek. "Answer mi, nuh?" she asked. "Yu too shy" she said, giving me a reassuring smile.
"She is down at the bottom a King Street", I finally answered.
"Yu know wha mi like about yu, pickney? Yu 'av manners."
I stepped back and stared at her deformed teeth. "And manners will tek yu through di world".

I closed my eyes and tried to picture myself travelling all over the world, but I came up blank, and so re-opened my eyes. The woman held her head and shook it. "Yu arite, Jasmine? Yu waan somting fi eat?"
I looked down to see the variety of food that was in front of her - mangoes, oranges, sweetsop and bananas.

"Mom...," I began, but the rest could not come out of my mouth. My mother would kill me if she knew I was eating from a stranger. She would rather know I dropped dead from hunger than was begging. My belly moved again. This time I made up my mind. I'd rather die with a full belly than without one. I nodded my head, "Yes". She handed me a banana and began peeling an orange. "Yu know, I know yu before yu born, pickney, but it look like yu nuh memba mi. Mi name Miss Joyce, man, Miss Joyce."

I managed to utter, "Sorry about that mam".

She pinched me on my cheek again, "Nuh worry yuself, but yu shudda dey inna school".

I nodded my head, "Yes."

"Mi nuh know wha wrong wid yu Madda. She nuh know she a destroy yu future? Mi a sell dung ere fi thirty years, but mi mek sure mi educate two dawtas. One is a nurse, a KPH, and di odda one is a teacha at George Headly Primary School. Now mi a sell by choice cause mi two pickney caan mine mi. Dem av dem owna family now an mi nah go ome go siddung, put up mi foot an watch soap opera. Mi use to mi workin, an a dat mi a go do till mi dead. But yu Madda too stubborn, Jasmine. Any time mi tell her dem tings dey, she cuss mi off. Ignorancy a go kill her".

I hung my head in despair. She rubbed my head and said, "Yu nuh worry yuself, Jasmine. Di Lord will work it out fi yu."

With those words I got up, thanked her, and continued on my journey. My siblings were much older than I am; the youngest being eight years older than myself. The four boys were born before the three girls. Barry is now serving a fifteen-year sentence at the General Penitentiary for armed robbery. My second brother, Steve declared he is a converted Rastafarian, "Bun Babylon," he would say. "Bun Babylon!" He moved to the country and began farming but from my mother's protestations, gleaned that he was planting more than food. "That blasted bwoy", she would often cuss, "Put imself inna trouble again wid di law, but if him tink mi a go bail him dis time, him run outa luck. Him a go stay dey an rotten."

My third brother, Raphael, opened a grocery shop in Rema, where we're from, but he and my mother cannot get along; they are like oil and water.

"Yu wild like a dog", my Mother often cursed him. "Yu an yu ooman dem always inna war, but mi a beg yu, nuh bring it a mi gate; I'm a very peaceful ooman now."

I would laugh whenever she quarreled like this as I can still remember the days when she used to block traffic dung a Princess Street when she and no one Downtown or where she lived would get along. I can still remember the name they would call her, "Jamintel", as you could hear her before you saw her.

My last brother, Courtney, was half Indian, but she could not afford to keep him, so she gave him up for adoption when he was two years old. From what I heard of him, everyone knew that he would be a brilliant young man. My mother found out that he is now a teacher, married and living in Williamsfield, Manchester. She wrote him a few times, but he replied that he wanted nothing to do with her and her family, and that we should respect his wishes. I could tell she was hurt, but like she always does when she does not want to face her demon, she lashes out - especially at me.

"Mi nah kill out miself fi oonu, cause pickney ungrateful." she told me one day. "as old people sey, mi a go wash oonu back but not oonu belly."

My first sister, Sophia, has just turned twenty years old, but she already has three children. I doubt if she knows all the fathers. Despite her flaws, she is very good to me, and she is not sitting down depending on any man, she is selling fish in the Coronation Market.

My last sister, Karen, moved to Mile Gully in St. Elizabeth a year ago. Holier than her you cannot find; always preaching to us about our shortcomings and quoting from the Bible. The day she left our mothers house she said "I will not associate with the heathen no more." As far as she was concerned, we are sitting at the gateway to Hell, and we are not going to draw her in with us; which I find ironic, since she moved in with a man and they are not married. The day she moved out was the happiest day of my life. It is not that I do not love her, but I sense she does not love me. When we are around each other, she would often verbally and physically abuse me, so the best thing we can do is stay apart.

I made my way through the crowd, sweat pouring down my face. School was over, and there were more people moving around. I maneuvered my way through the crowd selling, and in no time my supply of 'bag juice' was almost finished, but I knew I had to get rid of the biscuits too, as the last time I brought home excess goods, my mother gave me a fine beating.

"Mi know because yu walk an mek fren an idle chat," she shouted at me. "this is the reason why yu didn sell dem off. If yu tink yu a go put mi inna bankruptcy, yu mek a sad mistake." That night I went to bed without dinner.

By seven p.m., I only had two biscuits left, and I sighed with relief. Standing in front of a store, staring through the glass at the mannequins I noticed how elegantly they were dressed, I thought to myself, "It has been a while since I've got a dress or even a pair of shoes." The pair I had was from Karen, as ever since I knew myself, I would only get hand-me-downs.

"It look like a hoof yu born wid, yu a go walk wid yu plank," my mother said.

I bit my lips and turned from side to side staring at myself in the window. "I am not bad looking," I whispered to myself. Even though I am just ten years old, my shape has come into form.

I turned once more to my right, then I spotted him from the corner of my eye going into the lady's bag. I wanted to warn her with all my heart, but I knew from experience that your mouth can cost you your life. I felt so sorry for her, knowing that she might have kids and not be able feed them when she got home. I cannot believe someone who is healthy and strong would do that to another human being.

From the years I have been selling, I have come to know most of the thieves, and they know that I know them. But as far as I'm concerned, they do not bother me, so I do not bother them. I've seen enough violence that would last me a lifetime.

I will never forget when I was six years old, my mother sent me to the shop. There was a young man not older than eighteen years sitting on the sidewalk smoking a 'spliff' and drinking a beer. I saw when a car slowly drove up, and two guys got out. I will never forget one of their eyes pierced mine; frozen on the spot I could not move. I saw when the gun rose and the fire came from it. I could smell the gunpowder lingering in the air. I was deaf to the world. The next time I knew myself, I was inside the shop with the shop keeper touching me all over to make sure I wasn't hurt. Finally I began shaking like a leaf. "She inna shock," an old man said. Before I knew it, a bag juice was in my mouth.

"Drink up, Miss Kitty gal. Yu will be alright."

Within a few minutes I was well enough to look outside, staring at the crowd surrounding the young man's corpse, and a woman running down the street with her hands on her head wailing. My emotions got the better of me and I started crying uncontrollably.

"A fi ar family? "A man shouted. "Mi nuh know," answered another man. "Leave di pickney alone," the shopkeeper intervened, drawing me closer to her.

All that said and done, when the police came there was no one to give evidence. See and blind, hear and deaf, was the order of the day.

I sighed, remembering that time. I am longing for the day when drugs and violence could be a thing of the past in my community. Looking at the clock in the store, it was half past seven. I began making my way down Princess Street to meet my mother. I could hear my mother before I saw her. It amazed me. There are hundreds of people on the street, music blasting, cars honking, bikes revving, but in spite of all this commotion, I could still hear my mother shouting at me, "Gyal! Jasmine! Hurry up!". I quickened my steps, looking at the few items I had left. Relief washed over me when I realized I only had two bag juices and three biscuits.

Instead of greeting me, my Mother grabbed the bag and rummaged through it. "Yu couldn't even sell it off!", were the first words she uttered. "Mi try, Mam." I replied. "Mi feel sey a ramp yu a ramp, eenuh pickney;

but any day mi ever ketch yu, KPH (Kingston Public Hospital) nuh dey far fram ya so. Come, mi waan go home now," Miss Kitty said. "Mi hear sey war a gwaan weh we live, an curfew inna di area. Yu don't know sey if it get lata, wi caan go home tonight, because if Babylon nuh hole wi, di gun man dem will."

Without saying another word, my mother took off and I had to run behind to keep up.
While I moved through the crowd, tired, hungry and frustrated, I vowed my kids would never go through what I was going through. On the bus, people were talking. From what I could understand, I heard that two men were killed on Green Corner which sparked the incident. "Election a come up," an old man shouted from the back, "so yu doan know sey dem a go divide and conquor we." "Political warfare," said the lady beside me. "it happen inna every country. A we fi have sense fi nuh caught up inna it. Das why yu fi educate yu pickney dem. When dem av dat, nobody caan fool dem."

Feeling guilty, Miss Kitty objected. "Yu nuh a fi av education fi come outa dis, a jus common sense do it. Because mi nuh av it but nuhbody eva si mi rob, shoot and tief dem."

Everyone in the bus agreed with my mother, which seemed to please her very much, acknowledging it with a big smile.

When we came off the bus, a young man, Brian greeted us. "Miss Kitty, mi hear sey a tree dead dung dey. Nuh walk pon di road deh, tek di short cut tru di lane. Caw dem here bwoy nuh partial even though yu born an grow ya."

He said, "A mi little dawta mi a wait pon. Shi a do extra lesson. As soon as she come mi a cut, because dem bwoy ya blood a boil hot."

"Mi nuh business inna nutten," Miss Kitty replied. "Si wey mi business wid ya," turning to look at me, "but mi a pray fi yu dawta come and unoo come off a di street, for tonight look like it a go be a bloody one."

We continued on our journey home. I noticed the area was like a ghost town even though it was not yet eight p.m.; but from experience, I knew eyes were on us, peeping through windows and fences. Within seconds of opening our front door, we heard gun shots. I dived on the floor while my mother went to secure the gas cylinder. That night we decided not to cook, dared not light the stove.

It was after two a.m. when I jumped out of my sleep. I heard footsteps getting closer and shook my mother. "Mama," I whispered, "Somebaddy a come."
"Wey yu a say?" my mother mumbled. "Somebaddy inna di yard," I replied. Miss Kitty's eyes popped wide open. "Yu sure?" she asked. "Yes, Mam," I replied. She jumped off the bed drawing me behind her putting the lamp out. Within a second we were both under the bed, pulling boxes around us for extra protection. We had not had electricity for few weeks as my mother was not on speaking terms with the neighbours whom she was accustomed to receiving electricity. When they were friends, we have light, but when they were not talking, the light was off.
It was like time stood still in the darkness, but we both heard when the window pane moved and a voice saying, "Mi nuh si nuhbaddy. Yu sure smaddy live ya so?"
"Yeh man, sumbady mus dey ere so." The dogs began to bark harder. "Come," another voice whispered, "A soon daylight an wi nuh av no

more time."

I breathed a sigh of relief when I heard the zinc fence rattle. From their footsteps I knew it was about six of them. Then I heard it. The gunshots. I began to tremble, could not hold it in anymore, and I screamed out. My mother placed her hand over my mouth. "Shut up!" She whispered in my ear, "Yu waan dem kill wi off?" I did not know how long she was in that position, but when I came to myself, I heard the sounds I dreaded the most - the screaming and bawling, but we dared not go out because of the darkness.

It was after five a.m. when the crowd began to gather. Feeling safer, my mother went out with me by her side. They found out that the men went next door and killed two elderly brothers, Goldy and Robby, both in their seventies. Goldy's wife was battling for life in the hospital. Her son had to push her in a handcart to the main road, because no one would dare to drive into the community to pick her up. Everyone began to tell their terror story of what happened in the past night.

"A pon mi roof mi hear one a dem a come, yu nuh," said Brian who lived a few houses behind us. "De little buggas dem a try tek off mi roof, avoiding my Rottweiler in mi yard. Dem climb pon mi ackee tree next door an come pon mi roof. "Yu know from when," said Keisha, his baby mother, "mi a beg dem fi cut di ackee limb, an now it almost cost wi wi life."

Another woman shouted, "A nuff a unoo know di bwoy dem wey a do dis wickedness, but unoo nah talk."
"Shut up yu mout," Tracey intervened. "If yu nuh wa live, mi sure yu four pickney wan live."

"Lord Jesus," an elderly woman began to cry, "mi a ninety-four years old an mi neva know mi woulda live fi si Jamaica reach dis stage." Two young men rushed to her realizing she could barely stand up. "Arite, Grandma, wi a carry yu home an gi yu a cup a tea an put yu to bed." Without refusing, she went along with them. "Mi jus waan dead," I heard the old woman say, "Mi caan live so. Dis is not a life, dis is Hell," she moaned as her grandsons consoled her.

Raphael came on the scene. "Mama," he asked, "unoo arite?"

"Wey yu care?" our mother replied, "you know from wen mi nuh see yu?"

"Not because yu nuh see mi mean sey mi nuh care." Rubbing my cheek, "Yu arite, Jasmine?"

"Mi a try," I replied. "How yu mean yu a try? Yu av any care inna dis worl a part from eating and sleeping?" my mother probed.

"But mi help yu dung town, Mam...," but before I could finish the sentence, she hit me on my head. "Wey mi tell yu bout back answer? Shut up yu mout!"

I did not say another word. Turning to Raphael, Miss Kitty asked, "A wey yu a do roun yah?"

"Mi hear wey tek place last night so mi come check pon unoo, an now dat mi know unoo good, mi a go cut."

"A dat mi know yu waan do long time," Miss Kitty said. "Any time yu fine a new ooman, yu keep weh yuself. Yu nuh know if wi dead or alive."

"Mama, a dis mi nuh like, yu nuh every time we meet wi haffi argue. Wi a family, yet wi live like puss an dawg."

"A who yu a call dawg, dutty bwoy?" Miss Kitty shouted at him. " A mi bring yu come ya, an not di odda way aroun." Realizing that he would not get much further with her, Raphael turned and walked away. Determined to talk with him, Miss Kitty followed. "Not because yu av ole eap a pickney, dat nuh mek yu a man, yu know, Raphael."

He stopped and sat on the sidewalk, digging his toe in the dirt. It seemed it would take forever for him to speak again, but when he finally did, he said, "Mama, mi not styling yu, mi jus a sey wi can do betta as a family, an mi wouldna come roun here if mi neva love unoo." He got up, brushed the dirt from his pants bottom. "Mi a go leave before yu sey nuttin more."

"Turn yu back pon mi, dutty bwoy," Miss Kitty raged. "A dat mi used to." Hearing those words stung him like a swarm of bees. He turned and faced her. "Yu si yu, Mama," he began, "Yu mek it hard fi even the devil fi stay mongst yu."

"Yu just like yu wutless Puppa."

"How mi fi just like im an mi nuh know im?" he asked. She gave him one slap across his face;

so hard his head spun to the side. I suspected she wanted to do that ever since Raphael came on the scene.

He put his hand to his jaw and for a moment I thought he would hit her back. But when he spoke again there was no anger in his voice. "Yu a mi madda," he said, "so yu can do mi anyting, but before yu abuse mi, mi a go stay far from yu." And without another word he walked away.

I felt his pain, I was hurting too. He is a good brother to me, out of all of them, I love him the most. He is the type of person that will give me anything. I know within myself if he had it, I would be okay. He argues with our mother all the time to send me to school, but the most important thing I admire about him, he is a good father to his children. Even though our mother would curse him, asking him if he doesn't know condom, and if he is not afraid of AIDS; and how many children he got now, eight,nine? Mi stop count, but no matter what, you will never hear his woman curse him for maintenance.

For the rest of the day, I was worried about the elderly brothers who were killed. One of them tried to escape through the back window, and even though he was begging for his life, the young men who could have been his grandsons still killed him.

"At least when I'm Downtown," I said to myself, "mingling with the crowd, I still feel relatively safe." I could not eat, so I went to bed hungry. Most mothers would show concern, but not mine. "Yu damn lucky," she said. "If yu nuh waan eat mi will do it fi di two a wi." I watched her as she had her feast. This is why she is over two hundred pounds and climbing.

The next morning like clockwork, she purchased the goods and issued me my portion. "Jasmine," she warned, "Mek sure yu sell it off. Stop idle pon di road an go do yu job an me an yu will get on."

It was Saturday, which was a busy morning Downtown, everyone coming in from the country to sell their goods. Those who could not be accommodated in the marketplace vended their wares on the sidewalk. It was just after 9:00 a.m., but the morning sun had already begun to melt me with its rays. I could feel the summer coursing through my veins, and took out my rag to wipe the sweat from my forehead. Taking a deep breath, I was just about to leave my mother when a gentleman approached us dressed in a white shirt and black pants, sporting an identification badge on the left side of his chest.

"Are you the mother of this child?" he asked Miss Kitty.

"Wey dat fi do wid yu?" she asked defensively. He held out his identification card closer to her. I read it, Michael Clarke, Development Officer. "I got some information that this child is not attending school. Is this true?"

My mother did not answer. "Do you know that this is illegal here in Jamaica?"

Hearing this, she put down her goods and her hands akimbo. "Illegal?" she exclaimed. "Mi neva know sey fi mi pickney come help me, government waan charge mi fi dat! Tell mi sumpting, a who feed and clothe har? Mi tink is me an not di government."

"Listen to me, Mam," Mr. Clarke replied, "if she is not in school by Monday morning, you will answer to the authorities."

"Well if a mi or di authority," my mother replied, "…go dung a Jubilee fi hav ar, mek mi know." Realizing he could not get far with her, Mr. Clarke walked away.

Shouting at him she said, "You an di government come, mek mi buss di two a unoo ass." Even when he was no longer in sight she continued cursing. Embarrassed, I held my head down and began my rounds. From a distance I could still hear her voice, "If anyone tink dem a go tek mi pickney fram mi, dem can come. Mi wonder which johncrow go report mi, but mi haffi fine out a who, an when mi do, dog nyam unoo supper." I quickly made my way through the crowd not wanting anyone to associate me with her this morning.

Even though I was embarrassed about her behaviour, deep down inside I was happy. I miss school. I never wanted to give it up. Learning was my greatest joy, and I remembered my teacher saying one day, knowledge is the key which can open many doors for you. Looking up into the sky, I thanked the Heavens, and if I knew who saw my plight I would have thanked them too.

After a few hours, I was by my friend Ms. Joyce, enjoying my fruits as usual. "How yu look so, pickney gal? Yu arite?" "Yes," I replied. "Yu always sey dat even wen yu nuh arite." At that moment I wished she was my mother. She always showed she cared for me, giving me love and affection at all times. These basic feelings my mother lacked. "Monday morning, Mam, " I said with a smile, "I will be going back to school." "Really?" she asked in astonishment. "I found out this morning, Ms. Joyce. Mi happy."

"Mi happy fi yu too, Jasmine," she replied. "You are a beautiful gal pickney, mek di best out of life, an nuh mek nobaddy get yu dung."

"Yu know who report mi madda, Mam?" She smiled at me, and didn't have to say another word, as I knew then it was her.
Smiling I reassured her, "No worry yuself, Mam, I will never tell her. Thank you," I said standing up. "I will neva figet what yu do fi

mi."

For the rest of the day, it was the first I worked with joy in my heart.

Miss Kitty tried to put on a brave face for the rest of the weekend, but I knew deep down inside it shook her up. Even though she professes to be a bad woman, she did not want to get entangled with the law. "Babylon is nutten more dan trouble an di furthest wi can stay away fram it, the better off wi will be." The weekend seemed very long, like time slowed down just to punish me. I woke up early Monday morning and completed my chores. I went outside and my mother was still washing. She slowly held up her head and stared at me. For a second my heart stopped, thinking she would deny me my dream. The silence was intense between us. I could hear the breeze passing through the leaves making a whistling sound. Suddenly, I shivered as the cool morning breeze pierced my bones, and finally she broke the silence. "Wey yu a tan up a watch mi fa? Yu nah go school?"

Elated, she did not have to say another word. I headed back inside to get ready. There was no breakfast for me, but I did not care. Within seconds I was out the door, and for the first time in three months I was going back to school. I doubted if even my classmates remembered me. The moment I entered my school gate, I felt as if a burden had been lifted from my shoulders. I greeted everyone, three-quarters of whom I vaguely remembered. Standing in front of my classroom, I stared at the closed door. "Four B," I said to myself. "B" normally would represent the teacher's last name, but for the love of God, I could not remember mine. "What is it," I whispered to myself, "Bryan, Brown, Bennett?" Frustrated at my lack of memory, I opened the door. A wave of noise came rushing towards me. The teacher wasn't there. I felt relieved, but from the look of things, I could tell there was no one on board this ship without the Captain.

Bags flying through the air like airplanes; kids sitting on their desks with their feet on the chair; everyone seemed to be doing their own thing. I slowly made my way to the back trying to find an empty desk. Suddenly, I found myself on the ground. Everyone stopped what they were doing and focused on me. Then I heard the laughter, and opening my eyes I saw a young man standing over me. "Yu neva si mi foot?" he asked, "yu blind?"

"In the middle of the passageway?" I asked. "It nuh matta wey it did deh, a yu fi look, a yer fault. Apologize to mi before yu can get up."

"What?" I asked. "Wait dey now, yu not only blind, yu deaf too? Arite, apologize before yu can get up," he repeated. I tried to stand up, but he pushed me to the ground. This happened twice before another student ran over to him and whispered something in his ear. When he turned to look back at me, I could see the transformation on his face, as if for the first time he was realizing I was a human being. "Sorry, man," he said, grabbing me and my bag off the ground at the same time, brushing the dirt from them like crazy. "Hush. Mi neva realize sey a yu name Jasmine." I was curious about his sudden change of attitude, but it wouldn't be for long. "Yu know mi? " I asked him. "Nuh yu a Barry sista, man?" Bull Dog, everyone knows about my brother. He was the head of the Bull Dog gang, now serving time in prison. I was always ashamed of him and his lifestyle and what he had put our family through - everyone looking down on us being the relatives of a criminal. But for the first time, his reputation got me some respect.

At that moment, a boy ran in shouting, "Mrs. Benjamin is coming!".

"Dat's her name", I sighed to myself, "Benjamin."

Everyone dashed for a seat as if they were on fire, and in the confusion, she was inside the classroom before I could find a seat. Like trained soldiers, everyone got up and greeted her in unison, then sitting back down leaving me standing. "What is your name?" she asked. "Jasmine White," I replied. She opened her register, and used her finger to search for my name. Finally she found it, and staring at my name she said, "You look like a dry land tourist. It has been months you have not been in school."

"I am sorry, Miss." "Why haven't you been in school?" she enquired.

Not wanting to lie, I said, "I have to be helping my mother."

She stared at me for a brief time, as if she was contemplating what to do, and finally she spoke. "Ms. White, you'll have to find a seat." Instantly, the same young man that pushed me to the ground earlier, jumped out of his seat. "Here," he offerred, "Take mine." Without another word he ran out of the classroom as if he was on hot coals. When class finally began, Mrs. Benjamin might as well have been teaching in a foreign language. Nothing sounded familiar to me, but I was determined to make up the lost time.

For the first time in weeks, I felt like a normal child. I went through the day without a care in the world, catching up with old friends and finding new ones. I was so grateful for Ms. Joyce's intervention, I felt I could have given her my first-born as a reward. My dreams were dashed once more after two weeks as I was leaving school one afternoon. My mother was at the gate to greet me. "Put this on ova yu uniform. Yu a come dung town wid mi dis evening."

"But Mama," I began protesting; but before I could get any further, she grabbed me. "No badda tink becus yu a go a school now yu nah go pull yu weight round di house. Dat nah go work fi mi. Mi siddung a yaad di whol day a tink bout di situation, an mi conclude sey yu haffi come a town come help mi. Di man sey yu haffi go a school. Im neva sey yu caan sell."

Disappointment filled my heart, but I had no choice. Within the hour, I was Downtown once more selling on the streets. This continued for the next two years. She would often curse when I did not do my chores. "No man nuh want nuh wutlis ooman wey ongl dress an sport. Im waan a ooman wa can keep im house good an raise im pickney well. If yu nuh know how fi do dat, im wi ongl use yu an refuse yu."

One night when we were coming home, there was a traffic jam. Instantly, the crowd grew bigger around us. I was clustered and could hardly breathe. Over the crowd, I heard a man shout, "Dem kill two bwoy dung a Princess Street, an soldier an police a tackle di gunman dem."

"Jesus!" my mother screamed, holding her head. "Mi caan tek dis life no more. How wi a go home tonight?" she exclaimed. Scared, I held onto her for comfort. She pushed me away. "Stan up pon yu two fut nuh!" she shouted at me. I realized from a tender age that I had to depend on myself; but realizing that my Mother would not show me love and attention broke my heart. Later on in my life I realized that she did love me, but in her own way.

As if the moment could not get any darker for me, it started to rain. We rushed towards a plaza, fighting for space like hungry dogs after a bone. The same man who broke the news of the killing resumed his story. "Two truck load a man dem gone wid," he said. "Princess Street, Beckford Street, and dung a Charles Street block off." "But nuh dey wi tek di bus? All dem do is abuse poor people pickney," one woman shouted. "Mi a beg God my bwoy Junior nuh ina it." Another lady said, "Di las time dem pick up my bwoy Damion, a six months im get fi one knife and a orange im sell fi a living! Wey im fi peel it wid? Im han? Dat's why mi tell my own sey..." Another one interrupted "stay inna di ouse." "Like dat a go stop dem," my Mother joined the conversation. "Dem come fi dem from undaneth yu frock tail. Dis ya country come in like dere is no justice for poor people."

"Leave mi alone nuh!" I heard a young miss shout. "Yu dam tief yu! Wey yu a go inna mi bag fa?" and before I knew it they gathered around a young man and began beating him. "Mi know sey yu a pickpocket!" one man exclaimed, slapping him with a machete. "Mi mark yu face long time. Mi know yu a pickpocket. Yu use to do it inna Mandeville, an now yu come a town wid yu dutty slackness."

"A nuh mi" the young man pleaded, begging for his life. "Fram yu see im wid a puss eye yu know sey im is a tief!" a lady shouted. By the time they were finished with him, the sight of him made me want to vomit. The uproar drew the attention of the police, and they began running towards us, shouting randomly. The crowd began to disperse. My mother grabbed me by the hand and we began to run also. Panicking, I ran blindly, my heart pounding in my chest. Sweat washed me even though it was still raining. For a big lady, my mother could run fast. When we stopped to catch our breath, we were in an old building. In confusion, I asked my mother, "A wey wi dey,

Mama?"

"Shut up," she shouted, "you nuh see sey a inna di police station we dey. "Affisa," she said, "A bare war a gwaan out dey." "A wey yu waan mi fi do?" he asked. "But a nuh yu a di police?" my mother asked. "Unoo nuh dey ya fi protect wi?"

"Unoo need fi protect unoo self by stop breeding di criminals dem. Wen unoo si unoo bwoy pickney dem a go dung di wrong path, unoo nuh try fi curb dem, an wen wi kill dem, unoo same one tun roun and demonstrate. As far as mi concern, di ole a unoo a di same ting. Di ongl protection mi wooda gi unoo is wen unoo a go May Pen Cemetery ar Dovecot."

"Ah nuh everyone a wi a wicked," my mother began to complain. "Wi is good people com outta di inna city to yu nuh, an meybe yu tu?" With a grin on his face he shook his head. "A country mi cum fram!" "Yu look it," said a small boy who had run with us. Instantly, the officer hit him in his face with his gun, and he fell flat on his back. "Nuh kill im!" my mother shouted, falling on top of him and wiping the blood from his face.

"Mi a gi yu thirty seconds to com out," he

shouted at us; but before he could get up, a middle aged officer walked in. "Mek dem stay", he said, and there we spent the night.

Next morning when we got to our street, we heard a woman shouting from a distance, "Miss Kitty, Miss Kitty!" Getting closer to her, I realized it was Pansy. She is the only true friend my mother has, as she does not keep friends too long. Out of breath, she said, "Di soldier dem tek wey Raphael las night." Instantly, she dropped her goods at my feet. "Go home," she shouted to me, "Mi a go si wey dem do wid mi bwoy."

Even though they fight a lot when they are together, my mother generally cares about her sons/children. Struggling to carry the goods, I made my way home. Opening the door, I realized I didn't have to force it. It dropped to the floor. I stared in disbelief at the wreckage in our house - it was like a hurricane had passed through. Even though we live in one room, it was relatively comfortable. Overwhelmed, I began to cry. Finally, I gathered my strength and started cleaning up the place. By the time my mother got home, everything was back in place, but she was in a bad mood as usual.

"Di damn Babylon," she complained, sitting on the bed, "A go keep im twenty-four hours. Until wi start tun pon dem instead a each odda, wi nah go better."

In her temper, she did not realize that the door was off its hinges, until she looked at me for a response, she noticed I was holdin it in my hand.

"Mi nah sleep in ya tonite like dis," she exclaimed. "Mi get to understand dem search every house inna di area fi guns an drugs, and dem tink dem a go fine it in a my home" Miss Kitty said, "An mi caan hardly fine food fi eat. Mi shuda dey ya." She spun around sharply staring at me as if she saw a ghost. Instantly she climbed on her dresser, removed a piece of ply from the ceiling, pushed her hand through a hole and pulled out a plastic bag. I instantly realized that it was her money that she had been saving over the years. My mother wasn't a believer in the banking system, as she would often say, "Mi nuh tink mi shudda pay somebaddy fi keep mi money when mi can keep it miself." Having reassured herself that her treasure was still safe, she turned to me. "What yu staring at? Gwaan go ketch up di wata." On my way out I glanced back and saw her counting her money on the floor.

We spent the second night sleeping at our friend Aunt Mavis on her wooden floor. She was an elderly lady, in her late eighties who knew my mother from she was a little girl. Her husband died forty years ago, and she raised eight children on her own, selling in the market and doing domestic work. I'll never forget what she always told me; no work is degrading once you do it with pride and honesty. I've come to love and cherish her so much, often spending hours talking to her about the good old days.

Aunt Mavis lived on another street called Nature View, which is ironic, since not even grass grows around there. Sometimes the guys from my street and hers would clash, but I did not allow that to affect me. As far as I am concerned, as long as I am not involved in their wars, I am free to go where I want to.

When I woke in the morning, I was so surprised when my mother said that we were not going to town today. "I have to fix up the house," she said, "and look about Raphael. If mi nuh present miself dung a di station, im a go stay dey an rotten," she told Aunt Mavis. "Yu haffi show dem yu pickney av smaddy fi defend dem."

I was happy; not because of the situation, because I could get to spend the day studying. Exams were approaching, and I really wanted to do well. Within a few hours, my mother and I completed the repairs. After the carpenter completed his work, she turned to me, "Dis time, Jasmine, dem haffi bun dung dis fi get in, because mi caan go to di Government fi repair it again."

When she left to see Raphael at the station, I found myself moving swiftly to complete her demands, and by midday I was back at Aunt Mavis' home. Sitting comfortably in her rocking chair with my book in my lap wiping sweat from my forehead, I exclaimed, "I can't believe the time is so hot."
"Dem a mash up di environment," Aunt Mavis

commented. "In my day, yu wud wear sweater in di summer, even in di country." I stared at her in amazement, she had a great deal to teach young people. "In spite of my challenges" she said, "mi pickney dem turn out well, especially di girls dem."

Her husband died when she was forty, leaving her with eight children. Her first daughter, Pamela has lived in the States for the last twenty years. Kay, her second child, is a teacher at Wolmers Girls School. Angela is a secretary at a Law Firm on Duke Street, and Joy, her last daughter is a nurse at KPH. On the other hand, only Chris among the boys turned out well. He is an Insurance Salesman at Sagicor. Julien and John are twins, and are bus conductors. Peter, her last son, chose the way of crime. Prison is his second home, and as far as I could see, he seemed to prefer prison to anywhere else. It seemed as though three months would not pass before he did something foolish and went back to prison; it almost appeared that he was haunted.

She interrupted my thoughts by asking how old I am now. "Study yu lessons, because is di ongle way yu will elevate yuself from dis environment," she cautioned. "Mi neva get di chance to do dat," she continued. "I finish school at ten years old, an had my first pickney at fifteen. By the time I was eighteen, I was pregnant again, but my father wouldn't have none a it. Im went to Johnny's house wid a long machete, an a week later wi was married. Mi nuh regret it still," she smiled. "Im was a good man." Standing up, she grimaced in pain. "Arthritis?" I asked sympathetically. She nodded her head. I went over and began to massage her feet. She felt a bit better and continued, "When I was younger, Jasmine, everyone loved and respected each other. It was our community that grew me, not just my parents. Now we are like barbarians, not even the children have respect for their parents. But you are not to be blamed, we the adults need to be good examples, we verbally and physically abuse you, and we don't teach you the right things. If mi nuh live fi see yu tun woman, Jasmine, remember this, have manners and don't give up in life." Hearing her talk like this broke my heart. I cannot imagine my life without her. She knew my mother from the time she was a young girl, and knew me before I even existed. She saw the distress on my face and said, "Jasmine, seeing pickney like yu give me a hope for Jamaica. Yu help yu madda a town and at home, but nuh mek yu pickney dem come do this."

For the next three hours we continued talking, and I completely forgot about studying. It was when I saw the setting of the sun I realized how late it was.

"Jesus!" I exclaimed, jumping up and putting my things together; "Mi Madda a go kill mi, she waan di dinna ready by di time she come back." I began running and praying, "Do, God, nuh mek she dey dey." I guess Im neva hear mi when I burst the door open we met face to face. Out of breath I asked, "Raphael come out Maam?" Calmly she waved me closer. Hesitantly I went and in a split second I was on the floor. She stood akimbo over me shouting, "Next time mi tell yu fi do sometin, DO IT!" as she put her foot on me bracing me to the floor she said, "Is eida my way or di highway."

The pressure of her weight on my stomach

was unbearable. Through my tears I heard a voice shouting, "Mama, Mama, a wey yu a do?!" When I turned my head, I saw it was Raphael. In a flash he was by my side, pulling my mother off me. "A kill yu waan kill her?" he asked. "She a gal pickney," she retorted, "She must learn fi follow orders."

"Yu darn right," Raphael replied angrily, "she is a child, memba dat!"

"Yu pet har too much," Miss Kitty said. "A nuh pet," Raphael answered, "A love." Before she could respond, he went to the kitchen and started cooking. There was a deafening silence till Raphael said. "Mi av eight, an neva put mi hand pon nun a dem." "Yu gwine regret dat, Raphael when dem bruk out pon yu, yu gwine see. Pickney mus get discipline."

Raphael laughed out loud. "Fi once wi agree wid each odda, Maam, but your way Mama is against di law. Look pon wi," he said holding up his shirt to show a big scar across his back. "Look wey yu do wi an we nuh betta. Barry dey a prison an every minute yu affi bail Steve fi plant im ganga."

She jumped to Steve's defence, "a nuh weed im a plant. Di police jus love fi harrass im."

Raphael smiled, "Right, Mama, a nuh weed, a flowas." He continued, "Look pon Karen, Mom, shi finally married now, de pon choir a sing, an every time she an har husband quarrel, shi sleep out." "A Church Sister she dey," Miss Kitty said quietly. This time Raphael could not contain his excitement. Walking over to our mother he sat beside her rubbing her shoulder gently, "Mama," he said, "Karen's friend need medical attention." "Wey yu mean?" Miss Kitty questioned. He replied, "Her voice sounded masculine." "What yu implying, Raphael?" "Nuttin," he said lifting his hands in the air, "I'm just saying, beating don't change a person." She tried to interrupt, but he wouldn't give her a chance. "Mama, fi di love a God," he said, "mi just waan enjoy mi dinna wid yu an go home to mi ooman an pickney dem." Without another word he continued cooking. Dinner was excellent, as he was always the chef in the family. After dinner, we played a round of dominoes, but as usual, he always wins. Rubbing my head he said, "Later, Jas," and with that he was out the door. While washing the dishes, I vowed to myself if I make it in life before his kids, I would see to it they are alright.

Two years passed, and I was now fourteen years old. I did pretty well in my class considering I did not attend regularly. My mother, as usual, kept me sometimes three months from school. "Dem sey yu fi go school, but dem neva sey how oftin," she commented. "Mi need help, an wha di sense having yu an yu caan help mi?"

Within a week of celebrating my fourteenth birthday, I was Downtown when I met the man who would change my life. Standing under a tree shading myself from the sun, I felt a hand touch my shoulder. I looked up and saw a tall, slim, handsome young man smiling at me. "I am taking the ants off you, "he said, "You are too pretty to be bitten by ants. My name is Tony, what's yours?" Defensively, I said, "None of your business." "OK, none of my business. Can I buy you lunch?" he asked pointing to the Mother's fast food place.

If I was to be honest with myself, I was tempted to accept his offer, as I'd had nothing from morning, and I could feel the worms moving in my belly. It felt like they were starting World War III in there! Composing myself, I said, "No thank you." I could see the disappointment on his face, but he wasn't giving up. He glanced from my face to my hands, and saw the goods in them. "You know," he said, "I work at a wholesale, the one on Princess Street, right at the corner where the handcart men hang out. You know that one?" I shook my head in answer. "I can get you anything you want," he said, "I don't do it for everybody, but you would be special. I control the store room. Just tell me what you want and I'll get it for you, especially on a Friday."

I had been selling for my Mother ever since I was eight years old, but yet I have nothing to show for it. It was up to her as to when I get something, measuring the profit down to a tee. I can't even take a sweetie from it. This was an opportunity, I thought to myself, which I could not turn down. I know I have the ambition if given a fair chance. "Why me?" I finally asked. He smiled. "Look, nun of yu business." "My name is Jasmine," I told him. "That's a beautiful name," he said. "I have been watching you for a long time," he continued, "seeing you pass with your mother. I know ambition when I see it, but it's going to be between me and you. Not even your mother yu must tell, as I can lose my job."

By the next Friday, I took him up on his offer, both for lunch and the goods. It was very hard selling it for myself and keeping it from my mother; finding my own hiding place to stash my savings; but I knew if I wanted better it had to be done. We became good friends, meeting often Downtown, knowing that my mother knew everyone there even the devil himself. Within three months, he became my first boyfriend. Unfortunately for me, I did not know much about family planning, and within six months of our friendship, I got pregnant. I was fretting how to tell my mother that I was pregnant. She always cussed saying if mi nuh pull mi weight, mi can stay inna har place, and knowing her, it haffi go start sell from it drop outa di womb. I hid my problem from her for three months, but I could not do it for any longer.

One night we were at home when I said, "Mama, I have something to tell you." She turned to look at me, and before I could chicken out of it, I blurted out, " I am pregnant."

She came at me like a force not even Hurricane Gilbert could withstand her. Before she could grab me, I ran out of the house. I could hear her shouting, " Mi a go kill yu tonight, Jasmine!" But I ran and did not stop until I found myself at Mary Ann for refuge. Within twenty minutes she was there as if she knew exactly where I had gone.

Beating down the door, "Miss Mary", she shouted, "send di damn gal out. Mi waan talk to ar." "A talk yu waan, or yu waan kill ar?" Aunt Mary replied. "It no matter which one," my mother answered, "One a wi a go prison tonight, an one a wi a go margue."
"Well, Jasmine nah go neider," Aunt Mary replied from behind the door, using her frail body to brace the door. "Sen mi pickney out!" my mother shouted, beating on the door with more force. You could hear the whole house shaking from her force. I was so scared, I hid under the bed, trembling like a leaf. I knew she was capable of violence, but I had never seen her so angry in all my life. I knew without

a doubt if she held me tonight I would be dead. "Please, God," I began praying. "let her calm down." I was so terrified, I blacked out. When I woke up, Aunt Mary asked if I was alright. It took me a few seconds to realize where I was. Frightened, I jumped up. She rubbed my cheek with a reassuring hand. "Nuh worry yuself, she gone. Is afta two inna di morning. Not even di daag stay roun dis part dem hours yah. A wey yu get yuself inna, little pickney? Mi tink yu hav better sense dan dis. But nuh worry yuself, mi nah mek nobaddy do yu nuttin even if mi haffi tek yu in meself! As far as mi concern, yu a nuh di bes, but yu a nuh di worse." I felt overwhelmed and began crying, relieved to know someone was in my corner. I spent three days at Aunty May. When I returned home, three scandal bags greeted me on the verandah, and my mother was akimbo at the door. "Yu nuh longer live here," she cried. "Since yu a woman now, so live woman life."

Within a week, Tony and I rented a one bedroom apartment in Brack Bad Lane same place in Jones Town, but a good distance from where I had been living. That suited me because I did not want to see my mother too often. It was a big tenement yard. When we were moving our belongings into the room, which wasn't much, a bed and a stove; a young man greeted us. He couldn't have been more than twenty years old. "Welcome, man," he smiled widely, gesturing with a spliff in his hand. From the look in his eyes I could see that he had been smoking all morning. "A me name Woody, an me run dis place. Anyting yu want, just ask Woody an yu wi get it. Mi a run dis from me a fifteen," he said. "No bwoy talk to wi roun here. Once yu in Woody's domain, yu safe. Anybaddy violate, dem haffi answer to me an mi crew. We nuh deal wid Babylon roun here, we perform wi own justice. Babylon a part a de problem, not di solution."

"How old yu are?" Tony interrupted. "Me a nineteen." I smiled to myself, knowing I had been close to the mark, and making a mental promise to keep as far away from him as possible. There are some people you see trouble printed on, and his was visible a mile away.

Even though Tony was born and raised in Olympic Garden, another inner-city community in St. Andrew, him mek rat look like they are the bravest thing on his earth. I did not have to tell him about men like Woody. You could see from his expression that Woody shook him up. "Hurry up, Jasmine," he shouted, "wi haffi get di tings dem inna dis house before di rain come." Looking up, I could see the dark clouds forming, and then the thunder rolled. I got busy, and within half an hour, all our belongings were packed up in the small room.

That evening, while in the kitchen preparing dinner, it struck me for the first time in my life, that I was living on my own with a man. As bad as Miss Kitty was, she taught me everything such as washing, cooking and cleaning. By the time we sat at the table for dinner, there was a knock at the door. I opened it to find a stout dark lady with a round face grinning from ear to ear. "Me name Shirley. Mi live inna di back room, yu know di one wid di ackee limb ova it? Everyone climb pon my roof fi pick ackee," she continued, "mi a tell yu from now, mi nuh like dat, OK? If yu waan fi pick ackee, my girl, use di line stick, or else mi ago stone yu off a it. Di mount a hole inna di roof now is like mi ave a strainer ova mi head, an nobbady nuh waan help mi fix it. All dem do a oppress mi," she continued, but I realized her eyes were no longer on mine, but on Tony sitting at the table eating. "Well, I neva introduce miself to dis young man," she said stepping past me, and before I knew it, she was around the table helping herself. It took me a few minutes before warming up to her. "People sey mi mad, Jasmine, but mi ongle talk wey go so. When yu plain inna dis ya place ya, dem hav yu off, but mi no badda nuhbaddy, an mi nuh waan nun a dem badda mi."

After the meal was finished, she helped me wash the dishes, and before she left that night, we knew about the good, the bad and the indifferent people in our new community. "Stay away from One Foot Johnny," she warned. "Im a ole man now, but im love young gal, specially smaddy wey pretty like yu." "And Eshmel," she confided, "nuh mek she know yu business, or might as well yu put it pon bill board." "OK, thanks," I assured her, and then she was out the door.

The next morning I got up at five. It was dark, cold and windy, but I knew if I wanted space on the line, I would have to start early. The order of this community is first come, first served. Too many people in one space, and not enough facilities. By the time I put one piece of clothes on the line, I hear a commotion. Turning I saw a slim lady with braided hair using her broom to hit a tall, stout, dark gentleman. Trying to ease the situation, I walked over to them. "Every time yu go out to drink, yu do di same ting," she shouted at him. "Why can't yu lift di tilet seat before yu pee? Dis is why mi nuh like drunkard, yu know," she shouted. "Easy yuself, nuh Rita," he reasoned, using his hand to block the blow from the broom. "Good mawning", I intervened. "A who di hell yu?" "My name is Jasmine." "An so?" she questioned. "Mi live in di room a di corner," I replied. "So wey yu want? A welcome party?" Just easy, nuh Rita?" the gentleman said. "Why yu haffi behave so? Yu no si de pickney a try fi introduce harself? Mi name Frank," he said stretching out his hand, "an dis is Rita, mi ooman."

Reluctantly I shook his hand. Even with the distance between us, I could smell a mixture of sweat and alcohol on him. She tried to hit him again without success. "Nuh mine har," he said, "har bark is worse than har bite. Altho she behave so, mi love har. Mi get a nice dawta from har." When I looked around, I saw a little girl about nine years old standing in the doorway. From all indications, she had been there a while observing the proceedings. "Candice," he called, and she ran towards her father and hugged him. "Si mi baby here," he said to me proudly. "All mi a wait pon now is a son." "From who?" Rita shouted. "Mi ave five, an mi nuh waan nuh more. Ef yu waan a son, tek one outa mi four." "Do not lick mi Fada," Candice shouted at her mother. "Yu blasted lucky. Im spoil yu too much, dats why yu a defen im so." She held him tight around his waist and they walked inside holding hands. You could tell he was completely drunk, but that there was genuine love between them.

Rita turned to me. "Jasmine, a dat yu sey yu name? Sorry mi dear, mi did tink yu was one of Woody's streggy dem. Im use dem like ow im use tilet paper. Mi nuh know wey dem si pon dat mawga bwoy dey, an im not even good lookin. Im fava monkey a smile. Nuh get too friendly wid im yu ere? Cause if im si yu up to it, im wi tek full advantage a it." "Nuh worry yuself," I reassured her, "mi kno dat aredy."

After completing my washing, I was just in time to see Tony putting on his work clothes. "So wey mi brekfus dey?" he greeted me. "Yu neva see I was washing? Yu couldn't help yuself?" "Wey yu a sey, Jasmine? Wey yu tink me av a ooman for? Yu tink yu dey yah fi yu prettylooks? Yu sey yu nuh waan sell no more, an a mi fi go out an earn di bread, so di least yu can do is to prepare di food an put it pon di table." In frustration I hissed my teeth, which made him angry. He slapped me so hard across my face, I stumbled and held on to the table for support. "Look here," he said, pointing his finger in my face, "a mi an yu dey now, an a mi wear di pants inna dis place. Any day yu feel yu waan change di order a dis arrangement, inform mi. Yu caan get somting fi nuttin inna dis life, so yu affi go learn."

I felt tears running down my cheek, and the pain in my throat. Not wanting him to see my emotion, I turned and went into the kitchen, muttering to myself, "Mi madda always sey if yu nuh know how fi do nuttin inna dis life, man wi tek liberty wid yu. But yet mi can do everything an man still waan come tek liberty wid mi." I swore at that moment that a man would never use me as a beating stick, and turning around suddenly said, "Tony, if yu put yu han pan mi again, mi a go kill yu."

"Wey yu sey?" he asked with a shocked look on his face. This time I gesticulated with my hands and said, "Mi sey, if yu put yu han pon me again, me a go kill yu."

"But wait," he said, "Me neva know I tek up a bad gal?" With two steps I realized I was on the ground, and he was on top of me. All the anger that was building up both from my family and life itself erupted like a volcano. Using my knee, I hit him in the groin, and shouting, he curled up in pain. With strength I didn't know I had, I drew the pot cover and knocked him out. He was unconscious for a few minutes, and when he opened his eyes, I was standing over him with a knife in my hand. "For the third and last time," I said, "if yu put yu hand pon me again mi a go kill yu." Without another word, I fixed his breakfast. He ate in silence, took up his bag and started out. At the door he turned, stared at me, shook his head and left. That was the only time he put his hand on me throughout our relationship.

For the next few weeks, I tried to adjust to life in a new environment. As bad as things were in my mother's house, it was just the two of us. She inherited it from my Grandfather who died when I was six years old. Over the years, political promises of land reform and titles kept people from legally owning their properties, so generations would inherit without actually having a title. Politicians would promise you a ticket to Heaven if you give them your vote, and that is why I strongly believe in education. "My pickney," I told myself rubbing my belly, "my pickney will get it so they can think for themselves." Mark you, I'm not only blaming the politicians, some of the people are too complacent, or what my Grandfather would say "gravelicious", as dem love the word 'free'; free water, free light, free house, dem no matter what, as long as the word free come before it, they are all for it. And the Politicians know their weakness, so they will get their votes.

To prove my point, Woody was threatening the cable man saying HBO not working, an im caan come down til it fix. Even though I was born and raised in the ghetto, I will not have this mentality instilled in me or my children; only living for today and not preparing for the future.

For some reason, Candice took a liking to me and I returned it. When she got home from school, she would not leave my side until it was bed time. I was happy Rita took an interest in her schooling. She wasn't like my mother whose only interest was money. Frank came to me last night when I was sitting at my door. "Little girl," he said. "My name is Jasmine," I answered. "Yes, yes," he continued, and I could see he was drunk as usual. "I work at Seprod, an mi can get tings mi waan somebody fi sell dem fi mi, an wi share di profit. Would yu be interested? Mi hear sey a dat yu used to do."

"If it's at di gate," I replied, "dat's not a problem, but mi nah go back pon di street."
For these few weeks, I learned something.

You can never know a man until yu live wid im. When Tony and I just met, he told me he was nineteen, but I saw his driver's license and realized he was twenty four years old; and based on what I gleaned from members of the community, I was not his only baby-mother. "I wi tek forty percent of di profit, an yu sixty", I told him. After serious consideration, he agreed, and within a week I had my little business at the gate. Three days later, Rita approached and said, "Yu mek sure yu give mi my share, Jasmine before yu give Frank, cause all im a do a carry it go rum bar an Candice haffi get certain tings out a life." Without hesitation I agreed, not that I wanted to deceive him, but I know from experience if a man have a drinking problem, his family will suffer. Sitting beside me, she asked, "Yu know wey mi work, Jasmine?" I shook my head, no. " a Cherry Garden," she said. "Mr. and Mrs. McLean. He is a Doctor, and she work in a bank, but mi have a strong feeling sey im a fool roun im secretary. Mi believe im wife know, but shi no mine." This perked my curiosity, "Why, man?" I moved a little further away from her, as mi wonder how often shi bathe, no wonda Frank always drunk.

"You awrite?" she asked curiously. Holding my breath, I nodded, "yes." "Why yu tink di wife nuh mine," I asked finally. "Between di two a wi, it nuh look like she inna man much. She have good ooman fren dem too close fi comfort." "Wey yu mean by dat?" I asked innocently. "Yu nuh know areddy, likkle gal, di wife is a lesbian." When it finally registered, I asked, "How yu know dat, mam?" "But nay day shi move to mi, yu a go read bout dat inna paper." This time the look on my face gave me away. "Wey yu tink, Jasmine? Mi is not a good looking ooman?" She got up and started modelling in front of me, slapping her butt, she said, "Anybaddy wi want dis, man or ooman." This time I could not help it, I laughed until I got hiccups.

The next night we were having dinner when I heard a knock on the door. Thinking it was Shirley as usual, as for some strange reason, she seemed to have a built-in clock which goes off every time I take my pot off the fire; but when I opened the door, to my surprise, it was my mother.

"Mi waan talk to yu", were the first words she uttered, as she stepped past me and sat on the bed. Turning towards me she said, "Jasmine, me forgive yu. Mi ave time fi tink bout it an me cool dung. Any likkle young gal can mek mistake, so mi nah go hole it gainst yu. Mi waan yu fi still come help mi sell." "Mama," I replied, "mi a do a likkle selling fi meself now." "Lissen, Jasmine," she said, "family fi stick to each odda. A wey yu a go do wen dis ya man ya put yu out?" Tony got up instantly. "A wey yu a talk bout, Miss Kitty? Mi wud a neva do dat." "Shut yu mout bwoy! Mi know how di whole a oonu tan. Di whole a yu a Jan crow, unoo just use ooman an trow dem wey wen oonu no av no more use fi dem."

"A mi yu a call Jan crow, Miss Kitty?" Tony said walking towards her. Though I know Tony has a bad temper, im caan defend it. What I did to him a few weeks ago would be nothing compared to what my mother would do to him if he decided to get brave. "Tony," I intervened, "give mi a few minutes nuh? Go ketch di water cause yu know how it go if we nuh ketch it inna di night, we suffa di next mawning."

Reluctantly he gathered the buckets and headed through the door. Turning to her I said, "Mi a sell fi miself now. Mi six months pregnant an my pickney a go waan tings in life, an mi determine to see dat im get di best." She stared at me with those piercing brown eyes, looking right into my soul. "So, Jasmine, yu mean fi tell mi sey yu a abandon mi afta all mi do fi yu? A mi bring yu pon dis earth, mi wuk night an day fi feed an clothes yu, put a roof ova yu head." My blood began to boil. The anger that was penned up inside me for the fourteen years of my life spurted to the surface like a volcano erupting. I stepped up to her saying, "Lissen to mi. Di roof ova mi head belong to Grandpa, di clothes on mi back belong to Sophia an Karen, an di food dat mi eat mostly belong to di market people wey a go back a country an yu beg dem."

In the past, Miss Kitty solved all problems by hitting, and in a flash her hand rose up. Grabbing it, I twisted it to her back and she froze in astonishment. "Mama, mi nuh waan do yu nutten, betta yu leave." When I was satisfied she would not retaliate, I let her go. Without another word, she walked to the door, opened it, then turned to me. "Jasmine, from dis day mi hate yu like pizen," and slammed the door behind her.

I sat down and dropped my head into my hand while a few tears ran down my cheeks. If she had said that to me a year or two ago, I would have been devastated, but now I realize she didn't care about me, only herself. If she really cared about me, she wouldn't have treated me like this over the years.

Walking towards the door I was just in time to meet Tony with the two buckets of water in his hand. "She gone?" "Yes." I replied. "A wey yu woudda do if she neva gone?" "Wey yu tink?" he asked. "Tony, yu need anger management cause fi such a chicken yu ave a very big mout." "A waan yu fi know, Jasmine," he said, "A me wear di pants inna dis ya house, not yu or yu madda. A mi go work fi yu an yu pickney." "Excuse me," I interrupted, "A nuh yu pickney to? Mi neva know a mi alone get im."

"Look, Jasmine," he sighed, "yu haffi show mi likkle respeck." "Tony," I responded, "respeck is not demanded, it is earned."

The months went by so quickly, and before I knew it, I was at Jubilee Hospital delivering my first child. My daughter, Danielle came into this world on October 7th, 1987. When the nurse placed her in my hand, I thought she was the most beautiful baby ever born, and fell in love with her instantly. The nurse was at my bedside staring at me intently, then said, "You are a young girl. I don't want to see you back here for a long while." I promised her faithfully, not realizing then that the promise would be in vain.

When Tony came to visit that evening, he took one look at Danielle, then at me, and walked out without saying a word. Looking down at my baby I realized she had my complexion, and was the spitting image of me. I saw no trace of Tony in her features.

For the next few days, Danielle kept me busy, but to my astonishment, Tony had a three hundred and sixty degree change in his attitude. He often fed and changed the baby at night when I was too tired to do it. This is what I always wanted, I told myself, a man who will always be there for me and my children.

My little business was also doing well. I made

a lot of friends from my customers but I also made some enemies. Many people with whom I had associated myself started to distance themselves as soon as I started to make money, I guess you can never change people if they have 'bad mind'. I tried to stay off the road as much as possible, as I know anything could happen at any moment either by gunmen or the police. Then there will be demonstrations, blocking of the roads, burning tyres, and disruption of normal everyday life. At one of these demonstrations, Claris from down the road shouted, "Yow, Jasmine. Mi neva see yu out ya yet a defen wi, an di ole a wi live inna di same place, yet yu gwaan like yu betta dan wi!" "Dat's not true," I defended myself. "Mi nuh si di need fi a bun dung di place. Even if wi demonstrate, wi nuh haffi hender people from goin bout dem business. Afta wi nuh barbarian!"

"A Barbarian yu call we, wey a try fi defen wi uman rights?" "No," I retorted, " we jus need a betta way fi express wi self." "Like what?" she shouted back at me. "Like vote dem out! Dem politician dat doan have wi best interest at heart; den educate wi pickney so dat dey

can come betta dan wi an tink fi demself."
She hissed her teeth, and walked off with her
friend. From that day, I vowed to stay as far
away as possible from Claris. I realized she
was a warboat, and since we don't see eye to
eye, I planned to leave her alone.

One afternoon I was feeding Danielle inside
when I heard an uproar in the lane. Being
curious, I went to the window to investigate
what was happening, only to see it was Woody
who was accused of raping an eight year old
girl from Ants Lane, and half of the residents,
including her family came down on him. "Wi a
go kill yu Woody," I heard a voice shouting in
the crowd outside his room. Determined not
to venture outside, I tilted my window to get
a better view. "An if wi nuh kill yu, wi a bun
dung dis!," another voice shouted. It seemed
they were out there for an eternity but when
the crowd finally realized Woody was not
coming out, they set his room a fire. While it
blazed, another male voice shouted, "yu nah F-
-- off wi dawta an get wey wid it." Woody
shouted from the inferno, "Mi nuh touch di
likkle pickney. A lie she a tell." A woman
screamed, "So di Dacta a liad", to Woody. "I

knew it," I thought to myself, "Im too friendly wid di pickney dem. Always waan dem fi sit dung inna im lap." Woody realized he was trapped, so decided to shoot his way out. I heard the gunshot before I realized what was happening. He was determined to do or die. He jumped through the window, shooting into the crowd indiscriminately. It was a scene of sheer pandemonium as some onlookers screamed, and others ran away, whilst others chased Woody. After the ruckus passed, two people lay dead, including the little girl's uncle, whilst three were hospitalized in critical condition.

By midnight, police and soldiers overwhelmed the community; and Woody was on-the-run for murder. When the officer interviewed me, I assured him I did not see anything, as I was inside my house. "Oonu neva see nuttin yet," he complained to me. " Dat's why crime cyaan dun inna di ghetto. Until di violence tun back on oonu, dat is when oonu a bawl. Nex time maybe a yu mi a go pick up inna a body bag." There was some truth to what he was saying, but I also realized that I had no one to defend me, and I had a child to live for now. I was fretting about the situation with Woody for about three weeks. I had stopped selling at the gate, as I was scared of reprisal shooting. One morning I woke up and heard Woody was dead, apparently cornered by police at Three Miles.

I was relieved that the melee had finally ended. Although I was never fond of Woody, I felt disheartened that another young life was snuffed out. From the information I gathered, the family of the little girl hired a hit man to sort him out, and were instructed that if they couldn't find him, to take revenge on anyone that was associated with him. I decided it was time for me to resume business, because I did not want to depend totally on Tony. For a few days, I could sense the tension between me and Ms. Rita, but did not want to say anything to her. I let it go until one afternoon she came home early from work, and stopped and stared intently at me. I could not take it, so asked, "Is something wrong, Ms. Rita?" "Yu neva wash di bathroom dis mawnin," she complained. "Of course," I replied, "I always do when it's my turn." "Well, it neva do good," Ms. Rita said peevishly. "Yu can see sey yu madda neva teach yu," she sneered. "Ms. Rita," I said coldly, "is it the bathroom, or somting else yu waan sey? I consider yu as mi fren, so if yu av someting to sey, sey it!" She stared at me for a moment, then said, "Mi waan di money yu promise mi fi Candice. Mi an yu mek an arrangement." "But Ms. Rita, yu si mi dilemma? Mi nuh work now fi a few weeks, an mi jus a try get back mi foot on di groun. Av patience wid mi nuh Mam?"

"Mi like yu yu know, Jasmine. Yu av mannas, an anybaddy wid mannas mi respeck dem. But business a business, an fren a fren." Trying to be calm, I said, "Ms. Rita, wid all due respeck a nuh yu mi inna bisness wid, a Frank."

"Lissen to mi, Jasmine. Anyting belong to Frank, belong to mi." And as she walked away she said, "clean di bathroom tomarra, an dis time do it good." Shouting out to her I said, "A Shirley time tomarra, an di nex time mi do it, mi a go si if u a go drap dead if it nuh up to yu standard." She hissed her teeth as she went inside her house.

Folding my arms, I relaxed myself. "Inna some way, I like har," I told myself, "but shi remin mi so much of mi madda - cantankerous, an have a bullish attitude about har." I decided to avoid her for the next few days, hoping that she would be in a better mood the next time we talked. It was not long thereafter that I sent Candice with her money, and within a few minutes she was outside hugging me up. "Jasmine, gal," she began, "mi av story fi tel yu," acting like she neva disrespeck mi a few days ago. "It look like di marriage a go mash up!" "What marriage?" I questioned innocently. "Di people dem wey mi work fa, man. Di Dacta cum home couple days ago. Storming tru di kitchen an into im bedroom in a big uproar. It look like im ketch ar inna di act, as fram dat night dem sleep inna seperet rooms. Di man start drink. It look like im a tun Frank pan mi, an wen im unda im likka, im talk all kind a foolishness." She sparked my interest, and as I got curious I asked, "Like what?"

"Yestiday im was roun di dining table, drunk as a bat, im reveal dat a nuff patient im see and fram dem tell im dem symptoms, im know exackly wey wrong wid dem, but im caan cure dem just so, as im av wife an lifestyle fi maintain. Im jus buy a new Range Rover fi ar birtday. While im a talk, im a stare pon dem weddin picher, an get more depress. Mi had fi shet di balcony door fi protec im fram gwine ova. Di ole a dem a tief, Jasmine, wedda yu rich or yu poor, black or white, yu do it eida gun or yu do it wid a pen, a di same tief. But if dem tink dem a go mash up de marrige an lef mi outa job, outa compensation, dem av anneda ting comin. Dat is why me a go a Ministry a Labour fi secure mi rights." "Ms. Rita," I finally said, "Watch an look before yu leap. Do not confront dem an yu doan know what is happening."

"Mi a nuh trouble maker, yu kno Jasmine." I remember just about an hour ago, she almos lik dung Tony to sweep one part of di yard an leave di nex. "Mi know, Ms. Rita," I replied, lying through my teeth, "but mi jus nuh waan nutten appen to yu." This seemed to calm her down. "How di likkle one?" she asked. "Mi come in so late in a di night, mi hardly can see ar." "She's fine," I responded proudly, "striving well, almost creeping". "A hope yu nuh av nuh trubble wid ar in di future wettin bed," Ms. Rita said. "Mine woudda kill mi. Miguel stopped wen im a fifteen years, Carlos thirteen, and Johnny twelve. Not to mention sucking at di brest! All wen Johnny seven im waan titty. Mi haffi put single bible fi mek im stop. But even wen mi do dat, di bwoy lick it off an a suck same way. Mi haffi fight im like man an see it dey now? Im a teenager an nuh even waan walk wid mi pon di road." "Mi a pray to God Danielle nuh reach dat stage," I exclaimed. "Yu av a lot to learn, pickney gal," she responded, slapping me on di shoulder. "But nuh worry yuself, mi dey ya fi yu."

Tony began coming in later and later, even though the hardware closed at seven p.m., he wouldn't be home until eleven p.m. or midnight. When I questioned him about this, it would often end up in a verbal confrontation, so I decided to leave him alone. One evening he arrived home unusually early with a big grin on his face. "Jasmine," he greeted me, "mi jus quit mi job today, an di ongle ting mi regret is dat mi neva do it sooner." All the blood drained from my face, and I became red as a cherry. When he saw my features change, it was such a pleasure for him. He began laughing louder till the bag he was holding fell out of his hand. Before I could say anything to him, he said, "Nuh worry yuself, man, I got annoda one." "What?" I asked stupidly. He said, "I'm going to drive a taxi." "Taxi?" I repeated weakly. "Yu know sometimes yu on di road all day an doan mek a dollar, Jasmine," he explained walking towards me. "Mi av skill dat yu neva dream bout yet. I'm a survivor, an at least wid dis, I work at my own leisure." I know he did not have the money to purchase a car, but decided not to question him on the subject.

It took the landlord three months to repair and rent Woody's room. Typically, accommodation in Kingston would go very fast; the city simply did not have enough space to accommodate those coming in from the country. It took the landlord three months to repair and rent Woody's room. No one wanted to reside at a place where a gunman used to live. The new occupants consisted of a lady by the name of Sandra, her husband Keith and their three children. It took Rita only a few hours to find out all the family's business. From the moment of first introductions she stuck to them like glue, asking question after question until she felt satisfied. The next morning while we were washing clothes together, Rita informed me that Sandra is a cashier at a Supermarket in Half Way Tree, and Keith is a construction worker. They both come from Mile Gully in St. Elizabeth, but decided to relocate where jobs were available. Their three daughters were fourteen, thirteen and ten years old, and the man is a religious freak. "Yu an im av a lot in common, Jasmine, as from the moment mi introduce miself to dem, im nuh stop quote di Bible to mi like a dat mission de mi go pon. Mi haffi bite mi tongue a few times, cause mi just waan tell im fi shut up mek mi hear what im wife haffi sey. All wen mi a try fi leave, im a invite mi to Church."

"Ms. Rita," I said, "Dat's a good place to go. I started ever since I move in wid Tony. Wen I was by my madda, she use to behave like yu. Shi tell mi one afternoon as I was getting ready to go to Church, sey too much work inna di house fi do, an shi no si why she mus allow mi fi go sit dung fi hours a look inna people face, an pay man fi tell mi wey inna di same Bible we av at home. Ms. Rita, unda mi madda regime, mi cudden go a church, but now dat mi dey pon mi own, mi a mek full use a it, cause mi know how God good to mi."

"Yu can gwaan, Jasmine," Ms. Rita said, "because religion is a personal choice, an mi God a everywhere, even at mi house. Mi nuh haffi go nowere fi look fi im." I found it pointless to argue with her, so I decided to change the subject. "How did it go wid di Ministry of Labour?" "Dem sey mi entitle fi two week pay plus vacation. Mi mek sure mek dem write di letta gi mi, even doh mi nuh ready fi use it yet. But as mi Granny wud sey, prevention betta dan cure." I find myself getting curious about the McLeans. "What's going on between them?" I asked Rita. "Dem sey dem in counselling, as di husband tel im fren on di phone one evenin. Im waan rekindle flame back in di marriage. Damn fool," Rita laughed out loud, "Because if di ooman nuh inna yu, an yu a gi yu wife bun lef right an centa, a wah kine a flame up a go establish? An yu waan hear di man a boast to im fren, dis counselor is di best in Jamaica. Im fee is two hundred dollar US."

A week passed when I began to notice Rita's two oldest sons, Carlos and Miguel displaying an interest in Sandra's two oldest daughters Shantel and Vanessa. Miguel was eighteen years old, but short and stumpy for his age. Carlos, at sixteen, was bigger than his older brother. It became obvious to me, that as far as these young men were concerned, these girls were easy targets. I prayed that Sandra would have the common sense to keep her daughters safe, but when they thought no one was around, they would push fruit and letters through the window to the girls. I could not bear it any longer, and decided to speak to Shantel and her sister, as I would be devastated if something should happen and I hadn't said anything. If my madda had the courage and guts to warn me, I would not be here on my verandah now rocking a baby.

One afternoon, I was sitting under the ackee tree reflecting on my life when the opportunity presented itself, as both sisters joined me. Shantel was the older one, but was more immature than her sister, always smiling, even when you are trying to have a serious conversation with her. "Oonu know bout man?" I asked them. "Mi know enuf," Shantel replied giggling. "Mi nah talk bout the physical attribute of dem," I continued, "mi talking bout dem behavior, an wat some wud do to get a girl." When I realized that they did not understand, I decided to take a different approach. "I'm just a year older dan yu, I doan finish high school, but av a baby an living wid a man. Life no easy wen yu av responsibility, so di longa yu can wait, wud be better fi yu. Yu hear mi?" I warned them. "Listen to yu parents an tek in yu eddication because dere will be time fi dis later."

"Even if I have a child now," Shantel said, "a nuh sin." "But is a sin to bring dem an caan tek care a dem," I answered. "Beside a five a oonu in a one room, wey yu wouda do? Put di burden pon yu madda an fadda?" "My grandparents would often sey, Shantel, if yu caan hear, yu will feel." She got up and walking away said, "Yu caan tell mi wha fi do, Jasmine. One tief neva like fi anneda tief carry long bag. Yu grandparents neva tell yu dat?" and she turned the corner. I shook my head, and turning to Vanessa I asked, "Did yu hear mi?" She stared straight in my eyes, and without blinking, said "Yes".

When Danielle was eighteen months old, I got the news that Mary Ann, my old fren had a stroke, an was on the verge of dying. Without hesitation, I took the baby and headed towards her house. It had been ages since I had traversed this neighborhood due to on-going gang warfare but nothing, I told myself, would stop me from seeing her even for the last time. She was my best friend even though she was in her nineties. Bursting through her door as if the devil was at my tail, I grabbed her hand as she lay in her bed. "Aunt May," I cried, "don't leave me." But she only squeezed my hand as if to tell me that it would be alright. I placed the baby beside her on the bed, and I looked up as Angela, her oldest daughter joined us. She is a nurse at Kingston Public Hospital. "Mama," she said softly, "see your friend came to look for you and brought her baby." Aunt May smiled, put her hand on Danielle, and took her last breath. I was so distraught, I sat in the same rocking chair that had been a comfort to me over the years, and cried like I never cried before. Two weeks later, her funeral was so big, as everyone came from all over, even politicians, and for a few hours, everyone forgot political allegiance. No one cared that they were sitting or even talking to their enemies. Everyone had a kind word to say about Aunt Mary Ann. They said she was a great woman, and I vowed then and there, that's how I want to live my life. "It's how you interact with people," I thought to myself, "that will define the legacy you leave when you are gone." I walked home slowly, thinking about my past, and my hopes for the future. When I turned onto my street, I saw a large crowd at my gate. Everyone was excited, some shouting, "Kill di gal! Kill di gal!" I walked faster, thinking, "What now, Jesus?" When I pushed through the crowd, I realized it was Rita and Sandra fighting to death. "What's going on?" I asked a young man beside me. He told me that apparently Sandra came home early from work and caught Carlos and Shantal having sex in the bathroom. When she confronted him, he panicked and slapped her in the face, and she reported it to the police. Carlos is now charged with carnal abuse, and carnal assault, and is on a fifty thousand dollar bail. Even if he pays the bail, he cannot come to this house. When Rita got the call, she came home and confronted Sandra. "Mi an yu a fren. Wi cud a work it out. Yu neva haffi get Babylon inna dis!" But Sandra wouldn't listen, she said, "yu put up wid too much slackness wid yu bwoy pickney dem. Yu ignore dem dirty behaviour over di years an dis is why Carlos inna trubble now." Rita took offense to this slur against her son. "What yu know bout mi, Sandra?" she shouted. "Yu acting like yu dawta a good good pickney. Look how shi dress? Everybaddy inna di community kno dat Shantal is a likkle slut." This infuriated Sandra, and both of them started to claw and punch and rolled on the ground. When I arrived, both their clothes were almost completely torn off, but neither was giving up. Sandra seemed to have the upper hand, but then Rita would fight back. I realized something dramatic would have to occur to separate them. "Part them!" I shouted. "Yu nuh si dem a go kill dem one annada?" Biggs who was the designated referee, held his finger up to indicate he had everything under control. Peter, who I thought would help to separate them, only smiled. Realizing I would get no assistance from the men, I turned to the women. We got buckets of water and flung them on the two fighting women. This worked briefly, so I made use of that by grabbing Sandra's arm and pulling her away. She came without hesitation. Railing and kicking, Rita shouted, "A mus kill yu gal. Yu mus lef ya tonite." "If a yu rent mi dis room, mek mi lef now!"

"Ladies," said one of the men using a makeshift bell, "if yu ready for round Two, wi de ya fi unoo." Ignoring them, I pulled Sandra into my house and locked the door. This seemed to disappoint the crowd, and they began to disperse one by one.

For the next few days, the yard was so tense I could not bear it. Frank drank more and more, and would pass out by the roadside. It was the only thing he could do to avoid hearing Rita's whining and complaining. Keith, while sweeping the yard, or attending to the garden he made at the side of his house, would quote the Bible verse by verse, explaining generational curses and what will happen to hypocrites on the day of reckoning. Sandra stayed mainly in her house, and as for Shirley, nothing bothered her as long as she had Danielle to attend to. Whenever Sandra came outside, she would carry a machete. One morning while I was pinning clothes on the line she told me, "Jasmine, yu av a girl child. No mek no one tek liberty a har no matter how she stay. If mi drap di charge wid Carlos, it a go look like me in league wid it, an it a go look like mi nuh love mi pickney. She might be frisky, but even if she a gi im pon a silver platter wid knife an fork, im shudden tek it, cause she a just thirteen years old. Im shudda look someone im own age." I felt bad for Sandra. Even though I did not want to see Rita get hurt, Sandra was right. I felt as if I was caught in di middle. Wen Rita si Sandra an me talking, she wud get mad, thinking we were plotting against her, an dat I am not a true fren. Wen Sandra si Rita an me, shi also come to di same conclusion. So di bes ting I cud do was keep to myself.

Time went by, and eventually, the case started in court. During the trial, the tension between myself and my two neighbours magnified; our home felt like a volcano that could erupt at any time. The police made trips warning each party that any offence, it wud be straight jail, so most of what I heard was second hand, as Tony warned mi not fi get involve. "Mi neva climb eleven step yet, an mi nuh climb nun fi u." So I had to hear it from Mr. Junior, an elderly gentleman living down di bottam of my lane, retired ten years ago from di civil service. He wud attend court every day, since he didn't have nothing more to do, even though he lost a leg to diabetes three years ago. "Jasmine," he said one evening, "it look like Carlos is one of the saltest person pon God's earth. His defense all along was dat dem neva reach dat far, but dem fine out now dat Shantal is pregnant. Fram wat di Dacta sey, shi is two months pregnant, an dat is di same time dem was caught. As far as mi see, it look like a someting a gwaan di moment dat girl move in dis yard."

"So wey dem a go do?" I asked. "Di Judge order a Social Worka to cum to di house to investigate especially har living arrangement, becus if it not suitable, dem going to place har in State care."

"Yu mean tek har away from Sandra? Dat would devastate har!" "Di Judge sey if she an Keith is not a fit parent fi di girls, den is not Shantal alone wud be taken fram dem. All di girls wud go." "My God!" I exclaimed.

Within a week, di Social Worker was at mi

door. I was uncomfortable to talk wid her, but I told her di truth. As far as I was concerned, Keith and Sandra are very good parents. Dem work hard fi dem kids, and try fi provide di basic necessity fi dem, an I did not feel di incident was a reflection on dem parenting. A month later, di Social Worker complete har investigation, an di trial resumed. Unfortunately for Carlos, after six months of trial he was found guilty and was sentenced to five years for carnal abuse. As Mr. Junior infarm mi, di Judge told Carlos him was lucky, as im was looking at a sentence of ten years, but as di parents left Shantal unsupervised, im ad to tek dat into account. Dis broke Rita's heart, as in spite of everything she loved Carlos. I never spoke to her about Sandra and Keith again.

Shantal's daughter Ashley, was born one month after Carlos was sentenced. Sandra tried to ascertain through Frank, Rita's views regarding the state of affairs. Rita resolved that she wanted nothing to do with the baby or the family. Subsequently, Sandra and Keith decided to place the baby up for adoption. Although it was not my child, I felt distraught; I recalled what my mother went through with Courtney. The thought that the child would grow up not knowing her biological parents troubled me even more so.

Shantal spent two weeks in the hospital after giving birth, due to complications. Shantal was fourteen years old, but had the body of a ten year old. Sandra told me the Doctor's said Shantal had a slim chance of getting pregnant again. Nevertheless, Sandra felt they made the right decision, especially given their financial inability to support the baby. Sandra recognized however, that Shantal could not remain in the community. Persons whom Shantal had once regarded as her friends, had now become her enemies. Likewise distressing, were the stares she received as she walked through the community. She was willing to try with Shantal again, sending her back to school, but she knew she could not live there anymore, because those she considered her friends became her enemies, and she could not take the stares as she walked through the community. Most of the people blamed her for Carlos' imprisonment, and she had been threatened, so she was scared for her family.

"What?" I asked in shock, "Can't your Pastor help you?" Sandra smiled sarcastically. "My Church?" she asked, "most of the criticism is coming from the members. They believe as a Christian I should have forgiven Carlos, and leave the punishment and judgement to God."

For the first time since the incident, tears came to my eyes, and wordlessly, both of us started crying. "You're a good girl, Jasmine. Don't let anyone change you." I realized that things could not remain the same, so that evening when Rita was passing, I stopped her. "Sit beside me, Rita," I said. "A long time we nuh talk." "Wa dey fi mi an yu talk, Jasmine? Yu nuh av yu big time fren?" "Come on, Rita, di two a unoo a mi fren. Unoo a like mi madda. Unoo a de firs one fi reach out to mi wen mi dey pon mi own. Di two a unoo important to mi. Mi an yu can rap, an Sandra help mi wid mi spiritual beliefs. Mi caan choose between unoo, an it no fair fi yu waan mi fi choose." She tried to walk away, but I stepped in front of her. When she hesitated, I said softly, "It will get better, Rita." "Betta, betta?" she shouted at mi, an began laughing as if I'd told her the funniest joke. When she stopped laughing, she said, "Mi first pickney gone a prison, an yu sey it will get betta?" "Rita," I reasoned, "Yu are a good woman. Yu work hard to provide fi yu family. Carlos mek im own mistake, an im haffi live wid the consequences. Him is eighteen years old, im not a child, im a adult. Doan mek wey im do depress yu, yu av di res a yu pickney dem fi live far." "It nuh easy, Jasmine. People look pon yu bad. Even wen yu try fi grow dem di right way, people tink is your fault wen dem get inna trouble." Resignedly, she sat down, and I joined her. Shaking her head, she continued, "Yu nuh undastan". "Yu wrong, Rita," I replied. "Memba mi bredda Barry? Ow yu tink mi feel wen people look pon mi as a gunman sista? Pickney neva used to sit dung beside mi inna school, an di least likkle ting dem sey mi a mongrel. All mi life mi a live wid dis stigma, an mi pickney dem a come live wid it no matta if mi do good inna mi life, Rita. Cure AIDS, or cancer, an feed di hungry, dem still a go look on mi di same way, so mi jus haffi live fi miself an nuh bisness wey people tink bout mi. Mi know mi a good woman, an God kno it, an dat's all dat matta."

I realized she understood what I was saying. I squeezed her hand. "Our family mistake won't be yours. Hopefully Carlos will learn from his. But yu av to learn to forgive, Rita, both Carlos and Sandra fi dem stupidity. Sake of yu stubbornness, yu av a grandaughter who will neva kno yu. Even though yu don't av no love fi har now, wan day yu gwine regret it." "Mi couldn't bear it fi even touch or look pon dat chile, Jasmine, knowing dat shi is di result of all dis." "Dat's where yu are wrong," I explained, "Dat baby is di innocent victim of all dis. Is har parents is di cause of all dis pain. But mi a beg yu, Rita, "I spoke gently, "Nuh carry all a dis ina yu heart or yu will gu to yu grave wid all dis. Tink about it, Rita," I said, smiling reassuringly. She started to walk to her room, then turned and said, "Mi glad fi kno we still frenz, Jasmine."

Two days later, I woke up to find out that Keith and Sandra moved out the night before. She left a letter under my door informing me of their new address in St Elizabeth on Keith's family property. She promised to keep in touch, and apologized for leaving like a thief in the night. Heartbroken and depressed, I thought the day could not get any worse. I was wrong, as by the end of it I found out that I was pregnant with my second child. This caused a whole new upheaval in my house that night.

When I informed Tony, he shouted, "One more? It look like sey yu is a breeder, Jasmine." " Danielle is two years old," I answered, "An I tell yu fi use a condom at all times, an yu won't." "Fi wha?" he smirked proudly, "Mi a ital man." " Mi neva kno mi dey wid rasta. Di sun a reflect off a yu head top, Tony." "Yu nuh haffi wear locks," he said, "it inna yu heart. Besides a your responsibility fi nuh get ketch." Frustrated, I sat down. "Tony," I reasoned, "mi tell yu di pills dem mek mi sick, an mi caan tek di injection. If yu had mi at heart, yu wud help mi, but like mos man, yu ongl tink bout yuself. A mi an yu a lay dung, but yu put all di blame pon mi." "Shut up yu blasted mout," he said angrily. "Mi a go see a who a go carry it fi nine months, feed an clothes it." And with that he slammed the door behind him, and did not return until the next morning. It was the first time he slept out. I was hurt and confused, because I did not know where he was, and who he was with. To my surprise, he came back and assurred me he would be there for both of us. "Jasmine," he said, " a mi tek yu out a yu madda house, so a my responsibility fi help yu." "Mi nuh waan to be an obligation to yu," I said, "Mi independent from mi eye de a mi knee. As far as mi is concerned, yu a mi man. Di ongle ting wey mi nuh av a de ring, an I tink is time we rectify dat, as yu kno mi don't want to live this life." Defensively, he said, "Jasmine, mi nuh tell yu areddy mi nuh inna di married ting. Wi a live good areddy. A nuff people inna our position an rock di boat an tun it ova." "Tony," I pleaded, "Mi serious about mi Church, an mi waan yu fi serious wid mi. Mi waan us fi live as a respektable an loving family." He stared me straight in the eye. "A nat marrying", he said, "yu haffi tek mi as mi is." I could not change his mind, so I dropped the subject.

Over the next few weeks, things were going great for us. Tony was home on time, food was abundant in the house, and Tony finally began spending time with Danielle. When I got the ultrasound results that I was having another girl, he was infruriated. " All mi a beg yu fa is a son, an yu cyaan even do dat?" "Dis is nat my fault, Tony, is what yu put in yu get out. If yu did spen time inna school yu wudda fin dat out." "Mi nuh haffi go school fi know mi dey wid a bitch," he said, "An leopard neva change im spots," I retaliated, "But is my fault. Yu live wid dog, yu rise wid fleas!"

For the next few months we were like strangers living in the same house, even though he still brought in the food. He started coming in whenever he felt like, and I didn't care.

Miguel, Rita's second son, got a job at SuperPlus packing bags, and decided to rent Sandra's room as he quarreled with his Mother one evening. "Mi a mi own man, Mama, an mi need mi own place." "Mi know dat, son," she pleaded, "but tings tight financially, so it betta we pool wi resources togedda. Di money yu a go tek fi pay rent, wi can keep it in di family if we living all unda di same roof." Getting upset, he said, "Mi nuh business bout yu an Frank, a yu an im a fi mine di pickney dem, a nuh my responsibility. Mi young an mi money fi spend pon mi." Rita started to cry. "Yu is a selfish bwoy, Miguel," she said. "Mi neva know mi bring a bastard inna di world. Afta all a wey mi do fi yu fram birth...feed yu, clothes yu, an put yu tru school until yu reach dis stage, now yu a go tun yu back pon mi?" I thought Miguel would show compassion for his mother, but he only smiled. "Yu nah go mek mi feel guilty, Mama, mi dey a pond a swim an a yu an mi Papa come disturb mi, so a fi unoo responsibility fi tek care a mi. Now mi can do it fi miself, mi a go do it." And within two days Miguel was living in Sandra's room. Unfortunately for us, he used it as a brothel. Almost every night im bring in a different girl. The more wi talk to im, the more im ignore us.

I never thought I could love another child the way I love Danielle but I was wrong. When my second daughter, Toni-Ann was born, she stole my heart. I was concerned however about how Tony would receive her given his behaviour over the last few months. When the nurse placed her in his arms, he began smiling with her. Then I noticed for the first time that unlike Danielle, Toni-Ann had his complexion. As far as he was concerned, she was his little princess. "Tony", I said, "Is two yu have, nat one. Do not treat dem

differently, or yu might live to regret it."
"Nuh worry yuself, Jasmine," he responded.
But unfortunately, he did treat them
differently and this put a strain on his
relationship with Danielle for years to come.
The prejudice that I fought to overcome all
my life was now manifesting itself in my own
family. Tony would often take Toni-Ann for
walks, introducing her to all his friends. He
even had a picture of her in his wallet. If no
one knew, they would assume she was the only
child he had with me. He never had time to
spend with Danielle, and when she craved his
attention, he would send her to me.

One night we were sitting at home, and I tried
to reason with him about it, but as usual, he
got upset. "As far as I am concerned,
Jasmine, Danielle is your responsibility, while
Toni-Ann a mine. As yu always sey, wi a equal
partner in a dis relationship." He gave Toni-
Ann everything she wanted. I never even had
to ask twice. One night lying in bed I got a
call that I needed to come to the station to
bail Tony. He was caught on camera stealing
baby clothes from a store on King Street
Downtown. He tried to convince me it was a

misunderstanding, as he never knew he had so much in his hand, but I knew better deep down inside. Tony knew he would do anything for Toni-Ann. They had a bond I thought could never be broken, but I was wrong. After three weeks of trial, he was found guilty, and ordered to pay fifty thousand dollars or six months in jail. I didn't want him to have a record, so I helped him with the fine. I realized Tony showed little regard for Danielle and her feelings, I tried to compensate by buying gifts for her often, not letting her know I was the one purchasing them.

One day I was at my stall by the gate when Patrick, a little boy living at the end of the lane, ran up to me. "Aunty Jasmine," he shouted, "yu haffi come now. Di Police dem a tek wey Shirley." "Tek wey Shirley?" I repeated in shock. "Di bwoy dem down di road a tease har," he continued, "an shi retaliate by bussing one a dem head. Di Police dem sey dem naah let har go cause is di second smaddy head shi buss since dis year." I gathered my goods, and headed straight to the station. When I got to the door, I saw that Shirley had the better of them. It took four Officers to restrain her. "Who yu?" one of the Officers asked. "I am here for her," I replied in a stern voice. "If yu not har family yu can go back tru di door." " Mi an har a blood," I said, this time advancing towards them to reassure her that I was here. When she saw me, it seemed to calm her down. I held her hand and said to her, "nuh fight dem," and like a child, she obeyed. Turning to the senior Officer, I greeted him. "Look, Sir, even though I am not her blood relative, I am the only one she has in this world, and I am not leaving here tonight without her." A young Sergeant intervened, "a nuff time mi warn har, an she nuh hear. Dis time jail na miss har." "Yu a go av a fight dis time, because shi nat right in har head, an wen mi spread di word sey yu lock up a mad ooman, yu a go av a riot dung here." The Superintendent said that wasn't necessary, but while he was talking to me, his eyes were focusing on my breasts. I deliberately leaned back to show him everything, and he began salivating like a dog. "Tell yu what, Miss." "Yu can call mi Jas," I interrupted. "Even though the boy's family want me to press charges, I will try to convince them not to, since it is obvious that the boy was the aggressor, and I would have to press charges on him also." After reassuring him that it would never happen again, Shirley was released and we both left the station.

I know how the inner-city runs. Most people will bypass the law and take matters in their own hands, so we headed straight for the boy's family. I was scared that his family would bring violence to me, but when the Mother greeted me warmly, I began to relax. I offered to compensate her for medical expenses, which she gladly accepted. On our way home I tried to encourage Shirley to keep her temper under control. She was resisting at first, but I told her if she continued, she wouldn't be allowed to take care of my girls. This scared her, because without the shadow of a doubt, she loved them.

That night at home, she vowed to me that as long as she is alive, I would have someone in my corner. She began taking care of the girls more and more. At first I wanted to resist, but seeing how much she devoted herself to them, and the love they returned to her, I could never break them up. It was as if we all had a second mother. Tony began to get jealous, and often argued with Shirley. When I tried to intervene, he would storm out of the house. I never realized it then, but it was the start of him drifting away from us.

Two months later, we were all sitting outside talking when a van with two men drove up and asked for Miguel. The van side said Ministry of Health, and I became curious. "He is not here," I responded, "but I can take a message." "Please tell him," one of the men said, "to visit the Health Centre and ask for Nurse Thomas." When I told Rita that evening, a worried look came over her face. "Mi god, a wha now?" Right then, Miguel came by. When his mother gave him the message, he hissed his teeth. "You need to go," I said. "Maybe is someting important." "Mine yu business, Jasmine," he snapped at me. "Yu fi av manners," his mother shouted at him, but I tried to quiet her. "Man a gallis," Miguel laughed, "a tree a dem mi av a breed now, an si di next one a come fi ar fix yah." When I turned my head to look, the little girl coming to his room could not have been more than thirteen years old. "Yu sick inna yu head," Rita shouted, "yu nuh si wey appen to yu bredda Miguel?" "Im a fool," he scoffed, and went into his room and closed the door.

By the end of the week, I found out why they wanted to see Miguel. One of his baby mother's gave birth, and she was HIV positive. Rita tried to encourage him to get tested. "Even if you are positive, you can get treatment," she said. "Mi nuh av dat, Mama. Yu tink me gay? Look ow much ooman mi av. A gay man av dem ting dey." We tried to convince him that wasn't the case. Two weeks later I was expecting to see him in the morning at the pipe as usual brushing his teeth, but he wasn't out. I saw Rita crying, so I ran over and asked concernedly," What's wrong?" "Miguel tek sick las night," she cried. "About midnight, mi go see im in a pool a vomit an unconscious. Frank haffi carry im pon im back to di main fi get a taxi fi admit im to hospital." Fortunately, he recovered sufficiently to be released four days later. He came home with anti-retroviral medication. The doctor informed us, that he may have contracted the disease from the time he was fourteen years old.

When Miguel's HIV status became public knowledge, the whole yard was condemned. "A nuclear bomb mus drop inna it an kill all a dem. Nat even di cockroach mus escape," was one comment. Another lady said," A nuff young gal suppose to av it. Yu nuh si how Miguel used to run di place red?"

In due course, even my business became affected by the publicizing of Miguel's HIV status. Many people stopped buying from me. When Miguel came home from the hospital, his mother was right by his side. This same mother he had abused and disrespected was devoted to him one hundred percent. I was so proud of her, as she never wavered. She walked with him to the clinic even when people stared and jeered them. They also went to counselling as a family together.

I thought that Miguel was beginning to accept his new status, until late one Friday night when I heard a scream coming from his house. I rushed over to find Rita and Frank inside. Rita was lying over him on the floor, crying uncontrollably. Miguel had committed suicide by hanging himself with a rope on the wooden beam in the ceiling of his house. Throughout this ordeal, I was right by Rita's side helping her with the preparations for the funeral. Rita did not wish to delay matters and thus Miguel's funeral was held a week later. To my surprise, it was well attended. Even those who had turned their backs on him showed up to pay their respects.

In the months following Miguel's funeral, Rita was devastated. All the strength and bravery she showed while Miguel was alive had disappeared. As her friend, it was my job to be there for her. "Wey mi a go do, Jasmine?" she wailed, sitting on my bed one night. Carlos inna prison, Miguel now dead, an mi av tree more fi tek care a. Frank a drink more an more. If im sober one hour out a di twenty four, im sober lang. According to im, wen im drink, it give im more vibes, but mi too old an tired, Jasmine... fi go start life ova wid anneda man." I sat beside her and squeezed her hand. "Yu wi mek it, Rita," I comforted. "God wi se yu tru." "Nuh tell mi bout God, Jasmine," she said sternly, "Instead a im bless mi, im curse mi," she said angrily.

I know from experience not to say much when she is in this mood, so I stood up and said, "God is waiting on yu Rita, don't mek it too late." She got up and walked towards me. "Any day im can help mi fi come out a mi sufferation, an mi nuh haffi go a people ouse an wash dem clothes an even haffi look afta dem dag ten hours a day, an den come a mi yard ova tired til me feel fi drop dung, den yu can tell mi bout im." I looked her straight in the eye and said, "Your relationship with God is a fifty-fifty partnership. Yu cannot expec im fi bless yu wen yu don't put out di effort. Come a Church wid mi." "Mi nah go inna da place deh. Di ole a dem a hypocrite, mos a who condemn mi an mi family. A Church people now yu expec mi fi come siddung beside dem an shake dem han. As far as mi concern, if God waan fine mi im haffi come out a door." And with this, she left my house.

Over the years, my brother Steve and Tony became good friends. I was happy that he was getting along with at least one member of my family since Raphael did not like a bone in him. From the moment they met, Raphael told me he looked like a puss. "Im av a puss face, an mi nuh truss no man wid dem de face dey." Remembering how Tony and I met, I had to concur with him.

Unfortunately, I found out when it was too late that Tony was now smoking weed. When I told him he had to stop, he would get angry with me. "Lissen to mi ooman," he said one morning when I confronted him, "dis a di tree of life, an mi nah stap till di day mi die. I neva know sey mi did a miss so much joy ova di years." I hated Steve for introducing it to Tony, but I could not blame him alone. Tony was a big man, and had a choice of his own. "Yu waan fi si yu children tek up dis?" I quarreled. "If dem do dat, mi a go kill dem," he said seriously. " I have something to tell you, Tony," I said hesitantly, as I did not know how to break the news to him. "Anyting yu hav fi tell mi, jus go ahead," he reassured me. I didn't want to tell him I was pregnant, thinking he would be angry. I stood back, but he only smiled, saying, " so mi ganja child on im way," and started laughing uncontrollably.

Not wanting to put a damper on his good

mood, I didn't say anything. "Mi love mi gyal pickney dem, but so long as mi son a come, mi good." I started to pray that this time it would be a boy. I tried to reassure him that no matter what the sex of the child, we can make it as a family because I love him. For the next eight months everything went well, but when my daughter Alexis was born, I knew my life with Tony was over. He no longer slept at our house, often staying away for days. When I tried to speak to him, he would tell me to go to Hell, because as long as mi pickney dem a get food an shelter, mi nuh fi complain. I tried to reassure him that our girls were a blessing, but he would not listen. He started to neglect even Toni-Ann, his favourite. He had new friends and a separate life from ours. Heartbroken, I knew there was nothing I could do about it. I did not know who to turn to, and kept it bottled up inside me. Now I started missing Mary Ann. My own mother, after criticizing and condemning me, would tell me she knew this would happen. Depressed and alone, I stopped selling at the gate, often crying myself to sleep.

By the time Alexis was six months old, Tony

completely moved out. On several occasions, I went to the taxi stand Downtown to collect child maintenance money, but he and his friends would only give me the run-around. He would give me something only when he felt like. Ironically, it was Shirley who put me back on track. "Yu betta dan dis, Jasmine," she cajoled. "From yu a likkle gal, yu a work an av yu own independence. No mek im tun yu inna clown, an im an im fren dem a laugh afta yu." Deep down inside I knew she was right, so I stopped running after him.

Tony began dating the lady who owned his taxi. She was from Yallas in St Thomas, and her name was Pearl. I knew then that I had to become stronger for my kids, so I began selling at the gate once more. One year later, Tony informed me that he was getting married, and that he had a baby son. "Times is too hard on me Jasmine," he complained, "an mi wuk too hard widout success. As far as mi concern, mi an yu cud a neva mek life but if yu did gi mi a son, mi wud a consider fi stay wid yu. Even tho mi wife to be, Pearl, is twenty years olda dan mi, shi gi mi wey mi want." I thought that I would be hurt but at that moment I felt relieved. "Tony," I said, holding my head high, "If yu tink mi a go beg yu fi come back, yu ave annada ting comin. Good luck inna yu new life." I could see the surprised look on his face but he didn't say a word. When he walked away from me that afternoon, it would be a few years before I saw him again.

Sitting in my bedroom and staring at myself in the mirror that night, I realized I was in the same predicament as my older sister, Sophia. I was twenty-one years old with three children and no Father standing beside me. Unlike her, I would save my money - as Mary Ann would always say, "One-one cocoa full basket." I decided to withdraw some money and start my own business but I did not want to do it in my community, as I knew the mindset of some of them. They don't want to see you try. They will pretend they are with you, but behind your back they will try to break you down.

I opened a shop at Castleton in the hills of St. Andrew. This new venture involved buying goods to supply those who do not wish to come down to the city. Within seven months my endeavours bore fruit as I began to see a profit. Because of the distance to travel, I had to leave the girls with Shirley sometimes at night. "Yu is a good gal," she said smiling at me. "Don't give up pon yu gal pickney dem. Mi wi always dey ya fi help yu. If dem anyting like yu, dem will mek yu proud one day."

Ironically, I heard through the grapevine that Tony's son TJ was born on my birthday and I was happy for him. He had made his choice and it was up to me to provide for myself and the girls. Time flew by so quickly, I could not believe it was two years since my life had changed. Alexis had not been acquainted with her father since she was two years old when he got married and moved to St. Thomas. Tony was there for Danielle and Toni-Ann for a short while, but unlike them, she could only imagine what it would be like to have a Father to play with. I taught them to love him no matter what, and that it was not their fault he was no longer around. The last thing I wanted, was for them to feel the hurt that I was feeling.

One night I was sleeping soundly, and I dreamt that my old friend Mary Ann came into the room and handed me a piece of paper with numbers on it. When I looked at it, I knew immediately what it meant. She placed her finger over my lips so I could not talk. "A yu future, Jasmine," she whispered, and then disappeared. After calming myself, I wrote down the numbers that were on this seemly illusory piece of paper. For several days, I was torn, as my children and I were in Church. I believed it was wrong to engage in gambling. But when I looked at the poverty in my family and around me, I went against my beliefs and bought the ticket.

I knew that the lottery was scheduled to play in the evening. When it played that night, I was lying in bed with the girls, and I screamed so loudly that Shirley rushed in. Jumping up and down and throwing my arms around her I shouted, "Shirley, Shirley, I am a millionaire." "What!" she exclaimed, looking shocked with disbelief. When I repeated it, she 'peed' on herself. I forgave her instantly, even though I had cleaned my house earlier that day. I wanted to do the same but it wouldn't come.

"How much?" she enquired excitedly after she recovered. "Fifty million dollars," I replied, and she fainted.

Within three months I was looking for my dream house. At long last, I found an ideal home in Stony Hill. I paid twenty five million dollars for it – A tidy sum for a woman who had been living in a tenement yard just a few months ago. We moved in a month after purchase, and my business was still doing well. I enrolled my girls in a private school, then I purchased my former residence and gave it to Frank, Rita and Shirley, who became the new landlords.

After Rita lost her job a year ago, she became depressed. I will never forget the evening she told me about it. She came home, flinging her bag beside me on the sidewalk. She drew out a letter, and thrust it in my face. "Seven years of devoted service and now this is it? Two weeks pay and a thank you note?" She lifted her head to the sky. "If mi was a tief it wouldn't be so bad." "Rita!", I exclaimed, "Wha happen?" "Mr. and Mrs. McLean decided to divorce now, Jasmine," she said seriously, "Mos people inna Jamaica fight ova money, land, house and car. Dem dey two idiot a fight ova one poodle dawg, an it even reach a court now." I felt sorry for her, even though we were in the same economic situation, as Tony had moved out just two weeks prior and I was contemplating what to do with my future. "I have been thinking bout starting a new business, so why don't you take this one ova?" She sat beside me. "Mi look like a higgla to yu, Jasmine?" she asked incredulously. "There is nothing to it, Rita. I will try and help you as best as I can. Yu can stay home with Candice an still put food on yu table." She jumped up and said, "Only if Miguel wasn't so selfish. Im see wha happen to im olda bredda, an im still nuh willing fi help me. Frank alone caan do everything. A onle one pickney alone mi av wid im, Jasmine." "I know," I replied. "He is a good man, but Rita, mi sey yu caan dwell pon di past, yu onle haffi look to di future. Dat a wha mi do."

One year later I was a millionaire, with the ability to help not only my family but those around me. I expanded my brother Raphael's business, and later purchased and remodelled his house since he was determined not to move out of the area. "A Jones Town mi born an grow, an mi pickney dem also, but yu can leave, Jasmine," he said hugging me, "Mi always know yu doan belong dung ya so inna di firs place. Mi a king ya so, di old respec mi, an di youth dem rate mi." He was right, as from I was a little girl, everyone loved Raphael. I vowed not to leave him out and he only pinched me on the cheek. "Between di two a wi, Jasmine," he said, "Wi can mek a difference. No matta wey wi dey inna Jamaica, a nuff likkle yout pu dung di gun afta reasoning wid mi." I set up an education fund for my niece and nephews and gave it to him. "Raphael," I said, "I made a promise to help yu wen yu rescued mi fram our madda's wrath, an mi glad mi live to fulfil it."

Our mother was a different story. I found her selling Downtown and told her I could now help her but she refused and continued selling. Deep down inside I knew she wasn't a bad woman but she was just full of pride. "No sorry fi mi, Jasmine. Look how long yu no talk to mi, an now yu come a boast." I tried to explain but she flatly refused. "A yu disregard mi, so mi gi yu wey yu want, but mi neva stop loving yu cause a yu a mi madda." It took me three months, a mild stroke, and arthritis, for her to agree to accept my help and I gave her a monthly allowance for the rest of her life.

Surprisingly, it took nine months after winning the Lotto before Tony found out, and to this day I don't know how he did, but he showed up one evening at my gate demanding to see his daughters. "A now yu rememba dem?" I asked angrily. "A nuh dem alone mi memba, mi memba yu too," he answered smiling at me. "Alex has neva seen yu, how yu feel as a man? Shi is three years old now." "Give mi a chance, Jasmine," he interrupted, "Mi can mek it up to dem, please." Over the years I had known him, I had never seen him cry until then but I decided to hold my ground and not let him into my home. I vowed to myself, "The only man I'll take in my house, is my future husband." When I informed him of my decision, he stared me in the eyes and asked innocently, "Mi nuh can still be dat, Jasmine? Mi did tink dat life wud be greener on di odda side, but mi realise is not. Mi waan a second chance wid yu." I could not help myself and started to laugh uncontrollably. "Doan laugh," he said giving me the puppy look he always did to make me weak ova the years. "Pearl an I only married on paper, an because shi give mi a son, nuttin more, nuttin less. A yu mi love. All mi a do is drive taxi to support dem. Nuh matta wey mi do fi ar, Jasmine, she neva satisfy. Unlike yu, mi wuk twelve or fifteen hours outa di day, an wen mi go home, mi still feel miserable. Yu know, Jasmine, yu almos neva see mi again. Gunmen tek mi wey eight weeks ago. Dem carry mi inna bush an rob mi. Mi haffi beg like dawg fi mi life. Even mi clothes dem gone wid. An yu know mi always av a weak spot fi yu fram di moment wi meet." He put his hand on my leg and began massaging it. I was weak to him I had to admit to myself but I could not give in, not just for my sake, but also for my girls. The last thing they needed was a man to walk in and out of their lives. I got the strength to push him off. "Tony," I said, " all mi a ask is fi yu to be there fi yu daughters, nuttin more nuttin less. As fi mi an yu, it ova. Wey yu do to mi, Tony, di nex man inna mi life a mus God Himself drap im dey."

When he realized I wasn't giving in, he began walking away. I shouted after him, "Yu don't want to see your daughters?" but he did not respond, just continued walking. I watched as he turned the corner, then I sat down as the rain began and cried for the first time in a long while. I did not tell the girls their father came by, as it is best they do not know the type of man he is.

Sophia and I opened a hairdressing and barber shop together, where we trained the young men and women in the Jones Town area in these skills. "At least with a skill they can survive," I told her one afternoon in the shop. Each time a young person fell by the wayside it breaks my heart, as we know poverty breeds poverty. I tried to do my best for the next year, but it was hard on me alone. It was not easy to ask corporate Jamaica to help, but I was determined not to give up. My older brother, Barry, who was still in prison also found out about my wealth. One evening, Sophia and I were at our business place when a young man came in. He was dressed in full black, his head was covered with a hoodie, he sported a beard, and had a scar on his face. "A yu name Jasmine?" he asked. "Wey yu want?" I asked in a stern voice. "Barry sey money fi run di organization need help." "Yu mean di gang?" I asked. "Mi mean di family," he replied lifting his shirt to show his gun. "Yu av twenty-four hours. Barry sey a mi fi collect it." "Mi nuh owe Barry nuh obligation. Im mek im choice, an a im haffi go live wid it," I shouted at him. "Unoo haffi go kill mi. A so it a go, but mi nah give in." He took out the weapon and pointed it at me clicking it. There was silence all around. "Twenty-four hours," he repeated, and walked out the door. Before closing it he turned around, "Yu av balls," he said, "yu a really Barry sista. But memba mi tell yu if im nuh willing fi steer yu, mi nuh steer yu." When the door closed behind him, the shop was like a bee hive. Everyone whispering, moving around, some even crying. "Mi nah mek dem deter mi," I said loudly but Sophia interjected, "Yu av yu kids dem fi live for, Jasmine. Fram yu a likkle pickney mi know yu av strong determination, but memba yu is a madda now."

We closed the business early and talked all

night. "At least no one know wey yu live, Jasmine," she said, "an mi nah talk." I squeezed her hand. "But if dem caan touch mi dem wi get to yu." This is when we came up with a plan. Three months before, I had purchased a five acre farm in the country for Steve to run. We reserved an acre of the property to re-establish the business and to add a boarding facility for those from the inner city who wish to come. Sophia and her family will move there to be in charge of it. I was determined not to go back to my area.

Six months later, I startled out of my sleep at the sound of the telephone. Out of breath, I answered. Danielle ran into my room. Danielle had so matured through the years that now at the age of fifteen, she could easily pass for eighteen or nineteen years old. "Mommy," she shouted jumping into my bed shaking like a leaf, "Uncle Raphael, they killed him!" Jumping up I began screaming, and the room started to spin. It was half an hour later I opened my eyes to see my girls sitting around me staring into my face. "How did you know?" I asked Danielle. "It was grandma on the phone. She told me."

It was 3:00 a.m. in the morning. I drove like a madwoman, disregarding all traffic signs and bursting through red lights. I could hear a police siren behind me, but I continued speeding saying to myself, "Yu could have wings like di devil, yu won't catch mi." After being chased for two miles, I turned off at Ants Lane, and saw when the lights from the siren passed by. There are some places in Jamaica Police wouldn't dare go at certain times of the night.

When I arrived at the road where my mother lives, she was lying in the middle of the street crying uncontrollably with her friends trying to console her. "Mama," I shouted, but she would not acknowledge me. It took five strong men to restrain her so that she would not harm herself. They finally got her into the house.

I started crying again when Shawn came and hugged me. We grew up together, and just to have him at that moment made me feel much better. "Come with me," he whispered in my ear, leading me into a narrow lane behind my mother's house. It was so narrow he had to walk in front of me using his flashlight to guide my way from the rubble and old zinc in the walkway. "Do not allow anyone to see you, Jasmine. A nuff people a swear afta yu, sey yu get rich an swish, and wey dem wudda do yu if dem catch yu." Holding my head down, I entered his room. He turned off his flashlight as the moonlight was enough. "What happen to mi bredda?" I whispered, beginning to cry again. Rubbing my shoulder he said, "It was Barry. Even though he was in prison for the past fifteen years, he was still making our lives a living hell. Shawn continued. "Last week, Barry an annoda man got into a fight. During di squabble, Barry stabbed him to death. The man was a memba of a gang called the Rival gang. They decided to take revenge, and one of dem come an killed Raphael. He was in his shop as usual. He normally closed at ten but because there was a dance in the area, he decided to remain open. Jasmine, it was like a movie. Dem couldn't come through di crowd so dem decide to tek di gully. Wen wi hear di shots, everyone was flat on di groun, and people was running in all directions fi safety. I hear it was three of dem. Dem mek dere escape ova Mas Charlie. Wen it was all ova, we found Raphael behind di shop. He was peeing wen dem killed him." He squeezed my hand reassuring me, "Mi nuh tink im suffa, Jasmine, mi believe im go instantly. About ten minutes before yu came dem remove him body. Surprisingly enough, di Police removed him body quickly. Dem doan want to start no riot."

Raphael's death took a toll on my Mother. She spent the next two weeks in hospital while we made the funeral arrangements. After the funeral, I convinced his baby Mother Keisha to move to the country with the kids. I vowed to myself never to mention Barry's name again. Six months later, Sophia told me she received a letter from the prison officials stating that they found him in the bathroom dead. No one claimed his body, so the Government buried him.

With my family's migration to the country, I ensured that my kids spent holiday's with them. I encouraged them to stick together and never forget where we are coming from. As time passed, the kids fit into our new environment more than I did. The first time I was invited to a dinner party by Mrs. Thomas, the evening went from bad to worse. First, I bought a dress for Five Thousand dollars, which turned out to be the wrong outfit for the occasion. From the moment I entered Mrs. Thomas' home, everyone began staring at me as if I was from a different planet. It took me a few moments to realize that my attire was different from theirs. I wanted to leave, but she held my hand greeting me so warmly. "Come, Jasmine," she said, introducing me to everyone. As the evening progressed, I began to feel more comfortable, until it was time for dinner. She seated me beside her to reassure me she was there, even though we had not known each other a long time. In past conversations, I found out she was born in Britain of Jamaican parents. Her father worked at the railway, and her mother was a domestic helper, but they educated her and her sister, and now she is a retired teacher, living with her husband James here in Jamaica. All three of their children, two boys and a girl, live in England. One day while we were having lunch she told me, "It is so refreshing to wake up to the sounds of birds in the morning, and the weather is doing wonders for James' arthritis." I was enjoying the dinner so much I did not realize I had the fish head in my mouth sucking it. All eyes were on me and I felt embarrassed, so I asked to be excused.

I sat outside in the garden staring at the stars, and before long Mrs. Thomas joined me. "You have a beautiful garden," I told her. "I always loved a well-kept garden since I was a child. I will give you a start," she said smiling at me. "I realized, Jasmine, you felt uncomfortable all night, but you should not allow anyone to make you feel that way." "Most of the people here do not know me. If I did not have money or know someone who know someone, they would not be here. In England we had to deal with racism, in Jamaica it is class segregation. But if you educate your children, they will not have to go through it."

That was three years ago. Now Danielle is in Law School at UWI (University of the West Indies). The day she collected her acceptance letter was the happiest day in our life. She is now the first member of my family to be accepted in University. I am now contemplating going to evening classes so my girls will be proud of me.

Before I knew it, I realized that I had two girls now at university. With the help of Mrs. Thomas, Toni-Ann was now in London studying as a first year pre-medical student. It was hard letting my girls go but I knew for their benefit and my sake I had to. This is when I realized in order to keep up with them I would have to learn more. I started to attend evening class specializing in computers. As I said, it's the age of technology. Learning the basics, I started communicating with Toni-Ann which gave me peace of mind. Each time I saw her face on the screen made me love her more and more. My babies are growing up so fast. My heart leaps just to know that it wasn't long ago I was changing their diapers, holding their hands and walking them to school, feeding them, wiping their face, comforting them when they were hurt, kissing them when they needed it, but spanking them with discipline and love. Alexis was having a difficult time also letting go of her sisters. But I did not know it until one afternoon I was at home crocheting, when I got a call from her Principal, asking me to come there immediately.

Angels School for Girls in St Andrew was one of the best prep schools around. With my business doing well, I could afford to hire people, while finding time for them.

When I arrived in the principals' office, he introduced me to a young man by the name of Mr. Brown. "This is Alex's teacher," he said. "Well, where is Mrs. Grant?" I asked concernedly. "She is now on maternity leave," the principal said. "We sent a letter two weeks ago with each student, informing their parents of the change."

"Alex did not give me," I said. "That's understandable, most kids are neglectful," he said, butting in. "Repeat your name?" I asked. "Mr. Brown. Miss White, I think we need to talk about Alex. Today she slapped a student in her face."

"She's not really a violent child," I said reassuringly, "Her two sisters are now at University, and they are very close. Talking to them by phone and e-mail is not enough. Even though her older sister Danielle is just at the

University of the West Indies, she prefers to stay on campus because she said studying would be easier for her."

"What did the young miss do to cause Alex to hurt her?" I asked. "She took her pencil and broke it in two, but that's not the point. Alex should not have hit the child, she should have come to me."

"I know," I said. "Because this is her first offence, we will not suspend her, but she is on notice. Maybe you need to get her to talk to you more about her sisters." "I will try," I responded.

"Come to the cafeteria with me," Mr. Brown said, "and we will talk more." When he walked slowly ahead, somehow I felt I knew him. Even though we had never met before, his face was familiar to me .

Sitting in front of him, he ordered two burgers with fries and Coke. Then it hit me suddenly, he looked just like my brother Raphael. "Do you know you look like my brother Raphael?" I blurted out, as I could not hold it back.

"Really?" he asked. "Where are you from?"

"Rema," I replied. "Originally."

His mouth dropped open. "No way! You don't

seem like you're from Rema."

"Most people don't think that, but I was born and grew there. My brother and I came from a poor family. It was just a couple years ago my finances changed."

"Tell me something, " he asked, "Does Alex and her father communicate?"

This question broke my heart in many ways, and more than he knew. "Alex does not have a relationship with her father, " I said, "We broke up when she was just a baby."

"I see. Maybe it's not just her sisters, maybe she needs to have some form of contact with her father."

"I tried to get in touch with him a few times over the years," I said. "I know he got my message, but he chose not to get back in touch with me."

"Why not? It's his child," he said. "Are all three girls by the same father?"

"Yes," I replied, giving him a look that made him wish he hadn't asked. "Look Mr. Brown," I said leaning over to him, "most men in Jamaica, if you're not intimately involved with them, they do not want to have a relationship with their kids, as far as Tony their father is concerned, if it is not all of us, it is none. It is his choice, not mine."

"I apologise Miss White," he continued. "I do not want to seem like I'm getting into your business, I'm just curious. Alex is such a bright young miss, how old is she now?"
"She's your student, don't you know?"
"I've only been here for two weeks," he said. "I have not gotten a chance to know all of my students, but I suspect she's 13."
"Yes, you're right."
"This is the age," he continued, "that most girls and boys need a father."
"Do you have children?" I asked him.
"Yes, two boys," he replied.
"Are you from Kingston?"
"Why do you ask?" he said, looking straight at me.
"Well, if you know Kingston, especially in the inner city, fathers are few and far between. It is like winning the Lottery, if they are at home with you."
"I was born in Kingston, but raised in Clarendon."
This peaked my interest.
"Are both of your parents alive?" I asked out of curiosity

"My father died a year ago, but my mother is still alive."

"As I said, you look just like my brother Raphael, who is now deceased. If I did not know better, I would say you guys are twins."

"Well," he said after a long pause, "I was adopted when I was two years old." My heart dropped along with my mouth. "Tell me something Mr. Brown," I asked, "is your first name Courtney?"

"Yes." My food fell to the ground.

"Are you all right, Miss White?" he said concernedly, jumping up.

"I had a brother by that name, who was adopted."

"Really?" he said.

"My mother is Kitty White." I could see that he recognized something.

"Well unfortunately, Miss White, it's not my mother."

For the next few weeks I thought about it, but I did not want to pry into his business so I left it alone. As far as I was concerned if he is not willing to recognize our mother, then he is not my brother.

I began speaking with Alex more and more,

trying to find out what is going on in her life. One afternoon, we were at home when she came to lie beside me on the bed. "Tell me something sweetheart, do you miss your father?"

"How can I miss what I don't have?" she asked. A sharp pain ran through my pit of my stomach. She was right. She had only seen a picture of Tony. At least her sisters knew him. Over the years both girls tried to call and contact him. Each time they found a number and got in touch, he changed it. Toni-Ann was his heartbeat, and if he could turn his back on her, he could do it to anyone.

"I'm sorry." I said rubbing her cheek as she climbed over.

"Mom," she said do not feel guilty. It is his choice; he should be the one to live with the consequences. He rejected us not we him."

"I know," I said, "but I still feel bad."

"Maybe ....if I....."

"No". She butted in, "Do what? Stay with a man who did not love and respect you?"

She was just a teenager but she was so mature. We talked for hours that evening until she fell asleep where she was. It was the phone that woke me up. It was my mother on the line. "Talk to him nuh?" she said greeting me. "Talk to who?"

"Steve, your brother. You know say he dis Kerry Ann an a go to America tomorrow!"

"What?" I shouted, jumping up. This woke Alex. "I'm sorry", I said. "Sorry about what?"

"Not you, Mamma," I replied.

"Yes! Him claim there's nothing left inna farming again and all him a do is plant an a work han to mout. Im meet a ooman two months ago which wi neva know bout. Shi help him to get a passport an visa, dem call it fiancé visa; im a go ova to marry har. Kerry Ann is heartbroken along wid di two boys. Wey im dey now, God He knows. Wen wi fine out yestiday im moved out of di house! Wha wi a go do Jasmine?"

"I will try to call him," I said. "Mi a beg yu, talk some sense inna him. Him a di only boy I have left." I hung up and tried his number without success. The phone rang straight into voicemail and I left a message. I called back the next morning bright and early, but I heard he never went back there. "Mom, I called the airport after hanging up, but they wouldn't divulge any information, even when I gave them his name, date of birth, and explained that he's my brother."

The next time I heard about him it would be something I didn't want to hear.

Two weeks passed, and I was invited to a party at the school with the kids. Mr. Brown walked over to me. "It's nice to see you again, Ms. White."

"Same here," I said not wanting to look him in the eyes. But after interacting for a few minutes with other parents and teachers, I went back over to him. "Tell me something Courtney," I said, not wanting to be formal again. "I have a feeling that you recognize my mother's name, and I have a feeling that you're more than who you say you are."

"What do you want from me, Ms. White?" he said grumbling. "Are you my brother?" I asked, blurting it out. He turned his back and decided to go off, but I held onto his shoulder. "Just tell me the truth. I don't want anything from you, and I would never want anything from you, I just want to know."

Finally after a long pause he said, "Only on paper. I've never known your family, and I don't intend to know your family."

"So you do not feel that there is any

connection to us even though you're teaching your niece for the past few weeks?"

"Please do not tell Alex," he said. "Don't worry. I will never tell her that her uncle is teaching her. I would never want my child to feel rejection, as she has too much in her life already, and as for me, you will never hear another word about it." And with that I walked away.

Two months passed when one afternoon I got a telephone call from him. "Jasmine," he said.

"Well!" I said, "It's no longer Miss White!"

"I apologize. That evening I did not want to hurt your feelings. I have too much emotion welling up inside of me."

"Me too," I said. "Can we meet?"

"For what, Mister Brown? The only reason I want to meet you, is if it's regarding my child."

" I'm sorry," he said, "I want to know you more."

"What about my mother?" After a long pause he said, "She's not on my agenda."

"Tell you what, Courtney, if my mother, my sisters, my children, my nieces and nephews, are not on your agenda, I am not also on it."

And with that I hung up the phone. To be fair to him, I was so surprised that my child's grade was very high at the end of the semester. The principal informed me that Mr. Brown wouldn't be coming back to the school as Ms. Grant is now off maternity leave. That was the last I heard of Courtney Brown for the rest of my days. I never regretted it. As far as I was concerned, he was not the only one being hurt. My mother said it was poverty why she gave him away and nothing more. I see now that she wasn't that bad. She had a good heart. She would work us to death, but she loved us. She would climb the mountain for us, she would walk on sea, she would do anything just to make us survive. For years I've been bitter about her and growing up and having children of my own, I will never do what she did but I can understand.

A year passed before we knew what happened to Steve. My mother received a letter and showed it to me when I visited the country. When he went to the States, he and the lady got married. In order to support her, he decided to go into what he knew best, ganja selling. Unfortunately for him, he got caught with not only drugs, but with an illegal firearm and got twenty-five years in jail. When he was in prison he wrote his new wife, but she turned her back on him. He cannot help her any more, so he is no longer important to her. Kerry Ann who has his two boys, now has a new man. She moved out of the family house as she cannot get along with my mother. I do not think my mother hates her, but she could not bear the thought of not having Steve there and another man coming and going as he liked.

I did my very best to support my nephews. I invited them to my home every holiday and made every effort to get to know them better. They are little boys now, but by the time he comes out they will be men, and maybe have kids of their own. It made me realize the importance of family. Even though they know their father is now in jail, and by the time he comes out they will be men, and maybe have kids of their own, but they are still blood.

Karen called me one afternoon asking for some help financially for her daughter. I gave it to her, but she wanted more and more. I had to put a stop to it. So one day when we met, I asked her point-blank what she wanted from me, "What do you mean by that?" she asked.

"Karen you know from when I was a child we do not see eye to eye. You verbally and physically abused me. I will help you financially, but enough is enough."

"And you claim that you're Christian," she began. "No, Karen, do not bring Christianity into this, because you do not seem like a Christian person to me. You cheat on your husband, you defile your matrimonial bedroom but at the same time you're singing in the choir and being a deaconess in church. You claim that you walk on holy ground but you're one of the biggest hypocrites I know." The only thing she said was, "I knew you hated me."

"I don't," I said. "Yes, you do!" she said getting angry. I stood up showing her my full stature. "When I was five or six years old," I said, staring down in her face, "You could do it, but no more. Even though you are fifteen years older than I am, I am taller and bigger than you. Now you sit down," I said pushing her ass back on the seat, "and you are going to listen to me Karen." When I was finished with her, she cried like a baby. I took all of the emotions that were burning up inside of me all these years, and I let her have it all. I told her from Genesis to Revelation all the things she said and did that hurt me, hurt our mother, our sister, and even hurt our brother Rafael. From that day forward she did not come around me. I only sent her monthly income to her account to help my niece.

When she finally composed herself enough, she got up and walked out of the restaurant. I leaned back on my chair and composed myself. Taking a deep breath, "Yes," I said to myself, "Family is important but if they can use and abuse you, you have to let them go." At that moment, my cell phone rang, and Danielle was on the line. Hearing from her sent a sharp trigger through my blood.

"Mom" she began. "I have the greatest news!"

"What?"

" I met a guy!". Within three hours, she was at my home telling me all about him.

"The party was a great blast," she began, "but it was hot. Feeling nauseous, I opened my blouse, walking over to the bar to have a drink. "Hold on a minute," I interrupted her. "Don't worry, mom, it was orange juice."

"Continue," I said. I could not believe that my baby has become a woman now, staring at her across from me on the couch. "Having the drink," she continued, "...did not help. My head began to throb more than before, with so much people crowded in one environment. I guess the coordinator wanted all of us to get to know each other."

"All of us?"

" It was a party for the dorm."

"OK!" I said. "Then I saw him from across the room, dressed in full black staring at me. He looked like a dark Knight, Mom," she said smiling. "Slowly he walked through the crowd. When he came close enough, he said, "You should drink something stronger."

"I do not drink," I replied. "Good girl," he said in a soft voice. "Excuse me?" I replied, getting defensive. "I'm not a girl, I'm twenty-two years old."

"I can see that," he replied looking me over from top to bottom. I thought that he was so obnoxious, I walked past him and went outside. Taking in a deep breath in the night air I began to feel a little better. I looked up and stared at the stars. A slight drizzle began but I did not care. I sat down and began to reflect on my life."

"And what were you reflecting on?" I asked her.

"Oh, our life in Jones Town, and Daddy, Shirley, and by the way is she still coming to work here?"

"Of course," I said, reassuring her. I could see the concerned look on Danielle's face. "The day when she's not working," I said, "...is the day that she no longer exists. Shirley is a strong woman, she will work with us always."

"Where is she now?" Danielle jumped up looking around. It's been a while since Shirley had seen her. She loves the girls, and literally cries like a baby each time one of them goes away. "She's down by Jones Town for the weekend."

"You let her go?" Danielle said, out of concern. "She's a big woman," I said. "She has her freedom and choice. Anytime she wants to go, she has a room down there and all her furniture. I asked her a thousand times if she wanted to live with us, and she declined every time."

"Continue your story Danielle," I said.

"Well, before I realized it, he was sitting beside me."

"What's your name?" he asked. "Well, it's none of your business," I told him. "Well, none of your business, I'm John Kay." Without even asking, he grabbed my hand and held it. "Pleased to meet you." I drew it away. "So you're a second year student here?" he asked. "Yes." "And what are you studying?" "Law." "I'm Economics and Business. I want to own my own company one-day." "Good for you," I replied.

I closed my eyes and took a deep breath, once again, trying to engage with the salubrious atmosphere. The once faint drizzle soon took on a more blustery character. He said, "You can go back in." "When I leave I'm going straight to my bed." But when I opened my eyes a few minutes later he was still there staring at me. "What are you doing here?" I asked him. "Waiting on you."

"Look, John Kay," I said, "I'm not interested in either you or the conversation at this moment."

"You're a second-year student?"

"Yes, yes, please go away." I insisted. But ignoring me he continued like I wasn't even there "You know I'm from a rural community in St. Elizabeth called Green Acres. There you can either grow up to be a farmer, a fisherman, a wood maker, a furniture maker, a dressmaker or a barber. If you're lucky you can have either one or two of those skills. I knew by the time I was five that I wanted to leave that place and I worked hard for it."

"Five?" I asked. "Of course. By that age I was reading far above my age, and by the time I was ten I was accepted at Munro College. I left high school when I was 16."

"Impressive," I said mocking him, but he did not notice. "As a matter of fact, I'm doing my masters now in both Econ and Business. By the time I'm twenty-five, I want to complete my doctorate."

"And why are you telling me this?"

"I'm telling you this, Young Miss," He said, "Because I'm the man who knows what he wants out of life, and anything I want I normally get. I got up, straightened my dress and began walking away, but somehow I could feel his eyes piercing my body like a laser. That night I slept comfortably – much better than I had in the last two weeks. "And why haven't you slept?" I asked out of concern. "Mom don't worry, it's just the pressure of studying and working."

" Danielle," I said getting up, walking over to her and sitting down, "I told you that I will support you as long as you want."

"I know, but I want to work and study at the same time. I want to feel independent."

"But you can, with my support."

"Mom, we have argued about this a hundred times." She was right. Danielle was the type of girl who sought a summer job every year since the age of sixteen. She spent every summer working at a supermarket or wholesale. She was very independent, and I knew some of her independence was because of her father's rejection. She felt that she had to be on her own. It breaks my heart to know what Tony has done to her.

She saw the distressed look on my face and hugged me. "Don't worry Mom," she said reassuringly. The resemblance between myself and Danielle is remarkable. By the time

Danielle was fifteen people would mistake us for sisters. "I'm blessed," I thought. "Continue", I asked her with a gentle voice. "Well, the next morning I got up and to my surprise I was late for class. Hurrying, I ran right across campus to my classroom. Right at that door, guess who I ran into?"

"John Kay?" "Exactly! We bumped into each other so hard all of my books fell out of my hand. My instinct took over and I bent over at the same time as him and our heads hit. "Why are you stalking me?" I shouted out. "Stalking you?" he asked getting back up to allow him to pick up the books since he was the one that scattered them I realized he wasn't alone. A young beautiful dark-skinned girl was standing beside him. Putting the books in my hand he said, "I was just escorting my cousin to her classroom. But if stalking you is on my agenda I would gladly do it."

After this incident with John Kay, it was downhill all the way. It amounted to one of those days when you should never have gotten out of bed in the first place. To start things off, a young man stepped on my foot, stripping the leather off my shoes. Then, another young man spilled his drinks all over me. By mid-afternoon I had so many accidents that I just wanted to crawl right back into my bed. Later that afternoon, I went to the cafeteria for lunch. As I enjoyed my lunch, looking up briefly there he was. "Danielle Champagne." he said, "This is a very unusual name."

"How do you know it?"   "I have my ways." "And what ways are those" I asked. He went in his pocket and took out my ID, shaking it in front me. I was so angry I grabbed after it, but he withdrew his hand quickly. "Patience is a virtue," he said. "Are you going to invite me to lunch soon?"   "Leave me alone!" I shouted at him, getting more and more frustrated. "Danielle," he said in a calm voice smiling, "can I invite you to lunch?"   "I already have it, are you blind?" I told him. "Dinner?"   "No!" "Marriage and two kids?" "No, no!" I got up and moved to another table but like the plague he joined me. "Look John Kay," I said this time more sternly, "I'm not interested in your conversation, you, to be your friend, to be your acquaintance. I am not interested." But when I turned around, I realized the whole cafeteria eyes were on us. Feeling ashamed, I sat down out of frustration, but he just smiled. "As I told you before, Danielle, I'm not a bad guy. Please take the time to know me." And with this he stood up and walked away. I felt bad, embarrassing both him and myself, but at least he was gone, I thought to myself. But by the evening I was at my dorm, searching through my bag and realized my key was nowhere in sight. "This day cannot be over fast enough," I said. "Lose something?" I heard a voice asking from behind. When I turned around it was him. "Now I know for sure," I said to him, "you are a stalker." I need help to get rid of you. He came closer and put the key in the door. "If you weren't...."

"Don't you dare," I replied grabbing my belongings and heading towards the door.

I tried to snatch it out of his hand without success. When he opened the door I could never say another word but thanks. Walking in, I began closing the door behind me but he put his foot in the door way. "Are you not inviting me in?"

"What did I ever do in my lifetime?" I asked. "What do you mean?" "I must've done something awful to release the devil on me."

He laughed. He came in and sat down taking up one of my books. "Identity Crisis in a Complex Society," he read the title. "Well that sums you up pretty well," he said slamming it back on the table. "Please go," I asked. I actually pleaded and begged him, but his eyes roamed all over. "Is this your family?" he asked, getting up. "Your mother, she's very beautiful."

"And how do you know she's my mother?" "Look at you," he said smiling at me. Then he took up another book. "Econ. Up my alley. How well are you doing in this class?"

"To be honest with you." I finally said "I'm not doing so well. I failed it and have to take it all over again. "Well, Danielle Champagne," he said, "I can help you with that." How about me tutoring you."

"Well he's brave!" I interrupted her. "I thought so too. I could not pass up the opportunity. Mom, I decided to take him up on his offer since he wouldn't leave me alone. That was three weeks ago,"

"And why haven't I heard about him before?" "Mom, as I said I wasn't interested." "And are you now Danielle?"

"To be honest with you, I'm beginning to like

him very much Mom."
"What changed?"
"John Kay has a way of winning you over. When you meet him you will know, down right, Mom. He has this way of getting even his enemy to admire him whether for his boldness, his finesse, or his downright cockiness. Two nights ago we were studying when he said, "Look Danielle, I'm pretty much a straightforward guy. As I told you what you see is what you get and I told you from that night at the party that I like you. Please get to know me more than just a tutor." "We are having our first date tonight mom."

Tears ran down my cheek. Why are you crying?" Danielle asked out of concern. "I cannot believe it," I said, "It's just the other day I was feeding you and changing your diaper, now you come home to tell me you're going out on a date with a guy." Time waits on no one you always taught us girls that." "I wish it did for me," she smiled. Later that night I stood on my porch watching my first born heading out for her date.

During dinner, John Kay asked Danielle, "Why

were you so insistent on me leaving your room that night? Is it the fact that it was me?" "Haven't you noticed," she said, "that it's a female dorm?" So is it just because it was a female dorm or is it that you did not want me or any other guy there". "I did not want you there, John Kay," she said. "Okay, that hurt," he replied, "I thought I was special." "Only in the mirror," she replied.

They dated for three months before Danielle told me one afternoon while we were at the beach. "Mom I have something to tell you." "What?" I asked. "I think I'm in love."
I bent down slowly, removing some sand from the beach. I dotingly and carefully deposited these sheer granules of sand back to the even larger body of sand which they came from. So simple it was to observe, how the tide comes in and takes it out to sea. "Mom," she said holding my shoulder reassuring me with a squeeze. "He is great, he's smart handsome lovable. He has a way of getting under your skin."
I got to know John Kay very well over the last few months, as he would stop by often to have dinner with us. He seemed arrogant at first,

but as I got to know him better, I recognized that there was some metal in his character. Just like myself, Mr. Kay seemed to recognize that for one to be successful in life one must feel confident and exude confidence in order to have people feel confidence in you.

As he said, "This is a 'cut throat' business - the marketing. In order for me to succeed I have to make my client feel confident me." "Even when you do not know bull?" I asked him one afternoon. "Even when I do not know bull, Miss," he said. "Call me Jasmine." "Okay." As he said "Marketing is a 'cut throat' business. In order for me to succeed in myself Miss, I have to make my client feel confident in my abilities, even when I don't feel as confident."

For the next two weeks they were inseparable. Toni-Ann would complain that she could not get ahold of Danielle because she was always with John Kay. "Every time I call her," she said, "Mom, she's always with this guy John Kay. Do you know him? Do you know his background?" "Slow down, Toni-Ann. I am neither a prosecutor nor an investigator. I know as much as he has disclosed." "But you need to find out about his family, Mom" she would say "You need to know exactly how they live." "I am not one," I told my child, "...to judge people from their background given where I was coming from." "Mom, it's not where you're coming from," Toni-Ann said, "...but it's where you're going. Often the past can define and determine who you are in the present."

Although I felt that John Kay was an appropriate boyfriend for Danielle, Toni-Ann's words did elicit a tinge of concern in me that indeed I did not know as much about John as I should have. Some of these concerns were allayed in about a month when he introduced me to his mother, Hyacinth. Hyacinth seemed like a very respectable and loving woman. She told me she was a dressmaker from the age of fifteen, and by the time she was twenty, married their father William, and became pregnant with their first child. She had three girls before John. She wanted to stop, but her husband convinced her that they should try for another because he always wanted a son. "Jasmine," she said, "And John Kay is the apple of our eyes."

A few months later my fears were re-ignited when I noticed that Danielle's grades started to slip. I decided to take matters into my own hands, and invited them to lunch one afternoon. When I explained my concern to them he reassured me that he would never jeopardize Danielle's future, and they would limit their interaction for the time being. I told him, my daughter is twenty-two and I know she will have a boyfriend, but I do not wish this to become the centre of her life to the detriment of other equally important aspects of her life. He concurred. "We are young Jasmine," he said, "And in love but I know that future is coming for us to get married one day." The chicken that Danielle was eating fell on the ground when he made that statement. After a few months, Danielle's grades began to pick up, so my fear subsided. The year passed and John Kay graduated. He got a job as a marketing manager at Grace Kennedy. One afternoon out of the blue, he invited me to see him. I was puzzled and confused, but I decided to attend. "Jasmine," he said, "you know how I feel about Danielle. I want your permission to marry her when she graduates next year." "Do not ask her at this moment," I said. "I do not want her to think of anything apart from studying. But within a flash the year passed. He approached me again to ask for permission. John Kay did not seem like the type of guy who would hurt my child, so I said, "Yes." Danielle often said that he is not really a good saver, often spending his money on clothes and changing his cars, but I told him that Danielle needs a husband that will stand by her no matter what.

On the night of her graduation ball, Danielle looked so beautiful; dressed in a white silk gown with diamond threads all around it, and the diamond bracelet and necklace to match which I bought her as a graduation gift. I could tell that most of her friends envied her. To them Danielle and John Kay seemed to be the perfect couple. They interacted with all of their friends throughout the night, but decided to save the last dance for themselves. After it was through, John Kay went down on one knee, and in front of everyone proposed to Danielle. With tears running down her cheek she said, "Yes," as he slipped the ring on her finger.

The following week Danielle got a job at J&J International Law Firm in New Kingston as a junior lawyer. The new job involved dealing with litigation and tax fraud. Although I gave John the go-ahead to propose, I suppose ideally I felt that I would have preferred Danielle have more experience of the outside world after completing her studies before marriage. One day, while making the wedding arrangements I asked them "Why not wait a year or two before marriage". "Why wait, Mom? Danielle replied, "We are so much in love, we have been dating for almost two years, John Kay wants us to get married right away and I agree." "Are you sure about this Danielle?" I asked lovingly, squeezing her hand. "I am sure as the sun shines above and the breeze blows in my face, that he is the man for me, Mom,"

A month before the wedding, Danielle was driving home late one night and fell asleep at the wheel. When she regained consciousness, she was in the hospital. "Help me," I heard my baby girl crying out. I rushed over from the chair to her, holding her hand and squeezing it. "It's okay, Danielle, it's Mommy, I'm here." I said reassuringly. "What's wrong, what's going on?" "You're in the hospital, baby," I said. "Hospital," she said groggily, "For what?" "You've been in an accident," I said. She was so confused she started to scream, and I had to call the nurse to give her a sedative to put her back to sleep. Five hours later, Danielle woke up again, and I was there, never leaving her side for a moment. Each time she groaned in her sleep my heart melted. I felt it right through my body. They said that there is no limit on a mother's love, and I never thought I could feel so much pain at that time like I was feeling in that moment. When she woke up again she asked, "Mom?" "I'm here," I said still holding her hand not wanting to let it go. "What happened to me?" she asked. "Two nights ago, you ran a red light, Danielle, you went under a truck, it's the Grace of God that you are still with us, Baby," but I could never tell her the truth. "Why my head hurts so much?" I began to cry when Alexis came in and held me. "Sis," she said "it's OK, you will be all right."

Over the years Alex has grown up so beautifully. She is now studying accounting at the University. The way Alexis matured over the years, often I swear she was the mother and me the child. She squeezed her sister's hand gently. "What happened?" Danielle broke the silence in the room. I could not bear it. I started to cry so hard, but Alex took over. "You met in an accident, Big Sis." "Mom told me, but why my head hurts so much ? And this bandage? What is it doing over my face?"

"Honey, you underwent an operation," she said. "For what?" "For your facial damage, and..." "And...and what, Alex?" Danielle asked. "And your eyes," she said softly. "What's wrong with them?"

"Honey," Alex said, "you lost them." "Lost? Lost? What are you talking about Alex?" Danielle was getting irritable. This time I got the courage and went over, holding her other hand. "The windshield shattered and the splinters damaged your eyes. The doctor said there was nothing they could do. The splinters ruptured your retinas and so they had to take them out" "That means.....," Danielle said, but she couldn't finish it. "You guys are lying," she said finally. "No honey," I said, "Baby, you will never see again; at least not by sight." She started to scream. Alex held her sister and she cried and cried till she could not cry any more.

The next few days were difficult. Danielle stayed in her room, depressed. I got a social worker to come in to talk with her, but it takes two to talk. Danielle wasn't willing to talk to anyone, especially me. They say there are various stages of coping when tragedy strikes. First, I was angry, I was angry with myself for not being able to prevent my child from feeling hurt or pain. Then, I turned my anger towards God for allowing this situation to happen; then I grieved. I grieved for her future; I grieved for the loss of a precious gift, her sight. Then sitting on my porch that afternoon, I went into the stage of acceptance.

"Okay Jasmine," I told myself, "you couldn't prevent it from happening, but you can help her survive it, and with every breath within your body you will help her survive." Then I sat down resting my hand on my jaw. A turtle dove perched on the branch, then I saw him flitting to his nest. He had a family there also, I surmised to myself. The lizard that was nearby, made a hasty retreat down to the ground and through the grass. "My child will never see this again," I said to myself.

Lost in my own world, I did not see her until she was actually in front of me. When I looked up it was Mrs. Thomas. She sat down holding my hand. "It will be okay Jasmine." she said. "Danielle is a survivor, she's from you. Her world will not end, it's just beginning. Great things are ahead of her." I put my head in her lap and cried.

That evening, John Kay finally came by. "Where the hell were you?" I said to him angrily. "Please, Jasmine, I'm trying." "Trying like hell!" Getting bitter with each breath I took. He sat down on the couch. "I was working. I called her a few times but she won't talk to me." "You do not communicate with your fiancée over the phone, John Kay, you find your ass beside her." "Can I see her now?"
I hesitated for a while but as Danielle did not want to talk to anyone, I figured that if

anyone could get her to open up, it would be him. I was right. When I opened her bedroom door and he announced himself, she fell into his arms crying.

I was in the kitchen making tea when finally he came out. "Jasmine can we talk?"
Walking over, he sat on the chair in front of me. I took in a deep breath. I knew what was coming, but I still wanted to hear the words out loud. Rubbing his hands profusely, as if he was at the gallows and this was the only way he could plead for his life. "Speak, John Kay," I said in a soft voice. "I got a job in New York, Jasmine, and I am going to take it up."
"And what about Danielle?" I said, without raising my voice. "I need time. I have been placed in a new situation, I need time to cope, and adjust my life." "John Kay," I said, putting the cup on the table and walking over to him. He flinched, as if he thought I would hit him, but I only held his shoulder. "If anyone was going to cope and adjust their life, it should be my child. She is the one who has lost something here." He held down his head as if he was thinking about what else to say to me. "I love her honestly to God I do but

things have changed." "Changed?" I questioned finally releasing what he was trying to say. "I just need you and her to see this," he said pleading. "She needs time to adjust to her new life and I need time to see what the future holds for me." Sitting down in front of him, "John Kay, you said you loved her, but you are a heartless bastard. Within three weeks, my child has lost something precious to her, and now you. If you are willing to walk out of her life, do not walk back in." He got up, staring out the window for a few seconds, then finally turned around to face me. "I'm so sorry, Jasmine," and with this he was out the door and out of her life.

I went into her room and she was on the ground crying like a baby. Gathering Danielle into my arms I said, "If he was not willing to stay with you baby, for better or for worse, then he was not the man for you. You have not lost a great man."

For days Danielle wouldn't talk to me. When she did, I cried. "Mom," she said, "you were wrong, he was my life. Every day I woke up, I thanked God I was alive, but it wasn't for myself, I thanked God I was alive for him."

I drew her closer, squeezing her against me. She tried to fight without success. "Danielle," I said, "I did not raise you like this. A man should not be the centre of your being. You do not exist for him. You exist for yourself and God. Look what happened to me and your father. I survived without him and you can do the same." Later that night, I was in a deep sleep when I heard Alexis screaming. Jumping out of bed, I rushed toward the sound. When I entered Danielle's room, she was on the ground foaming from her mouth. "Mom", Alexis shouted, "It's this!" handing me her pain-killers. "She took it all, Mom, my God, she took it all!" Eight hours later I was in the hospital by her side when she woke up. "So, Danielle," I said, "you want to kill yourself? You did not hear anything I said to you earlier on?"

"You are my child and I love you so much". I cannot imagine my world without you in it Danielle," I said in a commanding voice. "Next time you choose to do such an act, please let me know so I can do it with you." "I don't want you to die," she said screaming, getting up out of bed. I pushed her back down. "You do not want me to die, yet you want to take your own life?" "You just don't understand, Mom," she said, getting back up once more, I pushed her back down, holding her this time. "Let me understand, Danielle, please let me understand ." Alexis was in the room pacing like a wild cat shaking her head, not talking to anyone. "I can't imagine my life depending on someone for the rest of it." Danielle said. I held her hand. "I carried you for nine months," I told her, "Gave birth to you, fed you, clothed you, I was with you when you were sick, wiping your nose - if you do not need me to depend on, then who else?" "Mom," she said in a whisper through the tears, "That isn't the point." "Then what is the point? What is the point," I said. "You are such a brilliant, beautiful young lady and you are willing to throw your life away because of what happened to you? Honey it's not worth it. You can achieve anything you want out of life. This is not the end for you baby." This time my emotion got the better of me and I started to cry. Somehow she held onto me and at this point Alexis came over. "Please, Danielle," she screamed, "Do not do that again. I can't....", but she could not finish her words, she just dropped on the bed and held her sister so closely.

"Danielle," I said. "Remember when I told you I was pregnant with Alex? You were just six years old. "Mommy," you cried, "I don't want another baby, I want a puppy." I reassured you that another sister would be better than a puppy. After your temper tantrum you fell on the ground, and finally gave in. When Alex was born, no one could touch her but you. Remember?" She smiled for the first time in weeks. "Yes, I remember. Actually, she did look like a puppy to me." "What?" Alex said tears drying up. "I didn't!" "Yes, you looked like a poodle dog, I remember!" With this, all of us hugged each other.

Shirley came to see her early that morning bringing breakfast. "Mi know how di damn hospital food stay. Not even dog want it." "You didn't have to," Danielle told her. "An mi daughter inna hospital, you mad?" For the next three days, Shirley visited her three times a day, taking care of her as if she was a baby again.

I was assigned a social worker as well as a counselor to work with all of us, because this tragedy affected us all. Toni-Ann came to spend three weeks with her sister, which seemed to help Danielle a great deal. They were always close. Confidence started to be reborn in my child and I could see from her demeanor that her independence was beginning to show. One afternoon I was sitting on the verandah when she summoned me. "Mom, she began, "I want to practice law still. I am a good lawyer and I can contribute to my society." Happiness and joy filled my heart to know that my baby girl is still willing to try. I hugged her. With the help of technology and some adjustment, within three months she was offered a position with J & J Law Firm on King Street Downtown. A year later she was offerred a senior position. At the banquet, Mr. Brown her supervisor told me, "Danielle is one of the best litigation lawyers I've ever seen. She knows how to summarize things without even trying."

Danielle and I started a non-profit organization called Independent for Life, where we teach persons who live with a disability to be as independent as possible in skills areas such as computers, woodwork, dressmaking, barbering, shoe-making & other skilled activities where they can earn a living for themselves. I tried to be there as much as possible for Danielle, but without trying I could tell that she would be alright with or without me.

One afternoon she was in her office when her secretary announced that there was a gentleman there to see her. She received a note from the Council for Disabilities a week ago asking her for her assistance in drawing up a proposal to submit to the Jamaican Government on the Charter of Rights for Persons who are living with a disability in the country. A young man walked in; 5 feet tall, dark and handsome. "Good afternoon, Ms. Champagne," he began, "My name is Cristan." From his accent, Danielle could tell he was either not a Jamaican or had been living out of the country for some time. As she told me, years later, the moment when their hands met, she knew that he would be someone special in her life. "Good afternoon," she replied, "You can call me Danielle."

"Ms. William at the Council told me that you were very attractive, but from what I can see, that is quite an understatement." Danielle blushed. It had been a while since a man had given her some attention. She remembered how it felt and she admitted to herself that she missed it.

Taking a grip of her emotions she straightened up. "What can I do for you?"

"Mr. Gordon," he said sitting down in front of her. "Cristan Gordon. You can call me Cristan." Danielle said, "As Ms. William from the Council told you, I am here to assist you in any area possible, have you done a lot of work with Persons with Disabilities?"

"As matter of fact yes, I have worked with them both in the States and since my return. I also did my PHD in social work and psychology," he responded.

"As I explained to Ms. William," she said, "I do not have much free time, but I am willing to try. Are weekends possible for you?"

"That will suit me," he said, "Because I often make a number of trips throughout the country areas." "May I ask for what purpose?"

she inquired. "For rehabilitation. Many people who have just become disabled, or who have been disabled for a long time, need assistance in learning skills that will enable them to become active, productive participants in their society. My observation has been that there are not enough social workers in the country areas, especially in the most rural parts that people often call 'outside of civilization'".

Danielle smiled, "Mr. Gordon...," "Cristan," he pleaded. "Cristan," she said, "Forgive me I thought we were living in the 21st century. I never thought we were still living in the 15th century. Jamaica is too small to have any place that is regarded as outside of civilization."

"I did not mean it like that," he said with a grin in his voice. "I meant that when a person becomes disabled and families are poor; living 5,10,15, even 30 miles from the nearest hospital, it is often a tremendous burden on the family to help that individual. Oftentimes, the only viable option is to leave them in the house. My job is to see that help comes to them since they cannot go for help."

Relaxing, Danielle understood "And have you

seen any improvements since your return?" I have been back for six months. There are one or two social workers who volunteer with the Council; funding is limited, but we are doing our best." "If there is any way I or my mother can assist you, let me know. We do not have much but we are willing to share what we have." "I appreciate it."

They made plans to meet the following weekend and for some reason without Danielle knowing why, she was looking forward to meeting him again.

Danielle mused over her encounter with Cristan that afternoon. Soon enough though, the voice of reason kicked-in to remind her that she was not some schoolgirl who falls head over heels for some man that she did not even know. Even more importantly she realized that, she didn't even know whether he was married or has a family. In a moment of panic, Danielle began to think that agreeing to work with Cristan may have been a bad idea. The first order of business, she told herself was to meet him in a public place. The more people that were around, the more they could focus on the thoughts at hand and nothing else.

The following Saturday morning, Danielle met Cristan at Burger King in Half Way Tree. For two hours they talked, putting their ideas together while Cristan jotted them down. "I believe," Danielle said, "that they should have a health fund for persons with disabilities, including sending them abroad for operations if possible." "We have come a far way Danielle," Cristan said, "but not that far. Jamaica is not that rich. It would also be a good idea Danielle, to have persons such as yourself with disabilities who have achieved a great deal in spite of their condition, speak publicly about their approach and their experiences living with frailty. When they see you Danielle, they will have hope for themselves." "I will think about it," she said smiling at him. "Anything else?" "I will plan it the next time we meet," he said. "So you have some ideas?" "Maybe, maybe not." "I do not understand," she replied. "Well, put it this way; if I gave you everything today, I wouldn't have a reason to see you next week." Blushing, she bit down into her Burger. "I could always tell you to jot it down and email me." "I am not good with computers." "I

think you are lying." "Maybe, maybe not."
"How long have you been blind, Danielle?"
Cristan asked. This seemed to upset her
somewhat. "I'm sorry, did I offend you?"
"Not really, I just do not like to talk about it,
about a year and a half. I think it would have
been much easier if I was born this way, then
I wouldn't miss it." "But at least you had the
gift of seeing." Cristan said. "What gift?" she
remarked, "How can being blind be a gift?"
"You have the best of both worlds," Cristan
rejoined, "The sighted and the dark. You can
tell people." "You are putting me in a position
to be a spokesperson, a champion for people
with disabilities in Jamaica?" "Really?" "Yes
and I don't like it. As I said, I will think about
what you said, and let you know but please do
not go around telling people that I will be
there for them."

Realizing that she was beginning to get angry,
Cristan changed the subject. "My parents
migrated to the United States when I was
just a toddler. I grew up in Jamaica under the
watchful eye of a loving and supportive
grandmother. When I was twelve, my parents
sent for me to join them in the States; I was

so angry and bitter, I cried for days. When I migrated to the United States, my best friend became a guy named Raoul. The first time I saw Raoul walking down the hall at school I didn't want anything to do with him. As far as I was concerned, he was an unkempt, bushy haired Mexican kid. What became even more noticeable to me, was his habit of bullying the younger students."

Cristan continued, "One day I witnessed Raoul remove some vodka from his bag and offer it to a younger boy. In an instant, it seemed as if I had summoned this courage to confront him. I grabbed the bottle of vodka from his hands and threw it to the ground. "Do you know drinking is bad for you?" I asked, "And if you do not know, you know now. If you want to kill yourself fine, but do not kill anyone else along with you." I could've told the principal, but I didn't. ." "If you want to have a fight," he said, "Let's fight." Feeling that I had nothing to lose, missing Jamaica, miserable all day, we fought and I won. From that day we became friends."

"Raoul was born in Cancun Mexico, and

migrated to the States when he was one. His father worked at a factory and his mother worked at a supermarket. For years we were inseparable and Raoul's behavior began to change. I introduced him to Christ, and to my surprise on his 16th birthday, Raoul was baptized in my church. Three years ago Danielle," he said without thinking, "Raoul was driving home. Some fool ran a red light and slammed right into him. His neck was broken and he was crippled from the neck down. It devastated me. I spent days, weeks by his bedside in the hospital, never giving up on him. When three months passed Raoul was sent to a rehabilitation center in Washington DC. I drove there every week for six hours back and forth to make him know that I was still there for him. He learned to write with his teeth."   "His teeth?" Danielle asked with a surprised look on her face.   "Yes, you would put the pencil in his mouth and he would write with his teeth. I'm telling you nobody could write better than him. Finally, he was taught how to use the computer. Eventually, Raoul and I decided to start a business together. Raoul was exceptional with mechanics, which we really needed for our venture."   "Me too,"

Danielle confessed. When I was growing up in Rema," she said, "my father had an old car that he used to work on in the yard. I used to assist him. What happened, Cristan?" she asked. "After making that plan, within six months Rauol died."

"Died?"

"Yes, organ failure. His kidneys and liver stopped working. It devastated me. It was then I decided to come back to Jamaica. Here I feel I can do some good for my country. I could've stayed in the States, Danielle, and earned as much as possible, but it doesn't make sense to earn it and not be happy. Raoul taught me to be happy. He never gave up, even when it was his last moment, the last thing he said to me the night when he died was ...*do what is best for you and everything will fall into place*." Danielle never believed she would hear her own thoughts echo from the mouth of another human being.

For the next few months Danielle tried to be as happy and fulfilled as possible. In due course, Danielle resumed her church attendance and started volunteering at the Golden Age Home. Soon, without any good reason Danielle would often feel herself smile - as if she had found a new and better approach to the world around her and her position in it.

Over the following months, they met almost every weekend. By the time they submitted their plan to the Council for Disability, Cristan realized that he was beginning to fall in love with Danielle. One afternoon, he came by her house to speak with her. Sitting down he began, "Danielle I want to ask you something. Please do not think it forward of me, but for a beautiful girl like you, why do you not have someone in your life?" "I did." She said. Without going into details, she told him it never worked between John Kay and herself. "Can I invite you to dinner?" She wanted to say, yes. Danielle had long recognized that the time had come for an intimate relationship in her life.

That night we spoke. "Danielle", I told her, "as your mother, I respect your wishes and so I am not going to tell you what to do. However, this Cristan seems to be a real gentleman, why not go out with him?" "For what?" she replied, "It will never work out between us" "Why do you believe that?" "Would he want a wife with a disability? Working with us doesn't mean he wants someone with a disability." "You're judging him Danielle, you do not know what he wants," I told her.

"Besides," I said, "he only invited you to dinner, it wasn't a marriage proposal." She smiled. "Come here, baby," I said holding her hand leading her to the bed. "Sit I have something to tell you. Three months ago I heard from John Kay's mother." Immediately, I could feel the tension in her body, "What did she want?" Danielle said in a frank voice. "John Kay got married, baby." For a brief moment there was silence between us. Finally I had to break it. "I did not want to tell you, but I feel it was the right time to tell you about it." "Why have you told me this now" she asked without changing the tone of her voice. "Because I want you to live, live for yourself, not for no one but yourself."

The following Friday they went to Anchovy's restaurant in new Kingston for dinner. From thenceforth on they were inseparable. Gradually, Danielle and Cristan developed a relationship. Eight months later, Danielle brought me the exciting news that Cristan asked her to marry him. I gave her my blessing and three months later my firstborn was married. A newlywed. After she moved out of the house to be with her husband, I missed her terribly. I had no idea I would miss her this much. I missed walking into her room and seeing her around her computer. I even missed the aroma of her food as she was cooking in the kitchen. As much as I missed her though, knowing that she was happy, and married to someone who cherished her, made me feel pleased and contented that she was moving along with her life.

Their wedding was a beautiful one. It was well attended by all of their nearest and dearest family, friends, and associates. Unlike so many other weddings where the ceremony starts hours behind schedule, this one went perfectly to time throughout the entire evening. As I waited for the wedding to start, it was strange, for some reason I could sense Tony's presence. My eyes searched through the crowd frantically. I spotted him in the corner dressed in full white. When he recognized that I saw him, he walked over. Even though he was ten years older than I, he looked like an old man. "Hello Jasmine," he began. "What are you doing here Tony?" I asked in a cold voice. "I could not miss my daughter's wedding." "How did you know? I never sent an invitation?" "I saw it in the paper." "And you just decided to show up after fifteen years?"

Smiling at me, I could tell that he did not take care of his teeth. "Fifteen years, eh?" he said. "It just seems like yesterday." "What do you want Tony?" I asked bluntly. "I just want to be at my daughter's wedding as I told you before." "You walked out on us," I said in a loud voice "and now you just feel that you have the privilege and the right to be here?" "Come now, Jasmine." Looking around, I could tell all eyes were on us. I did not want to spoil my daughter's day. I asked him to come outside with me. He obliged without protest. "Look, Tony," I said, "Your daughters needed you and you weren't there." For the past fifteen years you chose not to know anything about these girls; including what they ate, what they wore, how they slept." "I am not the one who can provide that for them," he said bluntly, "Since I wasn't the one who became a millionaire." "This is the reason why you didn't be a part of their life?" I asked.

"That's bull and You know it Tony. The fact is you walked out on us. You did not stay with your family during the storm. You chose your life, now you have to live with that. If you are the one that obtained wealth, would you turn your back on your girls?" "Jasmine," he said in a soft voice holding my hand. I should've grabbed it away, but for some reason I let him hold it, missing his touch. "I never denied my kids. I always accepted them and loved them. Yes, I made some mistakes, but which man upon this earth does not?"

"Tony," I said pulling my hand finally from his, "all your daughters wanted was a father's love, you denied them that. Now look at them now. Look, Tony." Turning him around, from a distance he could see Alex, dressed in a blue dress with a banner around her waist she looked like a goddess. "That's your last daughter, she is now 19 Tony, and the only thing she knows about you is what we told her. The only time she ever saw you is in a picture." Walking over to us, Alexis hugged me.

"Isn't this a great day Mom?" she said "The sky is blue, the birds are singing. It's a wonderful day for a wedding, don't you think?" At that moment she realized that Tony was standing beside me. "I'm sorry," she said apologetically, "You have a visitor."

"Alex," I said in a calm voice, "don't you recognize this man?" She stared for a moment then turned.

"No, should I?"

"Remember the picture you saw in Toni-Ann's room?" She looked back at him more closely.

"I'm sorry," she said, "Mom I have to go."

"Wait, Alex," holding onto her hand, I said, "Tell him how you feel. Do not walk away and let the unresolved feelings bubble up inside of you."

"I have no feelings, Mom. As I told you years ago, I cannot miss what I did not have."

"Alex," Tony said in a husky voice, "Let me explain."

"Explain what, Tony?" she said blurting out finally. "Explain that I wasn't good enough to be part of your life. Explain that the only father I know is my mother?" "Look Tony," Alex said frankly. "I do not want you in my life. Leave me alone, leave me out of your story," and with that she walked away.

"As I said, Tony," turning back to him, "all they wanted was you."

During the dance, Tony interrupted Danielle and Cristan. "Danielle," he said, "May I have a dance with you?" "For what Tony?" Danielle replied bitterly. "I want to talk to you." "You know what Tony?" she said turning towards him. "You walked out of my life when I was nine years old, but the truth too is that even when you were in my life you did not care about me. You showed me little regard, only spent time with Toni-Ann. It's like I did not exist for you. And if I did not exist for you when I'm four, I won't exist for you when I'm 24". And with that she held her husband's hand and then walked away. I never saw him when he left that evening, but I knew deep down inside he was hurt.

With Danielle and Toni-Ann away, and Alexis spending most of her time at the University; I found myself with time-on-my-hands. I spent my days reflecting on my life. Often, I would sit on my balcony overlooking the city of Kingston. Jamaica is so beautiful I said to myself. To my left I could see the Caribbean Sea, to my right the mountains winding up into the sky as if they belonged there, and in the middle the city, cars moving around like ants in a maze.

I could sense when Shirley walked up behind me placing my lunch on the table. "Yu alright, Jasmine?" she broke the silence. "Yes," I said turning around sitting to face her. Over the years, Shirley would hear something about Tony and inform me. Whenever Shirley went to the market Downtown, where most of her friends purveyed their goods, she would make enquiries regarding Tony. From what she gathered, Tony had not done badly for himself. Tony operated Pearl's taxi until he was able to afford three of his own. Thereafter, he opened a little shop in Mile Hill in St. Thomas. His son TJ, is now in high school and most of Tony's wealth goes into educating him. He wants to become a banker from what Shirley heard. "What's a banker,

Ma'am?" she asked one day. "It's someone who works within the banking sector," I replied, "Either as a manager, a supervisor, or an accountant. You just have to deal with money." "Bright bwoy," she said. I didn't tell my girls what I heard about their father, I did not want them to have high expectations or broken dreams because of him. I was right, not once did Tony stop by or call to find out about them. Even when Danielle had the accident it was in the paper, why didn't he show up at that time when she needed him? I thought to myself, slamming my fist on the table.

The saucer which was holding my tea spilled, turning over. Like a flash, Shirley jumped up. "Don't worry about that Ma'am, me clean it up fi yu." She was a good friend to us. I've known her for over twenty years and she has never done anything to earn my distrust. "Now Shirley," I said, opening my mouth for the first time, "Im showed up at mi pickney wedding! Look at dat!" "As so dem man tan, ya man, dem no mine dem pickney, den as soon as dem succeed inna life, dem try fi own dem. But no worry mek im come smile an gi yu likkle charm, him attitude rotten, just like him ways." I smiled. From the day Shirley and Tony met in our one-bedroom house, dem could not gree. "Picky picky head bwoy," Shirley often said, "Sweep up di yard betta nuh? Yu mumma neva teach yu fi do nutten? A waan Jasmine buss yu ass," but he would only kiss his teeth and walk away. "Look pan im," Shirley muttered, "Him mawga like a thread. Is like di more Jasmine feed him, a di more bad mine suck im out." I would often have to be the referee between them and it never changed. "He left hurt, yu know Shirley," I told her, "but I did not care. If he wanted to change his relationship with his daughters he should have done that years ago." "Same ting mi sey, Ma'am."

Watching her work so determinedly at cleaning up the mess I created, I asked one more time, "Shirley, over these years I beg you to move in and live with us, but you refuse. Please I'm asking you again, come live with me. As you can see, the girls them have a life of their own now, and I'm alone." I thought she would refuse as usual. "Yu still want mi come ma'am?" she said looking up from the floor.

"Arite, mi wi do it, but not until next month."
Joy came back into my life. "Why wait so
long?" I asked. "Dem a keep a convention a mi
Church, wan week worth, an mi waan attend,"
she said. "Okay," I replied not wanting her to
change her mind again. I regret that now. On
the last night of her convention Shirley was
on her way home. From what I heard, she was
happy, singing, with her Bible under her arm.
Crossing the road that night she did not look -
a truck hit her. When I went to identify her
body along with Rita, I fainted. Regaining
consciousness, I asked to speak with the
doctor. He informed me that she experienced
no pain. "From the impact, she died instantly,"
he said. The girls were devastated, especially
Danielle. For some reason, Shirley took a
fancy to her. When she was five years old I
remember boiling her soup, and gave it to
Shirley to feed her. When I bent the corner
unexpectedly, Shirley was having a feast with
that soup. I was so angry I began to curse
her, "How dare you Shirley, a eat out mi
pickney likkle lunch. Yu is a wicked ooman fi a
box bread outa baby mout." But Danielle
started to take up for her, "Auntie Shirley fi
eat my food, Mommy. Auntie Shirley sey, if I

poison, the two a wi a go dead and mi nah go dead lef har."

Throughout the funeral proceedings Danielle was inconsolable. I took her home and placed her on the bed in her old room. "Why Aunty Shirley," Danielle screamed, "Why her? Mi caan lose another person I love? No, no, no!" "It's alright Danielle," I said. She cried for hours until Cristan came to help me "Danielle," he whispered in her ear, "She's in a better home, she's with God and she was a Christian, so you know it's true." Kissing her he held her. Watching my daughter and her husband at that moment, gave me the comfort that if my eyes closed she would be alright.

Six months later, Danielle informed me that I was going to get my first grandchild. I was so happy. We spent weeks shopping for the baby's clothes, and what I did not buy, I made out of my own hands. "When mi grandson born," I said to her, "him a go put on dis first". She smiled, "and how you know it's a boy, Mom?" "Because me know," I would often tell her, "But if it's a girl me caan send her back, since mi caan put har from wey mi neva tek her from." "Neither can I," Danielle said laughing.

When Danielle was eight months pregnant, Cristan and her moved in with me. "Mom," she said, "you should be in your grandchild's life, and this house is so big, we do not want you to continue being alone." I could not contain my excitement. The night they moved in, all of us talked until dawn. The next evening Danielle went into labour, Cristan was at a retreat for the weekend. It was then left for me to take on Cristan's role as Danielle's support through this event. I took Danielle to the hospital. I remained with her as doctors prepared her for labour. I remained and supported her as Cristan would have done in the delivery room, and I was there too when my first grandchild Natasha met this world for the first time. I could not have been happier in my whole life than I was at this very moment.

By the time Natasha was three months old, I took her to meet my mother for the first time. Miss Kitty was very old and fragile now. Six months ago I found a housekeeper to take care of her. "You're doing well, Jasmine," she greeted me at the door. "Yes, Mama," I said, "this is my grandbaby Natasha," placing her in her arms.

"She look like you." I filled her in on what was going on with the girls and spent the weekend with her. It is funny, when I was a little girl, I told myself I wanted to run as far away from this woman as possible. Now, realizing that time was of the essence for me, I wanted to spend as much time with her as I could. Five months later as Danielle, Cristan, Natasha and I were gathered for Sunday dinner we received the news that my mother was no more. "She went home peacefully last night in her sleep," Sophia told me. I cried, I cried for having lost the chance to do more for her. I cried that she went to her grave without meeting her long-lost son Courtney. From the day I hung up the phone on him, I never heard from him again.

Feeling guilty, I decided to try and find him, to even offer him the opportunity to come to her funeral. When I finally reached him, he was working in Westmoreland at the Jerusalem School for Boys; a private school funded by the Catholic Church of Jamaica. To my surprise, he agreed to attend the funeral. I felt a sense of peace as they lowered my mother's body into the ground. No longer did my mother have to worry about her kids, and at last her baby boy acknowledged his relatedness to her.

Six months after my mother's death, Toni-Ann informed us that she had completed medical school, and was inviting all of us to her graduation ceremony in London. While there, Toni-Ann informed me that she wanted to come back home to Jamaica. Just like her sister Danielle, Toni-Ann wanted to give back to Jamaica. They both saw Jamaica as their foundation, a country that had done so much for them. I was so proud of her decision to work in Jamaica, she was so unlike many of her young, educated counterparts who leave Jamaica without looking back.

Toni-Ann had no problem obtaining a job at Kingston Public Hospital; working in the casualty department. However, within six months she felt the need to do more. With the assistance of an associate of mine, Toni-Ann started volunteering at the community center in Olympic Gardens. I looked forward to hearing stories from her visits. Many of the stories were so hilarious, they would send me careening to the floor with laughter.

"Mom," she said one afternoon, "Mr. Billy who is 97 years old, told me he wants a girlfriend. When I asked him what he would do with a girlfriend he said to pet her; so his great-granddaughter bought him a dog. 'Not because mi old,' he told me, Mom," she said smiling, "'Don't mean mi favor a mongrel' but the funniest thing is that he named the dog GeeGee. Everywhere Mr. Billy goes, the dog is 'pee pee cluck cluck' behind him, Mom, even in my office. Mr. Billy and the dog seem to be as one. Recently, when I asked him whether he wanted a girlfriend again, he shook his head. "No, women are nothing but trouble, Doc, he said, "at least GG don't answer me when I scold her, an shi do wha mi tell her." "Like what?" "Like carry the note to di shop fi me and dem wi put di sugar and di bread in a bag an tie it up an put it on har head an shi will come right back to mi an gimme without not taking a bite out of it." In addition to Toni-Ann's success at the community centre a year after the birth Natasha, Danielle and Cristan gave me my first grandson Joseph.

Happenings at the community centre however, were not always hilarious and rewarding. It had almost been a year into her tenure at the community centre when Toni-Ann came to me with a seemingly distressed look on her face. "What's wrong Toni-Ann?" I asked. "Mom, have you ever heard of cases where females abandon their offspring? I mean you all always hear about child abandonment in Jamaica, watch it on the television, and read it in the newspaper; but most of those cases are men." Instantly, my mind flashed on my own mother, but it wasn't abandonment, I thought to myself. She gave him up for a better life. Squeezing her hand, I said, "No, but obviously there are cases out there." "I know one. I met a guy three days ago, his name is Richard. He has a one-year-old daughter. Three months ago, his live-in girlfriend who he had dedicated three years of his life to, walked out on them, leaving him to take care of their child on his own. He asked his mother for help, but she said I quote "a no mi tel yu fi go out dere an breed ooman. If yu wan baby yu get baby." So he has to pay a little elderly lady in this community to take care of her during the day. "So he's working?" I asked. "Yes, as an insurance officer at Sagicor Jamaica. He has to work to pay himself. The more he puts in the more money he will get. He told me that most nights he comes home, so late the only thing he can do is take the child and go straight to bed. He hasn't had a cooked lunch in a long while, at least not by his own hand."

"Honey." I said holding her, "Please do not get emotionally involved with your patients; you're not a counselor to hear their sad story."

"I know, Mom, but this guy really seems genuine; he just needs a listening ear sometimes."

Finally she smiled at me. "Mom I'm a doctor, but I'm also a human being. Oftentimes, my patients only need someone with a listening ear to attend to them. People need to have their mental well-being cared for as much as their physical well-being." "I know," I said, "You are a good person, you wear your heart on your sleeve. This is why I'm scared," squeezing her hand.

"Of what mom?"

"Of you being hurt Toni-Ann. I'm sorry if I put you over the years in so much emotional distress."

"You haven't."

"As I said. you are a good person, I don't want you to change, but please take it easy."

Unknown to me, Toni-Ann and Richard became good friends. Toni-Ann introduced him to us as her new fiancé. I felt shock, disappointment, and concern for my daughter's future. In spite of my reservations, I knew the importance of allowing Toni-Ann to make her own decisions. I have seen where interference by parents in their children's lives has destroyed their relationship. All I asked her was to take it easy. "Mom," she said, "Get to know him, I value your opinion. I want you to know him like I do." Thereafter, Richard started to visit us. Often spending the weekend with his daughter Michelle, she was a beautiful little girl, and to be honest I fell in love with her.

I purchased a small town house for myself, and gave Danielle and her family my home. To be separated from them was very hard, but I knew their family was growing and they needed their own space. One afternoon, I was home alone crocheting when I received a very unusual call. It was Tony. He wanted to see me. My immediate thought was to refuse him outright, but my heart wouldn't let me. I have realized over the years that time is very special, and now I am a middle-aged woman and a Christian. I would have to learn to finally forgive and forget. I cannot teach my grandkids the way of righteousness when I do not know it myself. When he suggested that we meet at Mother's Downtown I burst out laughing, thinking that he was crazy. After thinking about it for a moment or two I finally said, "Okay." To go back to the place where we met when I was fourteen was suitable. To end it where it had started I told myself that night.

The next day I arrived at Mother's at exactly 2:30 p.m. Tony was already there enjoying a meal. Sitting in front of him I blurted out without helping myself, "What you want from me Tony?" thinking that he would get angry, but he just smiled. "Feisty as usual, Jasmine.

This is why I love you so much." "Tony you do not know what love is." "You're wrong Jasmine, I do," he said. "I want to ask you to forgive me for everything I put you and the girls through. The only way I can seek peace in my life is to let this happen," he continued. "I tried a couple of years ago at the wedding without success. I want to try again, Jasmine." "And you think," I told him, "You going to get a headway with our girls through me." "No, I do not believe that," he said, "but I believe I have to start with you."

I stared at him for a long while. All the hate, the disappointment, the pain, the hurt, drained from my body. Finally I spoke, "Tony, it took me a long time, but I finally forgive you. We are all human beings; we make our choices in life, sometimes good, sometimes bad. You've made yours, I've made mine. I have to learn to live with mine, but please do not make regret boil up inside of you till it bursts. Do not worry about it, life is too short and precious. Live every moment and every day to the fullest." Holding his hand without hesitation I squeezed it. "I forgive you," I repeated. This time he held his head down with my hand clinging to his and cried in front me like a baby. When he finally held his head up he said, "Thank you, Jasmine."

After the moment passed I finally asked, "How are you doing Tony?"   "I'm fine. I moved out of Pearl's home nine months ago." "I'm sorry to hear about that," I said.   "I'm not, I've served my purpose."   "What do you mean?" I asked.   "I was young at that time, I was able to take care of her three plus the one that she gave me, and her. Now I'm a middle-aged man with a lot of complications. TJ, my son, is now working at Bank of Jamaica." "That's very good."   "Pearl," he said without acknowledging that I spoke, "rented the houses that I built for her. She is well taken care of, and as for me, I'm surviving."   "I'm happy to hear about that Tony." I said.

We spent the next hour talking. I filled him in on the girls and their progress. Tony was happy that Danielle was thriving in-spite of her accident, and was even elated to find out that he was now a grandfather of two. Finally I said, "Alex is now working on a three-year contract in Toronto Canada at an accounting firm there." "Wow!" he said.

He mentioned that he saw me when he attended Shirley's funeral, but felt I would not wish to speak with him then. I was so surprised that he attended Shirley's funeral, they had always been at odds with each other. It was a large funeral, hundreds of people came. "I did not know," he said, "that she was so loved." "She was a good person, with a good heart," I said. My alarm went off on my phone. When I checked it, I realized I had a doctor's appointment. I told him that I would see him again and went outside but forgot my purse on the table. I was just in time to see Tony get up and realized with the shock on my face he was now a one-foot man. "I did not want you to know," he said sitting back down. "Why?" I whispered. "I don't want pity, Jasmine. I lost my foot a year and a half ago from diabetes. I figure that you can forgive me, a man, and not because I have a disability."

It took some work but I finally got Danielle and Toni-Ann to see him. I told them that evening when we met, "Despite it all, he gave me you girls, and I cannot imagine my life living without you three in it." Toni-Ann decided to treat her father, and with the help of her insurance company, he was fitted with a prosthetic leg. Danielle also helped him in his divorce and with her intervention he got all of Pearl's wealth.

Tony began volunteering at our organization Hope for Jamaica Downtown. His focus was on teaching young people mechanics. Danielle was impressed with his ability to communicate with inner city youth. He would often tell his young apprentices, "Only if you have a skill that you can use to survive you will make it in this life." I celebrated my forty-fifth birthday happy and contented with my friends and family in my life.

Toni-Ann told me that she was pregnant. I was so elated. One of the greatest joys a person could have on this earth, is to see their generation moving forward while they are still alive. Two weeks later, my sister Sophie invited us for a family reunion in the country. We all accepted the invitation. Everyone knows how important family is to me. I believe that it defines us and shapes us within our society, sometimes for the good, sometimes for the bad.

While we were at the family reunion, I observed Cristan. Cristan seemed to have an affinity with the country environment. He would take the kids bird shooting, fruit picking, and even to the river to fish. The children enjoyed themselves thoroughly, even when their hands and feet were covered in dirt. Danielle on the other hand would remind Cristan that he would have to wash the children's muddy clothing.

Through the years, my sister Sophie had done well for herself. It was just ten years ago that I helped her to open a little shop. Now, she not only has two of them, she also owns a supermarket. Sophie was so proud to show me her new empire. It's true, I thought to myself, you give a man a fish you will only feed him for a day; but teach him to fish and you will feed him for a lifetime. Likewise their children, in-spite of their humble beginnings all five have made substantial strides in their respective ventures. Each time I hear of the success of either one of them, it reminds me of the good decision I made to share my good fortune with others. It was not good enough for me to live for myself and my children, but for my wider community. The joy they were now experiencing redounded to me in a feeling of peace and contentment.

"I miss Stephen," I told her one afternoon when we were sitting on her veranda. "He is like a prodigal son waiting to come home. In the last letter Sophie received from him, he stated that he had only five more years of his sentence left. He was dying to come home. I smiled, "When Steven is here, the family will feel as if it will be alright." "He is the only brother I have alive," Sophie said.

The final night we had a party. We invited people from all over, not only our community but surrounding areas. We served fish, mannish water, curry goat, jerk chicken and pork; every food that you could think of. Every one present was having a good time. I saw him before anyone else. I blinked my eyes took a sip of my drink and blinked them again just to make sure he wasn't a figment of my imagination. I had to get to her before he did I told myself. He was fatter now, but yes it was him. Moving through the crowd I shook everyone's hand, and talked to them briefly not to seem rude. Finally, I found Cristan and Danielle in a corner talking and dancing together. "Excuse me," I interrupted. "What's wrong Mom?" Cristan asked when he saw the expression on my face. "We need to talk." We moved closer so that we wouldn't be overheard. "Mom," Danielle said holding my hand. "Sit down, Danielle," she complied. "John Kay is here." I could feel tension swell in my daughter's body. Cristan's instinct for protection kicked in, and he put his hand around her.

"Where is he?" Cristan asked. "Outside," I replied, "underneath the gazebo, eating and talking to some guys." I squeezed my daughter's hand. "It's okay, I won't leave you. If he has to face you, he will face all three of us." She sat silently for a few seconds. Finally she smiled, "It's okay Mom, I would have to face my demon someday. You have taught me to be strong, and trust me, I am." I stood there hesitantly, not wanting to move. Looking outside, I saw the clouds getting darker and darker; finally I heard thunder roll. "It looks like it's going to rain," I told her, "Let us go inside the house" I said, trying to protect her. She stood up and hugged me so tight, I wanted to cry at that moment. "You go Mom, if he comes to us we will face him but we won't run." I looked at Cristan and knew that my child was in good hands. I walked away. Minutes that seemed like hours passed and John Kay did not approach, more minutes passed and John Kay didn't approach. Finally, he slowly made his way towards them. "Hello Danielle," he said in a soft voice, "It's John Kay." "I know who you are," Danielle replied. "How are you?" "I'm fine," he said. "I did not know it was your family's place. A friend of mine invited me to this party. It's just a few minutes ago they told me of the connection. How are you doing?" Cristan cleared his throat then John Kay looked in his direction and saw him. "This is my husband, John Kay," Danielle replied. Hesitantly, Cristan put out his hand and John Kay shook it. At that moment the kids decided they wanted their parents and ran up to them.

Joseph who was now feeling the effect of running up and down all evening, tried to climb into his father's arms. Finally Cristan gave in and held them tightly. "These are our kids," Danielle said proudly. John Kay stared at them fixedly. Finally he spoke, "They're beautiful, Danielle, I'm proud of you. Can we talk privately?" "No," she said in a stern voice, "Anything you have to tell me, you can say it in front of my husband." He hesitated. Cristan realized that he needed privacy to 'say his piece'. Cristan squeezed Danielle's hand. "It's okay honey. I'll only be a stone's throw away." Cristan took the kids and went over to a bench. Sitting down he held the children in his arms, with his eyes transfixed on the man who eight years ago walked away from the woman he is now in love with. I realized what was going on and went over to Cristan rubbing his shoulder gently. "It's okay son," I said. "I know," he replied smiling at me. From a distance I could see John Kay and Danielle talking. Memories of the past flashed in my mind; how they used to run up to my home hand-in-hand, hugging and kissing each other. They had no care in this world only focused on each other, now they are complete strangers.

I sat down beside my granddaughter who crawled into my lap and began to play with my ears. Within a minute, her eyes were closed and she was fast asleep. Danielle used the ackee tree to brace herself. "You look good," John Kay said. "It's my faith in my family and God that kept me going over the years; they are my rock." Danielle replied. "As I said before, I'm so proud of you. I did not know that these people were your family members. It was my friend Keton who invited me to the party. It was just half an hour ago he told that it was your family's retreat. When Keton told me, my heart leaped." "For what?" Danielle asked. "To see you again." "Are you here on vacation?" she asked. "No, I moved back to Jamaica eight months ago and opened a store in Black River." "That's good," she said, "but why did you give up the States?" "It's a long story, but I wish to see you when I come into Kingston. Can I have your office number?" She gave him, not because she wanted to see him again, but because she now realized it was finally over. The feelings that she had for John Kay many years ago were completely gone.

As she was walking away he stopped her, "I must ask you something. Danielle." "What?" she asked without turning around. "I must ask you to forgive me. I was a coward and the biggest chicken you will ever know. I am so sorry." She took a few seconds, "Danielle did you hear what I said?" he asked. "Yes", finally she turned around. "It's okay, John Kay, I forgave you a long time ago. You never knew the favor that you did me by walking out of my life that day." "What do you mean?" he asked. "If it wasn't for you, I would never have found my soulmate in my husband. I could never hate you for that, John Kay," and with that she walked away.

I have seen Hope for Jamaica, grow from strength to strength since the seven years Danielle and I founded it. Both the public and private sector have increased their donations - but we needed more. Often, Cristan would go overseas to see Jamaicans in the diaspora for assistance. On these occasions, I would stay with Danielle. On one occasion when Cristan was abroad, I was cooking in the kitchen when

I heard the doorbell ring. When I opened the door I was so surprised to see John Kay standing there. "I'm sorry I came unannounced," he said. "Please," I replied, "sit on the veranda." When I informed Danielle that he was here, she did not say a word to me or act surprised.

"Did you know that he was coming?" I asked Danielle. She smiled, "No Mom, but I know the man. From what I remember of him he is very conceited, I knew it wouldn't take very long for him to present himself at my home." When both of us went outside I determined that I would not leave her alone with him this time. "As I told your mother, Danielle," he said, "I'm so sorry I came unannounced; but I was in Kingston. For the past three weeks each time I called your secretary, she informed me that you were either in Court or with a client. I just want to talk with you, nothing more." "You can talk now," Danielle said in a firm voice. He stared at me realizing I was a rock and wouldn't be moved, he finally gave in. "Danielle I want us to be friends. If you forgave me, we must be communicating as friends." "I don't see the need," Danielle replied. "Danielle..." he said, "When I went to New York eight years ago, I went with the intention of coming back to you... as there is a God, that's why I went. But when I looked at our life and how it had changed, I got scared. I wanted a perfect wife. I did not realize that life is not perfect. But look at you now," he continued, "You're married, you have your family."

"Are you married?" I inquired trying to decrease the tension between all three of us.

"I was but I am now divorced."

"Do you have kids?"

"A daughter, she is five."

"So why did you leave her?" Danielle asked, "Or is she here with you?"

"No," he said, "She and her mother live in the States; they're both Americans."

"What do you want from my child?" I asked doggedly of John Kay.

"I want to make peace with her."

"But she already told you she forgives you," I informed him.

He stood up and walked the length of my veranda staring at the cars on the road moving from left to right. Finally he turned around, "Jasmine, when I think of my life in Jamaica I cannot imagine it without Danielle. I know I've done her wrong, but I'm praying that we can be friends. Do you know that I'm a Christian now, baptized four years ago and it's all due to her. She was the guiding force in my life that changed it for the better. I want to walk into a room and talk to her without having this tension between us."

"Do you expect us to be friends?" Danielle asked finally.

He walked over and sat down. "Danielle I know you forgave me. I believe that with all my heart, but I'm praying that we can be friends. I donated to your organization since I've been back. I want to do some volunteer work down there."

"I will talk to my husband," she said, "We will have to make this decision together." When John Kay left that evening I implored her not to do it. "Mom," she said, "We are Christians. Forgiveness is the key - as he said we can never be more than friends."

Without hesitation Cristan agreed and for the next five months John Kay would often give up his Saturdays to come in for a few hours to counsel the boys. His impact was so great on them that they all wanted to be like him. By the time Toni-Ann and Richard's daughter Paris was born, I was beginning to wonder if I was wrong about him. One weekend I was by Danielle's home and Cristan informed me that something was not right with John Kay.

"What do you mean?" I inquired.

"Last weekend he was by the Center for four hours, and every 15 minutes or so he would take out some pills and swallow them. When I asked him about it, he informed me that he had rheumatoid arthritis and was prescribed medication."

"That's true," I said.

"But not like that mom," Cristan replied. "To me it appears that he is taking an excessive amount."

"I will ask him about it," Danielle said.

"Not without me being there," I told her in a stern voice. Thinking that she would protest I went over holding her hand, "Danielle I want to be there when you talk with him." She gave in, and two days later we were having lunch with John Kay. The meal was going well until I said bluntly, "John Kay, please tell me about the pills that you're taking. I heard it's for your arthritis."

"Yes, it was prescribed to me in New York."

"When were you diagnosed?" Danielle asked.

"Two years ago," he informed us. "This is one of the reasons I returned to Jamaica. When it's summer, it's fine for me, but winter is a hell. Often I can hardly get out of bed due to my arthritis."

"But are you not too young to have that?" Danielle asked.

"It's my curse," he said in a smiling voice, "My father had it by the time he was 35."

Feeling a little better, I excused myself to go to the restroom. As soon as I returned from the restroom, I could see from a distance that Danielle was crying uncontrollably. I rushed over to her. "What's the matter Danielle and where is John Kay?" Holding her she finally spoke.

"Mom, that bastard!"

"What?" I asked in a frightful voice, "Tell me."

"When you left, I told him I do not believe that he should use so many pills unless the doctor increased his dose, because I know if it's not done right he can become addicted to

it. He said, '...the only thing I'm addicted to is you Danielle. From the moment I left and came back I could not help thinking of you. I want you and I to spend a night together'."
"What?" I said, "if I ever..."
"Mom, I slapped him so hard I think I broke my hand."

For the next few days he tried to contact both of us to apologise, but we refused to accept. We did not hear from him for the next eight months. One afternoon we all gathered at my apartment to watch television. Cristan and Danielle were going to be featured on Profile with Ian Boyne. Richard informed Cristan he looked better in makeup and Toni-Ann agreed. "You look like beauty and the beast," she said smiling. Richard and Cristan began to roll on the floor like two young boys with the kids joining in. We were laughing so loud we did not hear Danielle's phone ring until she shouted, "Leave me alone." The room stopped as if it was frozen. Cristan jumped up at once off the carpet and grabbed the phone, "What the hell do you want, John Kay?" he demanded in a strong commanding voice.

While John Kay spoke to Cristan, I could see the tension in Cristan's body begin to dissipate and he began to relax. Finally he said, "You deal with me not my wife and I will see what I can do for you," and hung up the phone. We all stared at him with such intensity he sat down.

"John Kay needs help. He now knows that he's addicted to pain killers and needs some assistance."

"Do what you can for him," I said without hesitation.

"Yes," Danielle replied in a sad voice. Two days later, Cristan sent him information about some doctors and psychologists in the western part of the Island.

That very night I got a call from Alexis. I cannot believe time flew so fast and she was now a woman. I never wanted her to live so far away from me, but it was her desire to study and work abroad for a few years before returning home. I remember the days when she used to run around naked carefree, now she had responsibilities. "Are you alright?" I asked in a concerned voice. "Yes," but from the tone of her voice I knew something was wrong. My body stiffened, "Alex, what's wrong?" There was a silence and finally she broke it. "Mom I need some advice. You know about my new work at J and J International?" "Yes," I said smiling. I remember the day when I got the e-mail I was so proud of her. "Well from the moment I walked through the door there's a young Ms. Antoinette. She hates me."

"Hates you?" I repeated, "For what? Did you do or say something to her?" "That's just it mom, I didn't. I just do not know why she hates me."

"That's strange," I said.

"Tell me from the beginning."

She sighed, "Well from the first day I came into the office the Monday morning at 9:00 a.m., I had to do a proposal. The proposal was aimed at delineating how the Conquest personal computer could achieve global recognition in the next two to five years.

"What is conquest?" I asked curiously.

"It's a new form of PC which is smaller and lighter but yet carries more features faster than any of the other personal computer currently on the market."

"I still do not see what is special about them."

"Mom there are features that are the exclusive domain of conquest; it is artificial intelligence. I mean Mom it can learn with you and improve its software on its own. You do not have to update it. In fact you do not even have to charge it, it automatically charges on its own, feeding off the sun's rays."

"Wow!" I said.

"Mom I will send Danielle one, she'll need it. Anyway, as I addressed my colleagues, they fixated on practically every word I said. It appeared from the questions that were posed at the end that the ideas I presented were innovative and had never been considered before. While everyone else focused on what I had to say Antoinette on the other hand seemed to be taking copious notes throughout my presentation. However, to my amazement, when I walked closer to her she was drawing cartoons, Mom. I mean we were in a board meeting and she was drawing a cartoon of Mickey Mouse.

I did not want to say anything to her while everyone was present. I waited until the meeting was through then I walked over, but before I could say another word she walked past me as if I wasn't there. I found it curious that she did that, so I followed her till she was back at her desk. "Excuse me," I asked, "Is something wrong?" "No," she replied in a stern voice, "But I'm busy right now as you can tell time is money or money is time." "Whatever, I wanted to talk to you about the meeting to get your feedback." "I think you did an excellent job." "But from your reaction I did not notice that," I said, "you were drawing." "I had nothing better to do. Now can I get on with my work?" And mom for the whole day she did not say another word to me. This has gone on for two weeks now, Mom. She only speaks to me if she wants some information, or if she wants something from the filing cabinet, seeing that my chair is in front of it."

"Thank God she is not your boss," I finally said.

"I know," Alex replied laughing for the first time in the conversation. "If she was, my ass would have been out of here a long time ago."

"Alex", I said in a stern voice, "Be careful, it's not everyone who will like you."

"I know, Mom," she said sadly, "But it still hurts. If I did something to her I would understand,"

"Honey, it's a cold world out there. I'm so sorry I'm not near you to help you go through this, but keep me informed, I want to know what is going on.

"Mom," she said before I hung up the phone, "I love you."

Another week went by and I believed my life was beginning to fall in order again. I was in a deep sleep one night when I heard the phone ring. This gave me the news that shook me to the very core of my being.

"Danielle," I managed to whisper through my sleepiness.

"Mom," she said in tears.

Jumping out of bed "What's wrong?" I asked in an eager voice.

"It's John Kay mom, he's dead."

I wanted to say something, to scream, to talk, but my body could not react. "Dead?" I managed to scream.

"Yes mom, he died last night, overdosed on pain killers."

"I'm so sorry baby," I said falling down on my pillow. I know despite it all she still cared about him; he was her first love and she will never forget that. "I will be there," I told her looking at the clock on my bedside.

"No, it's after two in the morning. I do not want you to drive alone."

"Honey, when my kids need me," I said to her, "I will move heaven and earth." Within two minutes I was in my car heading to her.

"Oh John Kay." I said to myself. The darkness seemed to stand still, just for me, it was as if time would not move. At the same time, the road seemed to be saying it's yours, you go. I hit the accelerator; turning on Hope Road and onto Halfway Tree and then Constant Spring, heading towards Stony Hill towards Danielle. "She needs me." I whispered to myself. It's like I could not reach there fast enough. When I finally did, I saw Cristan and Danielle sitting in the living room. She was crying on his lap. The moment I walked through the door, he got up and hugged me. It's like he was saying, "be there for her" without saying a word, then he headed towards the bedroom. I went over to Danielle and held her.

"Danielle," I said, "it'll be alright."

"If only I could help him a little quicker, Mom."

"No, it's not your fault Danielle," I replied to her. "You could never have predicted this. You tried to help him."

"Oh mom," she cried holding onto me for dear life. "First off Shirley, then grandma now John, John...." but she could not say his name. I kissed her.

"Danielle it's okay baby. John Kay is in a better place now and he is a Christian, he will see God. Think of your faith hold onto it and never let go."

"Yes mom," she finally said, "He is in a better place now, but it still hurts Mom." She began crying again. We cried together until the crack of dawn when Cristan came out and made us breakfast.

"I'm going into my office today," she said.

"Honey take a day off," I advised her. "No, John Kay wouldn't want me to have pity on him. He wasn't that type of a guy, he would want me to get on with my life and live it the best I can." I smiled for the first time - I know my girl has the strength of a lion.

Two weeks later we were at his funeral. I met his ex-wife and his five-year-old daughter. Upon meeting the little girl, Danielle told her that her father was a good person. Danielle explained how they met in college and were good friends. But I noticed that she did not mention anything about their personal relationship. On our way back into Kingston I asked her about it. "It doesn't make sense Mom, to tell her that we were once engaged and that he walked out on me in my darkest hour." "You're right Danielle," I said to her.

To a little girl, her father is a superhero and can never do anything wrong. He would climb the highest mountain, swim the deepest sea just for her, and for me to shatter her dream would only devastate her. For the first time, Cristan spoke throughout the trip, "If Natasha would look down on me, it would break my heart. I do not think I could live with that." Danielle smiled "This is one of the reasons I give you guys moments to spend time together. Even though Joseph needs you, Natasha is now at an age where she needs your influence," she smiled at me. "Why are you smiling at me Danielle?" I inquired. "Mom Natasha thinks Cristan is a God." "Not a God," he said rubbing her hand, "Just superman." "Oh, this is why you always try to do things that you cannot manage?"   "Like what?" "Like climbing the tree and swinging on it like you're flying." "When Natasha looks up at me and I see her little face saying 'Go Dad', I think I can do anything," he replied.

When I arrived home, I got an e-mail from Alexis, the caption read "problem solved". Curiously I called her.

"Mom," she said in an excited voice, "You will never believe this. Antoinette and I are now friends."

"Huh?" I asked.

"Guess what? I found out what was between us. She applied for the same position that I got. Antoinette was angry towards me because she had been working there eighteen months before I did. For Antoinette, this job would have meant better pay for her, and would greatly assist her and her family, since she is now helping her brother through college. Last week we were at a party when she started to choke on a bone. I remember all the training than Toni-Ann used on me when we were kids, when we used to play Dolly house, and I went into action saving her. Now she and I started to talk. I conclude, I do not know what the future holds for us, if we are going to be good friends, but at least we are now talking and in the office I'm a hero," she said gloatingly.

I laughed out loud. "At least those experiments that Toni-Ann used to do on you paid off, although it scared me sometimes when I used to come home and see you bandaged from head to toe. Toni-Ann would look at me with those innocent brown eyes, I just did an operation on her mom she said."

"Mom it's not you alone," Alex said. "Sometimes when she would mix up all those concoctions in the kitchen and force me to drink them it would scare the life out of me."

I laughed again, "Hurry up and come home, Alex."

"Okay mom," she said.

A few months went by and my brother Stephen returned home. When he came to visit me I realized that he no longer had locks. I questioned him about his new conversion. He said, "Sis even tho I am much older I'm a little bit wiser. I had to trim to save my soul." I laughed uncontrollably for a few minutes until I adjusted myself. "Tell me why you said that?" I asked him.

"Well while I was in prison, I caught head lice so many times I cursed uncontrollably. So to solve my problem I had to get rid of the locks."

"I miss you," I told him, "you're like a prodigal son that's returned." When he realized the sadness on my face, he sat down.

"The only regret I had was not seeing my kids grow up sis, and not being there when Miss Kitty went home." I rubbed his hand. He stayed with me for a few days before returning to the country.

As the years rolled by my grandkids increased and my children grew more spiritually. On my 50th birthday, I was scheduled to accept an award at Independence Park for my work with Hope for Jamaica. Standing in front of my mirror, I stared at myself. "I cannot believe I'm now this age," I said. Turning from side to side, I realize that my figure was still there and I smiled. At the award, I sat down beside an elderly man named Mitchell. He informed me that he is a returning resident who came back to live in Jamaica five years ago from England. He was a supervisor at a law firm. When I told him about Danielle, he wanted to meet her. That was their first encounter, and over the months we became good friends often going to church together. At my 53rd birthday Mitchell asked me to marry him, and the day I walked down that aisle, my kids, grandkids, friends and family cheered. I could not believe it had been so long but I was finally a wife.

Footnotes...
Frank died from cancer of the kidney because of this excessive drinking, but his daughter Candice became a teacher; lived and worked in Montego Bay, married a policeman and had a son and daughter. Carlos, Candice's oldest brother after returning from prison, started to date women who were 10, 15 even 20 years older than him, he never looked at a younger girl again. Rita tried to find out about her granddaughter without success, which broke her heart for years to come.

Finally, at the age of 95, before Jasmine closed her eyes for the last time she told her kids, grandkids and great grands who gathered at her bedside, that she had lived a very fulfilling life and did not regret any of it.

"The hard times," she said squeezing her first-borns' hands, "Taught me to be stronger but yet wiser. It also taught me to show everyone respect, for I do not know what the future holds or what they can achieve out of it. Live by the Bible," she told them "And you will never go wrong." As the breath left her body, her girls hugged each other and knew without a shadow of a doubt their mother was a great woman.

~The End~

Blood Type

I am Cristal Alexandra Gay, but my friends call me Crissy for short. A lot has happened to me over the past two years, so before I tell you about the present, let me tell you about the past. I was born on the 25th of December 1977 on a cold wet Tuesday morning. I came into this world so quickly that my parents did not have time to go to the hospital for my delivery. Ever since I was a little child they made it clear to me that I was really special. This had to do with the fact that I was their only child along with the circumstances of my birth.

My mother Annmarie had been a very 'sickly' (unwell) child and because of that, when she and my father, Noel got married, the doctor told them that there was a possibility that they wouldn't be able to have children and, any chance of conceiving would be very slim. Countless visits to the doctor drained them financially. This is when my mother turned to her faith. She prayed, fasted and got to know her Bible more and more. All her efforts proved fruitful as two years after their marriage I came.

My father is a teacher and a very good one too. Although he prefers to deal with adolescents he got a job teaching at a basic school and found it very enjoyable. My mother is a social worker and I treasure her with all my heart. She has a passion for looking after street-children and shows a great deal of passion towards her work. My dad always tells me, "You have your mother's heart." From the day I could go to school by myself and come home without any assistance I took home every stray animal I could find, even if it's a goat. My father jokingly calls his house "a refuge for animals."

Education-wise, I was very brilliant. I got into high school at age ten and by the time I was 15 years old I had eight CXC subjects with distinctions. I went to Sixth

Form and completed it before my 17th birthday and got four A' Levels, also with Distinctions. I took a year off from studies before applying to university. My passion for law inspired me to get a job in a law firm, where I would be able to learn more about the field first-hand before continuing my studies.

I treasure the relationship I have with my parents. My mom is the stern one. She always complains that I wrap my Dad around my little finger (so to speak) and this is why I get away with stuff.

"Crissy," she said one day. "Being a disciplinarian doesn't mean I don't love you." "I know Mom," I said.
"You do? Then why is it you always go to your Dad when you want to get something that you know I will not approve of."
"I do not," I said, smiling.
"When do you not go to your father to get approval for something I have disapproved?" Mom asked sarcastically.

"How about all the time for example," I replied.

She laughed. "Last week you wanted to go out with your friends. I did not approve of you driving on the highway as yet because your licence is young, but somehow you convinced your father that it was a learning experience," my mother retorted.

"But it's true," I said grinning my teeth.

"Yeah right!" she said, rolling her eyes.

"Do you want another example? There are more. In fact, there are hundreds of them, honey," she said on a more serious note. By the time she reached six examples, I had gotten the picture. Getting up, I grabbed my bag to hurry to class, kissed her on the cheek and said, "Mom, at least my life is balanced." Before she responded I was out the door.

I don't keep a lot of friends but the few I have, are very close. I always wanted a sister. I often find myself daydreaming about what it would be like to have one. My best friend, Michelle has two sisters and sometimes I feel jealous of their relationship. That is until I see them fighting and change my mind.

I just completed my first year at law school and was looking forward to going down to the country with my parents for the annual Christmas visit with Grandma, who is a retired nurse. I am so proud of her, especially of how people speak of her in her community. In her 36 years of nursing she has delivered over five thousand babies. Before she retired, everyone I knew would say she had some influence on their lives one way or another. Every visit to my grandmother allows me to get know her more and more, not only by speaking to her, but to others around her. Somehow she manages to make an impact on every life she touches. I have met teachers, nurses and politicians who told me it was my grandmother who delivered them and even helped them to attend school when they were small.

I got home that night and dinner was unusually quiet. Normally, this is the time where my dad would ask about our day and even the week as he often says that he wants to be involved in the lives of his two women.   After dinner Dad said, "Crissy, we need to talk." I looked at mom for some clue as to what was going on.   But instead of a sign, she took her bag and headed for the bedroom, leaving us to face each other. "Crissy, you don't know much about your old man, do you?" I told him I knew everything I need to know about him. "What do you know?" he asked. "That you are a good man, a devoted father and a great husband. You're a hard worker, a good provider and a good son to your mother." I answered. "Yes," he replied, "But I was also a young boy and a teenager." He made space beside him on the couch, and said, "Come sit with me baby," then he began. "Growing up in the country is just as sweet as growing up in the city." "I know," I said, reminiscent of the summers I had spent there, swimming in the river, climbing the trees, running down the animals and away from some. "Yes," he said, "My mom wanted the best for me and my sister but when I was five and my sister just one year old, my father died."

I didn't know much about my grandfather but hearing my dad talk about him I could see that it still hurts him. I reached to hold his hand.

"What killed him?" I asked.

"He got a heart attack," dad replied, "But mother had both of us to hold on to and her work which kept her busy. When I was fifteen years old my sister and her friends went to the river to swim. She got into difficulty and drowned.   This broke my heart."

I said, "I'm so sorry," because I didn't know what else to say or do to comfort him at that moment.

He paused and then said, "Let me take you to when I was 17 years old. I was going to school but often I would skip class and go to a bar where we would smoke and drink."

I looked at him in surprise, "You use to smoke and drink Dad?"

"Yeah," he said, shamefully. "I was trying to be big and to fit in with the crowd at that time. Anyways, I met a lady who was working at the bar I was hanging out in. I would change my shirt so as not to get recognized in my uniform and hang out at the bar all day just to see her. She was 26 years old and even though I was only 17, I thought she was the sexiest thing on earth. She took an interest in me, and by getting to know her I found out that she had two sons and her husband was living in the States. One afternoon she invited me home and I could not believe it. I felt I had died and gone to Heaven. Without hesitation I took her up on her offer. That night I had my first sexual experience with a woman. This went on for months until I found out she was pregnant with my child."

I jumped off the couch! "What!" I said at the top of my voice, "A baby?" "Yes," he said sadly. "Sit back down honey."

Reluctantly, I did and he continued. "Becoming a father at that age wasn't something I wanted, but I didn't believe in certain things, like abortion. I was still going to school and I was not working so I could not support her and the baby. Fortunately, before my father died he had a trust fund for both my sister and I which grew over the years. My mother often said it was my father's dream that we go to the highest level of education. I forged my mother's signature and drew out a large sum of money. Ironically, it was my mother who delivered the baby, not realizing that it was her own granddaughter. While filling out the paper work my mother asked, "What is the baby's name?" I don't know the mother, Ruth, replied. "Ask your son.""

"At home that night I was pacing the floor, sweating through my teeth when I got the news that my mom wanted to see me at the hospital. I prayed all the way and when I arrived my mom came out of the waiting room and asked, "Noel, are you the father of Ruth McKenzie's baby?" Nervously I answered, "Yes mother." She slapped me so hard across my face I saw stars. She was so angry but she didn't want to express it in a room full of people. She told me to go back home and wait for her. That was the longest night of my life. My mother came home after finishing up at the hospital at two in the morning. She called me out of my bedroom and told me to sit. "So, you are a man now," she began. "I send you to school and you go to school between a woman's legs! Don't you know that she is married?" she shouted. "Mom, I didn't know 'til it was too late," I replied. "Too late, too late! Didn't I teach you something out of life?" she said. "Didn't I try to be the best mother I could be to you, Noel?" "Yes, mom," I replied. I saw the tears rolling down my mother's cheeks and I felt so bad. I wished the earth would open up and swallow me that morning. "What are you going to do, Noel?" she asked. "I'm going to move to the town where I can get a job and take care of the baby." I replied."

"Between going to classes in the evening and working during the day I could not visit home often, but, I wrote Ruth frequently to find out about our daughter,

Sarah, and how she was doing. One afternoon I got a letter that changed my life. Ruth's husband had filed for her and his sons. Apparently, he found out about the baby and added her to the file. Ruth insisted that she is not leaving without her daughter and there is nothing I could do about it. She finally convinced me that America is a better place for her to grow up and she will always let her be a part of my life. Reluctantly, I agreed because I wanted to get my life back on track and to be someone that my daughter would be proud of. However, after a few letters she stopped writing. I was so scared and frightened I didn't know what to do. I went back to the country and found a few of Ruth's relatives, who wrote on my behalf, pleading to her that I should be in touch with my daughter. Finally, after a year, she wrote back to me telling me that I was still a boy and her husband wanted to adopt my daughter and raise her as his own. He forgave Ruth for her transgression and wanted to make their marriage work. Ruth told me that I should get on with my life and become a man and get a family of my own. That was the last letter she ever wrote me. I was depressed and started drinking again."

"My mother visited one weekend and saw that my life was going down the tubes. She dragged me to church and asked the Pastor to pray for me, and he did. She also pleaded with me saying I was the only child she had left and if I killed myself, or anything bad happened to me, she would die inside. That is how I got the courage to continue my life and finish school. I went to Teachers' College and continued going to church. That's where I met your mother and my life changed for the better."

After it seemed like we had been sitting for hours my, father finally turned to me and said, "Look at me." He took my hand and said, "Crissy, I've made mistakes in my life, but marrying your mother and having you were the best things I ever did." Not knowing how to respond, I broke down and cried. He held me and let the tears flow from his face also.

Finally I said, "If you do not know how to get in touch with her, why have you told me this story?"

"Because, honey, she is in Jamaica. Sarah is here and she wants to meet both of us. She got in touch with grandma and that is how I found out."

A few seconds passed before I asked, "Does mom know all of this?"

"Yes, I told her everything before we got married."

"Dad, you waited 18 years to tell me?" I asked with a new determination in my voice.

"Honey," he said, hugging me, "I never thought I would meet Sarah again and that is why I didn't want to rock your world by telling you about her. She was just a baby when she migrated and also, when she was adopted by Ruth's husband. Knowing Ruth, I didn't think she would tell Sarah that her husband was not the biological father. It's been 24 years, but I have to face her and apologise to her."

"For what?" I asked. "It's not your fault that her mother took her from you. You did not send her away."

"I know", he said, "But I made lots of mistakes. It was not only Ruth."

For the next few days the house was very quiet – every one of us in our own thoughts. I was thinking "I have a sister, but do I need one? Hell no!" It had been 18 years and I'm practically a woman now. Maybe I wanted one when I was little, but not now. Why is this girl coming into our lives after 24 years? I saw that my father had not even met her and yet it was taking a toll on him emotionally. He spilled juice, bumped into furniture and talked foolishness to himself. Just the thought of her name sent chills down my spine.

I wished the drive to the country would go on forever. When we arrived at Grandma's home, it was drizzling. My father and mother got out of the car leaving me in the back seat. While getting my things together, I took the opportunity to put my thoughts into perspective. "I don't hate this girl," I said to myself. "How can I? I don't even know her. But I do not want her in my life." I asked myself, "Is this wrong?" I got out of the car and walked up the driveway. Instead of going through the front door I went around the back and opened the kitchen door. I could smell the sweet yet spicy aroma of baked chicken and rice and peas. There was also a cake in the oven. My mouth instantly filled with water. I went over and hugged my grandmother from behind and kissed her on the cheek. "Hi, baby," she said without turning around. "I miss you too."

"Do you really Grandma?" I asked.

She said. "Is it just my cooking you miss?"

I smiled and asked, "Can I miss both?"

"Where is Dad?" I asked.

"He went into the living room," she answered.

"I'll be back," I said as I patted her on her head. As I passed through the hall I was just in time to see my dad standing at the living room door. Behind him was a girl standing at the window looking out at the rain. She turned around.   She was beautiful.   She could have passed for a model.

"Hi Daddy," she said. My father who was 6ft 5 inches tall and weighed 210 lbs. was wobbling towards her. He seemed to be shaking at just the thought of meeting his daughter. I could not believe my eyes to see a man that I thought was the bravest person on earth could be so vulnerable at the sight of this girl.

When I was 12 years old there was a robbery at our home. My dad confronted the thief and there was a struggle. My mom became hysterical, screaming and holding me in the corner. There was an explosion and a bullet grazed my dad. When mom saw the blood she fainted. Before it was over the guy lost five teeth and three went down his throat. He also got a broken hand. By the time the Police came, the robber was begging for his life. After all this it was dad who was driving us to the hospital to get my mother and myself checked out. "No matter what," I thought to myself, "as long as Dad is beside me, no one can hurt me even if they have ten guns." When I watched action movies, no matter how great or fantastic the star is, I always say they could never be like my daddy. Now, I see my hero in front of me shaking like a scared little boy and all because of her!

When they finally met in the middle of the room they melted in each other's arms. She was crying and tears were rolling down my father's eyes. I just wanted to get away, and think things through. Their interaction troubled me. I didn't know what I would say or do if I remained there. I started to run across the field, towards Mr. Jones property, through his cow pasture and headed towards the river. I ran until every muscle in my body ached and I could feel my heart beating through my chest. It was two miles to the river and I arrived with shaking hands and took off my clothes and dived into the river to cool my body down. Although it was now raining harder than when I started swimming, everything around me felt so peaceful, I felt my body and mind relax. I did not want to venture too far out because whenever it rains, the water level rises and it can get out of control.

Through my thoughts I heard a voice breaking the silence, "Hey baby. Can I join you?" When I looked up I saw it was Kirk, Mr. Jones' grandson and my biggest enemy as a little girl. Coming here for the summer, I remembered one particular time I wanted to get some mangoes. He convinced me that he would help me to get some big mangoes. He tied a rope around my waist and helped me to climb the biggest tree on his grandfather's property. It felt so good eating the mangoes but before I knew it he was on the ground and I was left in the tree. Laughing he said, "Hey Rugrat. Come down!" He knew I was scared. Then his friend joined him and they started to tease me. I started to cry. Pleading and begging didn't help me because the more I did is the more they laughed. Then Kirk took the rope and started pulling it. The more I screamed was the more excited they got. Finally Mr. Jones heard the commotion and came to rescue me. From that summer I avoided him and his friend. They had played other tricks on me but none as scary and cruel as that day. I was scared of heights but I wanted those mangoes so bad and I guess my greed got the better of me.

My mind came back to the present when he said "Skinny dipping in the rain is my favourite pastime."

"What do you think you're doing?" I asked him when I saw him taking off his top and throwing it to the ground.

"I already told you," he said smiling.

"I'm joining you."

"Are you crazy?" I asked. My phone began to ring. "Please," I said, "let me get out and put on my clothes. I have to get the phone."

He started to laugh in that voice I have hated over the years. "Are you crazy," he said. "I can see you naked and don't join you for a dip. Come on now Rugrat, do you take me for a fool?" He started to unbuckle his pants. My phone rang again. "Come on, Kirk. You'll get both of us in trouble. Now let me answer my phone. It's my father." Hearing this statement he stopped in his tracks. Just mentioning my father was near was enough.

"Are you telling me your father is here with you?"

"Dah!" I said. "Did you not see his car in the driveway? I know you are a spy."

"Your grandmother told me last week that you started driving and I just assumed that you drove the car."

"No." I said sharply. "It's my dad and if I don't answer the phone he will come looking for me."

He picked up his shirt and threw it over his shoulder and, turning his back he said, "Hurry up, Rugrat. I don't want to keep your father waiting. After all he will soon by my father-in-law."

"Over my dead body," I said getting out of the water.

"That could be arranged," he laughed.

With trembling hands I put on my clothes. I answered my phone on the last ring. "Hello Dad," I said.

"Where the Hell are you?!" he asked angrily.

"With a friend," I said, not wanting him to know the truth.

"Well, get home!"

"I'm coming," I said. Before I could continue he hung up.

Heading back through the path I caught up with Kirk. Turning to face me he says, "Merry Christmas sweetheart."

"I am not your sweetheart," I snapped back.

"Not yet," he smiled. "By the way you said you hate me from I was small. You're not a little girl anymore," he said looking at me with dreamy eyes. "Listen," I said, "I don't like you. Never have, never will!"

"Time can change things," he said.

"Not my feelings towards you."

"Can a man dream?"

"Only reality, not fantasy." He smiled. "I can find my way home and I don't need any company or any bodyguard," I said angrily. "You know, Kirk, for some strange reason I believe you do not take insults." I picked up my pace trying to outpace him but stride by stride he kept up with me until I reached my driveway. My father greeted us on the verandah and from the look on his face I saw he was angry. "Good evening Mr. Gay," Kirk said, but my father only frowned at him.

"You're wet," he said to me.

"Yes, the rain caught me."

"Go and change. I want to see you in the dining room." Without saying another word I passed him and headed for my bedroom. I almost felt sorry for Kirk. Some other guys would bolt when they hear news, but like a lap dog, Kirk keeps coming back for more and more punishment, not only from me but from my dad. Taking off my clothes I fell on the bed. I ached all over, even in places I don't want to mention. I've never run such a distance in a long while and my body was screaming for help. It needed assistance from a doctor.

With some difficulty, I managed to change and headed towards the dining room. My father was standing beside Sarah. "Hi," I said. "Honey, this is your sister." On an impulse I went over and held out my hand. When she took it I groaned.

"Is something wrong?" she asked.

Reluctantly I said, "I was helping Kirk remove some of the animals from low ground. I guess it took a toll on my body."

"Well," she said, "maybe I should hug you instead."

Without another word her arms were around me. The emotion that ran through my body scared the hell out of me. I was expecting to feel angry or even hatred towards her, but what I felt I could not explain to myself. The room was cold but I felt very warm. Then I realized her warmth was coming from her tears, from her eyes to my neck. Without thinking my arms went around her and we embraced each other. Finally she pulled back, looking at me. "You look like him," she said. Everyone said so. Dad interrupted, coming between us, looking from one to the other with a big smile on his face. "Dinner is getting cold," he said. "Let's eat."

Dinner went off okay. Everyone seemed to be getting along. Sarah looked comfortable and at home. I looked at my grandma and noticed there was some contentment in her mannerisms. I realize that she got what she always wanted – her family together. Gosh, I thought, it must have killed her over the years not to be able to tell me about Sarah. For a brief second Sarah's eyes and mine met across the table and I notice something I couldn't put my finger on. Was it longing? Fright? I thought I did not know but there was something wrong. After dinner we sat in the living room watching television. Grandma and my mother excused themselves, complaining of being tired and fatigued and wanted to go to bed early. The three of us were left. My father asked Sarah, "How did you find out about me?"

"It was by accident," she said. "I found out about a year ago when my older brother, Mark, and I got into an argument."

"What was it about?" my father asked.

"Before I tell you, she replied, "Let me tell you about my family's situation. As you know, I have two older brothers and then two younger brothers. They are twins, David and Kevin. Being in the middle and the only girl I guess they thought my father treated me very special. I got a job in Atlanta, Georgia and I moved there. My father paid for my apartment for the first six months to get me on my feet. He also bought me a car and I guess Mark felt jealous. He found a girlfriend a couple of blocks from me. One Friday night, he came by my apartment wanting to borrow my car and when I refused he went away and came back around midnight, drunk as a bat. "I just wanted to borrow your lousy car. Anyways, I don't see anything special about this shit," he said. "You think you're very special because of Dad and you not being his own child." "What?" I said. He realized what he had done but it was too late. I asked him to explain but he refused and ran out the door. So, I got in my car and drove back to Orlando where my parents lived.

I arrived there about three in the morning. I opened the door with my spare key. My parents were still up watching a late night movie and were surprised to see me. I asked, "Am I your child?" My father was staring at me like he was surprised at the question. "Of course," he said. "No, I don't mean like that," I said, getting angry. "I mean am I your biological child?" My mother's head lowered and I realized Mark was right. My dad put down his beer and got up. I stepped back. "Am I? Tell me the truth, damn it! I am twenty-four years old and I want to know!" My mother could not control her emotion anymore. She started to cry. My father grabbed me. "Listen," he said, "You are my child." "Am I your biological child?" Our eyes met and his seemed to be staring into my soul searching to find out how I would react when he speaks again. Finally he said, "No."

"Are David and Kevin?"

"Yes."

"Are the other two?"

"Yes." I looked over at my mom. She was still sobbing uncontrollably. He drew me closer into his arms. "Baby," he said, "You are everything I always wanted in a daughter and more. Your mom made a mistake."

"Am I a mistake? Am I a product of a mistake?"

"You are not a mistake." he replied. "Listen, your mom and I were not together. I was here and she was in Jamaica. It was an honest to God mistake but I am not sorry because you are perfect." After what seemed to be an hour of crying, he finally left the room giving me time to speak with my mother. I went to her on the couch and said, "Look at me mother." She finally got the courage to hold her head up. "Who is my biological father?" I asked. Then she told me about you. I was so shocked to find out that you were a school boy at the time. It took all of my control not to call her a slut. Finally, she said I must not hate you. I said I didn't hate you but didn't know how I felt about her. For the next few months we hardly spoke to each other. Then I came down with a terrible flu and she came to care for me." Slowly, Sarah turned around and looked at our father and I saw that there was something terribly wrong in her eyes. "Dad," she said, "I have leukemia. I was diagnosed two months ago. I was supposed to be on radiation but I know the system. There might be a possibility that I would need a bone marrow transplant. This is the reason why I am searching for every family member just in case I need it. My doctor also informed me that, if this is necessary he would place me on a list but I was told hundreds of people died. Without being the first on the list the best chance I have is to get a match from a relative."

I saw my father's shoulders droop. He finally found his daughter and maybe he might lose her. I think it was too much for him. He put his head in his hands and started to cry. I leaned over and hugged him but didn't cry. "Dad," I said, "Do not cry." Sarah also began to console him. After a few minutes he said, "Where should we do the test?" The mention of the word sent a chill through my spine. Ever since I was a little girl I hated hospitals and needles. My parents had to literally hold me down and drag me there, kicking and screaming all the time. I recall once when I was ten years old I fell off my bike and bruised my knee. My dad took me to the hospital to get it dressed. When I saw the nurse take out a needle, I fainted. I remember another time I got injured playing wrestling with Michelle. Instead of telling my parents about my arm, I bore the pain for days until it got infected and started to swell. It took all of my parents' energy over the years to get me through my phobia and now my father wanted me to go through all that again for something that may be unnecessary. "I don't think so," I thought.

That night I could not sleep. I tossed and turned in the bed all night. Finally, when I drifted off to sleep, I dreamt I was in a taxi heading towards an unknown place. When I arrived and the driver turned around to collect my fare, I realized the driver was a man in a surgical mask with a cutting tool and a big needle in his hand. "It is time," he said. I got out of the car as fast as I could and started to run. He started to chase me. When I looked back there were others joining him, all dressed up in gowns with masks. I ran inside a building screaming and asking for help. A lady came to my assistance. She told me they wouldn't find me but it was a trap. She led them to me. They turned on the light and I saw a big, lonely cold room with a bed in the middle. They tied me up and placed me on the bed. Immediately, all types of machines surrounded me. The man that was the taxi driver came over to me with two knives ready to cut me up...... I jumped out of my sleep screaming with sweat pouring down my face. Before I knew it, my grandma was in my bedroom, beside me, touching me and trying to calm me down. She said, "You are trembling." After a few seconds, I regained my composure. "It's OK Grandma," I said. "No its not," she replied looking at me with concern. "I just had a nightmare. What time is it?" She turned and looked at the clock on my nightstand. "It is just after six. Do you want a glass of water or a cup of tea?" "Do you mean chocolate tea?" I asked with a smile on my face. She kissed me on the cheek. "For you, my baby, anything."

"I am 18 years old Grandma. I'm no longer a baby."

"You will always be my baby," she said.

For the next two days Sarah tried to speak with me but I always avoided her. On the day we were leaving for Kingston she finally caught me alone. I was in the kitchen washing the dishes.

"I want to get to know you better," she said.

I turned around and asked, "Why?"

"Because we are sisters."

"Half-sisters!" I said sharply.

"There is a big difference."

"Not to me," she said as she came closer. After a few awkward moments she finally continued.   "Dad told me you are in law school."

"Yes," I said.

"That's good.   What do you want to specialize in?" she asked.

"Criminal Law."

"Oh, to get the bad guys?"

"Something like that." I said, putting away the last dish and attempting to walk away.

She held me, "Crissy," she said, "I am the only sister you have and you are the only one that I have.   Please give us a chance."

"Tell me something. If you didn't find out that you were sick, would you seek out Dad and me?"

She stared into my face. "Yes," she said.

"I don't believe you," I said, walking away.

Under dad's supervision that evening, I reluctantly gave her my email address and cell number. She informed us that

Dr. Grant, who is based at the Kingston Public Hospital, would do the test for us and send the results to Florida. After pictures, hugs and kisses and well-wishes, I got in the car. Before I could close the door Sarah stood between me and it.

"I have not gotten a goodbye hug," she said leaning over the car door.

"Look," I said sharply, "We are sisters. That doesn't mean we are friends." Before she could reply my parents got in the car.

"Is everything OK?" my dad asked.

"Sure dad," Sarah said. She went around to where he was and gave him a final hug.

The journey back home was filled with most of the conversation being between my parents. I, on the other hand, was staring through the window, lost in my own thoughts. "If this girl thinks she can come into my life and turn it upside-down, she has made a sad mistake." I thought to myself. "I will never put myself through unnecessary pain just because of her – especially for her," I muttered to myself.   "Not even if they pay me a million dollars.   Hell, this is the 21st century.   Forcing someone to do something against their will is not only immoral – it is illegal!" There and then I came up with a plan.   Avoid, avoid and avoid some more - her, Dad and the topic!   Leaning back in the seat I felt better.   "After all," I said to myself, "What I don't know won't hurt me."

A week passed before I got the first email from her.   When I did not respond to it, she called. I saw her number on the phone screen and I waited until it went to voicemail. After a few minutes I retrieved it.   "Hi Crissy," she said, "I hope you are OK.   I wish I could talk with you.   We need to talk."   Finally she continued, "We have some unfinished business," and hung up.

In order to avoid my dad, I tried studying on campus or at a friend's house, therefore arriving home very late and tired most of the time. When I got home

I would head straight to my room. After a few weeks of this, Dad waited up for me one night. When I turned on the light in the living room he was sitting in the dark. "Crissy...," he began, "Why are you avoiding your sister?" My mouth dropped open.

"What do you mean Dad?", I asked innocently.

"I said your sister told me she's been trying for weeks now to get in touch with you, as I have...come to think of it. I hardly see you..., so what's up?"

"You know university Dad," I said trying to reassure him. I tried to explain to him that it was very demanding and I wanted to do well especially since I'm in my first year. He was staring across the living room as if he was trying to analyze in his mind exactly what I was saying.

Finally he said, "Come here baby." I went over to him and sat beside him. He put his arm around me.

"Do you know how much I love you?"

"Yes," I replied.

"And, do you know that you're still my baby."

"Yes," I said.

He took out his cell phone and dialed a number. When the other party picked up he passed the phone to me and said, "Speak to your sister. I want you and her to get to know each other. Please honey. Do it for me." All my life I knew my father as being a proud man. He didn't beg or borrow or bow down to anyone. But at this moment I could hear him pleading with me and my heart broke as I put the phone to my ears.

"Hello," I began.

"Crissy," Sarah said, "How are you?"

"I'm fine. You?" I asked.

"OK... but the radiation treatment is taking a toll on my body and that I feel so weak."

"I'm sorry to hear," I said. "Maybe we should talk some other time."

"I'm not too weak to talk, Crissy. I've wanted to talk to you for weeks now." Without saying another word my dad got up and walked towards his room. "I'm sorry," I said. "I have been busy."

"Can I ask you something, Crissy? How can you hate me when you don't even know me? You formed an impression of me in your mind and you decided there and then to hate everything about me."

"I don't hate you," I said.

"I believe you do, Crissy, but think of this. How would you feel if someone treated you the same way?" I couldn't say a word because I knew deep in my heart she was right. Finally she broke the silence that was between us. "Another thing, Crissy," she said. "You claim that we are half-sisters, not friends but that doesn't matter. We come from the same man, so if you hate me you hate a piece of yourself also." I felt so ashamed. I wished the earth would just open and take me in at that moment.

"Are you still there, Crissy?" she asked.

"Yes," I said. "What should we do now, Sarah?"

"Let's get to know each other then we can form an impression of the other and see if we get to like each other or not. But, I can tell you this, Crissy, I could never hate you."

My heart melted. Finally I said, "I'm sorry."

We spent the rest of the night talking and learning about each other. Surprisingly, we had a lot in common. We both liked karate movies and, like me, she is a sucker for romance! We each found math difficult and until this day she said she cannot do anything without a calculator. The more we spoke, the more I relaxed and I found myself telling her a lot about my childhood days. She laughed uncontrollably when I told her about the incident when I was eight years old, playing hide and seek with my friends. I had hidden on the roof but the roof was so hot I shifted right off the edge and landed on top of Rex, the dog. Fortunately he was not hurt but I, on the other hand, was so shaken by my feelings of guilt that in the evening, I gave Rex my dinner. I felt better when I saw him wagging his tail as he was getting down in my chicken leg! By the time I told her two more of my childhood adventures she was begging me to stop, saying she would burst if she did not stop laughing.

When she got her composure back, I asked her to tell me some of her stories. She said when she was ten her mom wanted her to stop eating sweets. When she bought some candy, not wanting her to find it, she hid them in her undies. Unfortunately, she went to bed with them there and ants took them over and started to bite where the sun don't shine! Her mom decided to come into her room at that moment to search for a pen and saw her digging. "What's wrong," she asked. Not wanting to tell her about the candies she said, "I was praying Mom, and the Spirit got a hold of me." The more the ants bit her, the more she shouted, "Amen!" Finally, she couldn't take it anymore and she jumped out of the bed and dropped her panties on the floor, scratching and slapping, naked as the day she was born. The sweets were on the floor, with the ants covering it. She thought her mom would be angry and punish her, but she looked at her pitifully and said, "I think you have punished yourself enough."

I started to crack up, picturing that story in my mind. By the time we got off the phone, it was three o'clock in the morning. The last thought I had in my mind before sleep got a hold of me, was that finally I had a sister. With that realization I said to myself, "I don't want to lose her." My God, I did not want to lose her! I got out of bed and for the first time in a long time I went on my knees and said a special prayer to the Lord for her.

For the next few weeks we were in touch constantly, e-mails, texting and phone calls. She completed the chemotherapy treatment and from all indications, she was doing well. She even had a plan to visit Jamaica for our Dad's birthday. I was happy everything was going well in my life and our relationship was getting closer. My parents and I were perfect and I even met a new guy, Fabian. He was studying medicine. From all indications I was on cloud nine and didn't want to come off. But my world came to a stop one Friday night.

I was expecting to hear from Sarah because she usually called at the start of the week. Waiting all day and not hearing from her, I started to get anxious. Finally, in the night the phone rang. It was Sarah's mother saying that Sarah had fainted and they had to rush her to the ER. The doctors said she had a negative side effect from the radiation and definitely would need a bone marrow transplant this time!

"Ruth, Ruth!" I cried. "Is she going to be alright?"

"I don't know," I heard her saying through the sobs. My dad was pacing the floor like a wounded animal. Instantly, I ran into his arms, not only to comfort him, but to comfort myself as well.

"What are we going to do?" I asked.

"I don't know, baby," he replied sadly.

"Dad," I said finally, "I want to be tested on Monday to see if I am a match." He looked straight into my eyes, recognizing my courage, knowing well my phobia towards hospitals. My mom came and joined us. When words could not explain our feelings, our tears did, as we all embraced each other.

On Monday morning, my parents accompanied me to the Kingston Public Hospital. Doctor McLean conducted the examination, it was so difficult for me. I even begged him at one point to put me to sleep. He laughed and said, "It will be alright. I'm just going to draw some blood." I looked ridiculous, with both my parents in the room with me, holding my hands! When it was all over my dad insisted on taking me for ice cream. After arguing with him about my new status, becoming an adult…we finally settled on pizza and fruit juice. The doctor said he would put a priority on the test since it had to go to the States. Hopefully, if we were lucky, we would get the results in three days.

I had never prayed so hard in my life. I made a list of the things I would give up if everything would be okay. Sitting at the computer, I began: 1) no more self-satisfaction for myself. I will try to think of others first; 2) no more lying especially the unnecessary ones; 3) try not to insult people so much, even Kirk. I drew a line under his name and wrote *more prayers*; 4) think of what is more important in my life, my family, my faith and my education; 5) I will try to appreciate everyone and everything around me because when its gone it might never come back; 6) do not put a price on emotion, love, happiness, joy. Express it freely before it is too late. I continued writing for about half an hour until my cell phone rang which startled me.

"Hello," I said with a trembling hand, as a voice said, "Honey, its dad." My heart stopped. I did not want to hear any bad news. I didn't know how I would cope.

Finally he said, "Are you still there?"

"Yes, still here."

"What's the news, dad?"

"It's a perfect match!" I could not believe what I was hearing.

"Say it again."

"You are a perfect match!" he shouted excitedly.

For the next few days I was so busy. Dad looked after my documents to visit the States and I was organizing my lectures to try to keep up with my class work. Fabian was a sweetheart. He insisted that he would be the one to take notes for me in class.

When I finally arrived at the Miami airport it was Ruth who greeted me. She was not as beautiful as my mother, I thought, and she was quite plump. But the embrace that she gave me and how she interacted with me made me like her instantly. When we were in the car on our way to her home I looked at her more closely. I thought, this is the woman who turned my father's life upside down all those years ago. I could see how he would have been attracted to her. She must have been a very beautiful woman when she was in her twenties, and to a school-boy, an older woman would be picking the forbidden fruit. She insisted that I stay at her place and not a hotel. "After all…," she said to me, "You are part of the family."

In the morning I arrived at the hospital to see Sarah for the first time in months. Standing at the door, I hesitated before I went in. She opened her eyes. She saw me and said, "So come give your sister a hug. I hear that you have come to save your favourite sister's life."

"You are my only sister," I said.

"Damn right," she said. We started to laugh and I realized that made her uncomfortable.

"Are you OK?" I asked.

"It could be worse," she replied.

Not wanting her to get depressed I said, "I met your father, Lloyd, last night. He is not as cute, dynamic or sexy as mine."

"Really!" she said smiling at me.

"Yeah," I said, "But he's OK."

At that moment, the doctor entered the room. He was a middle-aged, bald, Caucasian man with strikingly dark blue eyes. He explained that I had to complete a battery of tests before the surgery could begin and the tests had to be done right away. Immediately Sarah sensed my anxiety and held my hand. "Doctor," she said, "My sister has a phobia about hospitals and everything in them. Would it be possible for an extra bed to be put beside me?"

He looked at one and then the other of us, "This is not hospital policy but I can speak to the supervisor in charge and we'll see what we can do. Now, ladies do you want me to explain the whole procedure to you?"

I quickly said, "No, the only thing I want to know is if you will put me to sleep." He smiled and nodded, yes. I let out a sigh and thanked God. After that, I asked to be excused, to call home. Leaving the room I heard them in conversation about what will happen.

To my relief they granted us our request the night before surgery. I got to stay with Sarah. I was starving because they told us not to eat anything after 5:00 p.m. I tried to take my mind off food by studying.

"I have a big exam at the end of the month," I told her, "And Fabian will take notes for me. Oh, I forgot to tell you about him! He's really a cute guy and a medical student, but sometimes he sits in class with me when he's not studying for himself."

"Really," Sarah said.

And, trying to change the subject I asked, "And what about you? Do you have someone special?

"Yeah," she said.

"Who is it?"

"Andrew. We were high school sweethearts but then times and things changed. He joined the army and has just come back from Iran."

"Really," I said. "Yeah, I guess old fire stick catches easily."

She looked at me blankly. "I don't understand what that means."

"Oh, I forgot you are not a real Jamaican. What it means is that there is still a spark between the two of you that can be easily re-ignited."

She laughed, "Go to bed, Crissy." Turning her back to me she said, "And, for your information I am one hundred and ten percent Jamaican."

The next morning, at 6:30 a.m. the nurse came with the porter to take Sarah and me to the operating room. The room was cold, and although there were many lights, it seemed very dark. I wanted to scream and run out, but I knew that if I had a nervous breakdown they would not be able to do the surgery. Fortunately, the doctor whom I met upon arrival, came to my bedside and said "Miss Gay, it's okay, close your eyes". His voice was reassuring and I did what he told me. He lifted my hand up and I felt a sting. The next thing I remember is waking up in the evening with the nurse offering me some soup. The first question I asked was, "Where is Sarah?"

"She is recovering," the nurse said with a smile.

I tried to turn on my side but she held me down. The pain rushed through me. "It's OK," she said, rubbing my hand.

"What did they do?" I asked.

"They took the marrow from your hip. Now let me feed you your soup."

I closed my eyes at those words and wished my mom was with me. When I was a little girl getting the flu was a nightmare but having my mom's chicken soup and her comforting me to sleep was the best thing I could ever have in my life. Lying in this hospital bed, I felt homesick and yearned for both my parents. I am 18 years old I thought to myself, but I still needed their support and affection.

Thank God, the week went by quickly, and before I knew it I was at Ruth's home again, with strict instructions to take my medication and stay off my feet for another two weeks. Ruth treated me like her long lost daughter. She was so grateful to me, I believe she would have given me the world. I told her that it wasn't a duty but a pleasure for me to help Sarah. I had developed such feelings of respect, love and appreciation towards Sarah as my sister.

I returned to Jamaica shortly thereafter. My family, including my grandmother, was waiting for me at the airport. It had been several years since Grandma came to Kingston. To think that she did this just for me filled my heart with such joy. She spent two weeks with us. Grandma became sort of like my conscience, always reminding me every time I forgot to eat right or take my medication. Fortunately, I didn't fall back in class, and was able to keep up with the other students.

Sarah was discharged from the hospital and was recuperating very well. Everything that had troubled me seemed all right again. I thanked God that everything was going so well, not only with my family but with Fabian as well. He finally met my father and he, being a Christian, was accepted. But there were strict guidelines concerning where we could go and what we could do. Fabian seemed to accept everything my father put down as law. I appreciated this because most guys would have run away. Fabian unlike many other guys was determined to be there for the long haul.

Months passed, and with my final exam out of the way, I completed my first year with good grades. I wanted to celebrate with Fabian that night. I was on my way to his home and I picked up my phone and called him. "Hi, Baby," I said. "I want to go see a movie tonight. Are you game?"

"Yes," he said.

"I'm on the way to your home – get ready."

"Sure, Honey" he said.

I hung up the phone and put it back in the glove compartment. I looked up, and the only thing I can remember were the two lights that were heading towards my car. Immediately, I was transported to another world. It was a beautiful garden. I could smell the lilies and the violets. It seemed that every flower under the sun was there. A handsome gentleman, dressed in a white robe came to greet me, smiling and reassuring me. I felt at peace and strangely, at home. There were other people there, walking around and looking so happy. He wanted me to come with him and so we began walking.

As we passed a stream, he filled a cup with some water. The water tasted like the sweetest water I had ever drank in my life - pure, perfect, and cool. We continued on our journey and arrived at a big gate made of gold. He lifted up his right hand and the gate automatically opened. Then he turned to me and beckoned me to enter. Then I heard the voice say, "Crissy!" But I ignored the voice and started to walk to the gate when I heard the voice again say, "Crissy baby, come back. Come back to me!" I knew that voice but he still beckoned me to enter and then I heard the voice again say, "Baby, baby I can't live without you." Then I realized that it was my mother and I turned to him. He understood, and turned to walk to the gate by himself. The gate closes behind him and I wake up.

The first person I saw was my mother with tears running down her cheek. She was holding my hand and when she saw that my eyes had opened she cried out loud, causing the nurse to enter the room. She turned to the nurse and cried, "She's awake, she's awake!" The nurse came over to my bed and picked up the telephone, I guess to inform the doctor because a few minutes later he was at my bedside examining me, pointing a light into my eyes.

"Can you hear me?" he asked.

"Yes," I replied slowly.

"You were out for a while – actually three days." He could see the surprise in my eyes and he smiled. "Don't worry, you'll be OK within a few hours." My dad walked into the room and kissing me on the cheek, he lovingly said, "Hi, baby, I have a surprise for you." When I turn my head I saw Sarah. "I just picked her up at the airport," Dad continued.

She came over and hugged me. She said, "So how is my favourite sister?"

"I'm your only sister," I replied.

She smiled and said, "Don't you ever forget it."

I turned to my mom. "What happened? I don't remember much."

"It was a truck which was speeding," she said. "The truck ran through a stop light on Marcus Garvey Highway and headed straight into your car."

"Is the driver OK," I ask concernedly.

"Yes," said my dad, "He's at the police station, lucky for him because I would kill him if I got the chance! He will be charged for speeding and driving under the influence."

Seeing our dad getting angry, Sarah interrupted him. "Hey, the doctor tells me that you will be here for at least a few days more. Lucky for you I've brought my portable DVD player with some of your favourite movies and some romance novels. This will keep us busy for the few days."

It was then I realized, with surprise Sarah *was* in the room! "What are you doing here? Did the doctor give you permission to travel so soon?"

She laughed, "I don't think he had a choice. Not even the jaws of death could stop me from coming."

For the next few days, Sarah rarely left my side. Not only did we watch the DVDs together but she read the novels to me. Fabian came to visit often bringing me my package for my second year. He met Sarah and both of them hit it off so well that they even started to gang up on me when I protested saying two on one is murder. They laughed. "Luckily I'm a doctor," Fabian said jokingly, "I could make it look like a heart attack."

As soon as I was well enough, Andrew who was Sarah's love joined us in the island and the four of us went around Jamaica getting to know our country. We spent the rest of the summer together until Sarah and Andrew returned home and I resumed classes at the university. By the time the Christmas holiday arrived, Sarah and Andrew were engaged to be married! Fabian started his internship. I was settling back into my routine and doing well in my discipline. I was looking forward to going to Barbados the following year. I would miss Fabian but from what I realize, our relationship is very strong and we will make it through because we really care about each other.

Sarah, over the Christmas, came back to visit our father. While having dinner she said, "Dad, as you know I'm getting married. Please understand that I've really grown to love and care for you but my father Lloyd was the only dad I had ever known for 24 years of my life and I really want him to walk me down the aisle." We looked at his face for some type of disappointment but what I saw was understanding and care. "It's OK," he said. Turning to me and smiling he added, "I would feel the same if it was Crissy." Sarah came around to his chair putting her hand on his shoulder she said, "Noel Gay, you are a wonderful man. I am proud to be your child. I would be proud if you would attend my wedding."

~The End~

Betrayal

Putting my hands to my face and wiping the sleep from my eyes. I rolled over in bed thinking that this was another day in my life that I was unsure of. Depressed and alone, I thought, if only I could just get through one more day.

I wondered about my past. I looked to see David sleeping beside me. He looked so innocent, but I stopped fooling myself, he was a cheater, and I knew deep down inside that it might be happening to me once more. Getting out of bed, my feet touched the cold floor. What happened to me a year ago, suddenly hit me. I stumbled into the bathroom and splashed cold water over my face. Squinting the sleep out of my eyes, I stared at my pale face in the mirror. Leaning on the basin for support, I wondered how I got to this stage.

I grew up in a small farming community called Friendship Cross in Western Jamaica. The Carbarita River flows between the Georges Plain to the south and the Dolphin Head Mountains to the north. This river originates in Hanover and crosses Westmoreland, supplying water to the sugar lands and factory at Frome and ending at the sea at Carbarita Point in Savanna La-Mar. We loved the river as it was not only our playground, it also provided irrigation for the farmers, and was our life source during the dry period between January and April.

The Dolphin Head Mountains grew acres of bamboo. Young men cut down these bamboo trees to build rafts for tourists that would traverse the rivers. The tourists reveled in the surrounding natural beauty; it was so different from their own homelands. This mountain also produced world famous coffee grown on the high altitude slopes. When the ripe beans were being roasted, the aromas would drift down into the valley with scents everyone could enjoy. I was only three years old when I had my first taste of our famous local bean.

Most of the farmers planted everything, including tomatoes, scallion, and watermelon. The famers supplied hotels in the surrounding areas, like Jakes Paradise on the north coast and as far as Coronation market in Downtown Kingston which is hundred and twenty miles away. Those who did not farm the land, reared animals such as cows, goats, pigs and chickens. Due to the remoteness of my community, many farmers used wooden carts drawn by donkeys or mules to transport the produce from their farms to a central collection area where they were picked up for the various final destinations. By the time I was five years old, I could tell by the sound of the horn, whose truck was approaching the collection area. Such as Mr. Smith, who drove a 1966 Toyota pickup. His horn sounded like a cow calling her young but his truck was more reliable than some of the newer models.

Friendship Cross was a close-knit community, everyone in the valley knew each other, and if you traced the families back, many of us were related. I am the youngest of eight children. My father's name is Joshua Ezekiel Daublin and my mother is Mary Catherine Daublin. As I said before I am the last child for my parents and this is how their story goes: They had five boys, one after the other and decided to try for a girl. Well, my sister Johan was born. My father claimed that his family was unbalanced with five boys and one girl, so they decided to try again and had Michelle. My mother wanted to have a tubal ligation at that stage, but my father, being very conservative and (as far as he was concerned) religious, claimed that it was not necessary because she was going through menopause. So, baps! I came and as my father would say, I am the wash-belly, being the last for them. I act just like it because he claims that when my mother was going through her pregnancy cycle, she was very miserable and I was born miserable.

My name is Susan Catherine Daublin. My first brother John, is now a farmer like my dad. John is married with three children, all girls. My second brother Desmond, is a teacher at a basic school in the community. My other brothers Rohan, Rupert and Tyrone are plumber, carpenter and technician, respectively.

From ever since I was a child I knew I was not meant to be a farmer's daughter. I never felt I belonged in a farming community. My father would often jokingly say that the only way Susan's hands would ever touch the ground was if she stumbled and fell on her face. Or he would say that Susan was allergic to animals. Even though I would get angry when he made those comments, I knew deep down inside he was right. I can remember when my father would slaughter an animal I would get sick to the stomach because of the blood. By the time I was seven, I became a vegetarian so while my relatives and friends were enjoying curried goat and jerk pork with their meals, I would have salt fish with mine.

My sister Johan was 25 years old when she got married and has one daughter. As far as my father was concerned she was a virgin until her wedding night. But I knew that she and her husband Peter were together sexually for many years before they got married, as I was their look-out girl.

Michelle was 21 years old when she got engaged to Jack; a guy with great standards and value in his community at Grange Hill. His father owns several properties, including a garage. Jack managed the garage, and trained young boys in the vocation without charging them. Being the only son, Jack would inherit most of his father's wealth. But Michelle has a secret, that no one in the community knows, not even our family, except me. She does not have any feelings for men, only women. She often tells me when we are talking, being that she confided in me ever since I was small. When we talked she said she felt that I was her priest, and she did not need to confess in Church. I felt it was an honour and a privilege that she had such trust in me, and I was determined not to betray her trust. We knew that the truth would kill our father, and before he died he might just kill her for bringing shame and disgrace to our family. For many years she took great care not to show signs of her sexual preference, even though I knew deep down inside it was tearing her apart. She introduced me to her girlfriend Janet who happened to be Jack's younger sister. They went to Westen High together and were inseparable from the first day. They would go hiking, swimming, the library and cinema together, and often spent nights at Janet's home with my mother's blessing. Ironically, it was Janet who introduced Michelle to Jack. My family thinks nothing strange of their friendship, as they think of them as sisters. I guess being engaged to Jack is the only way she can be close to Janet without arousing suspicion. Our Father Joshua, and Jack's dad Moses, knew each other from their early twenties, drinking in the local bar together and playing dominoes. Their relationship grew over the years and they often boasted that with their kids coming together, they would be bigger and better as a result of the union.

Chapter 2

I was an excellent high school student. My favourite subjects were History, Geography, Art and Psychology. My mother would often give me the privilege of studying instead of doing chores, which I hated. My father complained that my mother spoilt me, and if she wasn't careful, I would grow up thinking I was better than them, including her. I had to travel fifteen miles to use the parish library, often begging rides with the farmers as they took their produce to and from the collection centre. Due to the close knit nature of our community, I had no fear of driving with the farmers.

Returning home was a challenge. I often travel home late at night when taxis were few and far between; but I was determined so I would frequently walk. By the time I arrived home, dinner was already eaten. My father would threaten that one day none would be left for me, but my mother always ensured that dinner was waiting for me when I arrived home. My father would chide me saying that I should be glad I lived in an age of technology, as in his younger days he never knew electric light, much less computers. He would say, "I don't know what those boxes are teaching you, but for your sake I hope you get off your high horse." As far as I was concerned if I was on a high horse, I would ride it straight to the finish line. When I remember waiting three hours to do an assignment at the library and how slow it was to connect to the internet, compared to now, I smiled to myself. If my father had to be forced to use a tablet or kindle now, maybe he would have a heart attack. He is one of those men who is comfortable in his own space, and does not see the need for change. One of his favourite sayings was, "Why fix it if it isn't broken?" The worst thing you could do was to try to impose your belief or opinion on him, or try to argue with him when he had a view on something, so I learned over the years to leave him in his space where he is most comfortable. We get on better that way.

I finished high school at the age of eighteen and got a part scholarship to the University in Kingston. My challenge now, was how to survive out there, when I had never left my parish in my entire life. I have never been on my own for more than one night. Packing my suitcase and getting ready to leave for the city, my parents sat me down and said "Now listen, you are going to that place for I don't know how long." I said "Three years, mommy." "Well, three years is long enough", my father said. He continued, "don't give nobody your books because you nuh know weh dem wi do wid it people hand no clean." "No wear nobody clothes", my mother remarked, stuffing my last pair of jeans into my suitcase, especially them shoes. "They will give you big foot," she said. I smiled. "Big foot mother? This is modern time. I do not believe in such bull!" "Excuse me", my father interjected, "Weh you tell your mother bout bull and cow?" "No, I mean I do not believe in superstition," I replied.

Well coming from a poor family, I could not be driven to the city. I had to take the 'country bus' as they would call it. When we arrived in Savanna-La Mar at the bus depot, I saw this huge dirty yellow and gray bus that looked ancient. Some of the windows were missing, and cardboard had been placed in the spaces to block the passengers from the elements. The driver saw the apprehensive look on my face, and reassured me he would take good care of me and would get me to Kingston safe and sound. He assured my parents that he had been driving for forty years and had never been in a serious accident. "Anything me lick stay lick", he said with a big smile printed on his face. A woman who weighed at least three hundred pounds sat beside me, placing trays of eggs underneath her seat and in her lap. "I sell in the Papine market", she said, "An a dis mek my children go a school," pointing at the eggs. Trying to shuffle her huge body in the seat to be more comfortable, one of the eggs slipped from the tray in her lap, and fell breaking. She hissed her teeth and said, "Cho, mi profit gaan down now." This seemed to make her angry not only at me, but at the driver, and she began cursing continuously. In an effort to block out her tirade, I removed one of the pieces of cardboard from the window to take in the scenery. I could see my parents waving goodbye, and I waved back feeling as if I was five years old again, and leaving home for the first time for primary school.

At first the road followed the coast and we drove through Black River then passed women selling shrimp in Middle Quarters. The bus then went inland through Santa Cruz and the cool hills of Mandeville, coming down Spur tree Hill towards May Pen and Old Harbour. At one stage, the hill was so steep, the bus began crawling like a snail, but as soon as we reach the peak of the hill top, it takes off like a rocket. I held onto the seat in front and prayed, as I was still not fully confident that this contraption would bring me safely to my journey. This motion caused the eggs to shake precariously, and the large lady cursed loudly. Because of traffic, the bus slowed as we drove through Old Harbour and into May Pen. The driver navigated the traffic with ease, while on-lookers in passing vehicles looked at the old jalopy and shook their heads in amazement.

When we arrived in Papine later that evening, I was fortunate I had no troubles during the journey. I was surprised that it was so quiet, hardly anyone was on the street, only cars passing by. I asked a young man nearby to direct me to my Hall of Residence, but he replied, "If you can read, you will find it." So I followed his advice, and in a short time, I was walking through the gate to Irvin Hall. After my coordinator interviewed me and gave me my key, she escorted me to my room. She opened the door to show me where I would call home for the next three years. It was a ten by twelve square foot room with a balcony located on the second floor. Two single beds with a lamp on a side table beside each, and on either side a matching chester drawers and a built in closet with five foot mirrors on each door. I squinted my eyes, as I realized the entire room from ceiling to floor was painted pink. The coordinator informed me that my roommate would soon be arriving, and we could put pictures on the walls to make it feel more like home, but I cannot dismantle or change the colours of anything, as it is the property of the University. I was not really taking in everything she said, as I was mentally and physically exhausted, and just wanted some quiet time alone. I felt so relieved, when she left, I did not even unpack, but fell on my bed and closed my eyes. How long I lay there I did not know, all I could hear were students outside greeting each other, and moving around like swarm of bees. Upon arriving, after only two hours I already missed home. It is so funny, I had hated my environment from the day I 'have sense'. I hated the smell of animals, hated the wet dirt, the gloomy windy days, the rainy nights and the same old people I saw every day; Mr. Charlie with his old horse that he still used to plough his land and refused to be modernized and buy a tractor, even one-foot Greta with her nine children.

I was normally the one cooking, because all my other brothers and sisters were living on their own, except Michelle. Usually, I would portion the dinner at 3:00 p.m., but one day I decided to prepare the dinner much earlier as my mother was home and my father was not feeling well. As soon as I finished cooking, there came beggy beggy Bobo, "Good afternoon Mr. Joshua." I was just passing to go to the bar but I smelled the sweet aroma coming from your house so I have to investigate", Bobo said. As usual, my mother decided that she would give him almost half our dinner because I guess one drumstick couldn't satisfy him. Being a Christian woman she claimed that you must give to receive and you must treat others as you would like them to treat you. I understood where my mother was coming from, as I too liked to help the less fortunate, although it didn't make sense to me to give away your only pair of shoes.

Sitting up, I began to unpack my things from my suitcase, and at an instant, I began to wonder what I was doing there. For the first time in my life I felt lonely. Although, there was a party atmosphere around me, it did nothing to assuage my feelings of loneliness. I wished that I was back home in bed curled up, having no cares in this world. I unpacked as fast as I could and realized that my father had packed yam, banana, sweet potato and everything in one suitcase. I thought both my suitcase was packed with clothes, but then I remembered him saying

"Mek sure you eat good you know, and no go to no fast food restaurant ca mi no want you over fat." To emphasise his feelings on the matter he said, "Mi no want you eat no dry food for mi know how you love sweets, dats why you full of worm". I thought to myself, leave it up to my father to remove necessities such as books to make space for ground provisions; from ever since my father did not recognize the worth of books.

Just the thought of explaining to my Professor why my books did not arrive with me made me laugh so loudly that I never realized my roommate had been standing at the door watching me. Seeing her reflection in the mirror startled me, and I turned around. Seeing the look on her face, the only thing I could say was, "I am not crazy." Reluctantly she walked towards me stretching out her hand. "I am Chelsea", she said greeting me. I could see that she was also nervous, like a hesitant bird leaving the nest for the first time. "Where are you from?" I asked her. Sitting down on her bed she replied, "I am from Comfort Castle in Portland." Relieving she was a country girl like me, I began to feel more comfortable, until she admitted she had been living in Kingston for the past five years, and attended Wolmer's High School for girls. She boarded out when she passed her Common Entrance Exam. Feeling disappointed that I am still the one wet behind the ears, she reassured me that by the end of the week I would know everywhere that I needed to go to enjoy myself in the City. "I am here to learn," I said. "But you also have to enjoy yourself", Chelsea replied.

"Look, Susan," she said, "I am a bio-chemistry student with number one passes at A Levels, and most of my friends consider me the perfect nerd, but no one parties more than me. Slapping me on the back, she said, "I will convert you, this I promise." I never took her seriously at the time. Before falling asleep, I made a mental note to get in touch with my mother to send me my books.

The following morning I jumped up realizing I was late for an 8 o'clock Sociology class. Not listening to my father, the first young lady who sat beside me asked to borrow my book; I lent it to her. Another girl asked me if I could take notes for her because she had a clash between classes. Well, by the time class was over she was at the door. I did not have time to make two copies of the notes, so she grabbed my paper and said "I will copy it and bring it back to you." Well, for three days I did not see her.

Chelsea and I quickly became best friends. We did everything together, spending most of our free time with each other. I majored in Psychology and she majored in International Relations. Being first year students we took several classes together. She was the same age as I, eighteen. I was born in October, while she was born in September. Sometimes when I wasn't doing things her way she would point out that she was older than me, as if a month made a great difference.

I was very popular in high school, and had a lot of friends, but I never had a close friend I could share my secrets with. I never had that friend with whom I could share my fears, desires or ambitions in life. I was close to my two sisters but being the youngest I guess they didn't think I had problems. Often, they would tell me their problems but somehow they never had the time to listen to mine. Chelsea changed all that. We shared jokes, laughed, cried and talked about our situations. We were inseparable.

True to her word, she did convert me. Almost every weekend we were at a different party, but at the same time, she encouraged me to do my work. "You've got to learn how to balance life, Susan," she said, "There is time for everything under the sun, as my mother would say," she told me laughing. I felt a little bit guilty as I knew my mother would be shocked if she could see what I was doing. I reassured myself that once my grades were okay, there was no point being a recluse, as life was depressing enough. I started to drink but realizing I lost control easily, I limited myself to one glass per night. I did not take it seriously until one morning I woke up after a night of partying, and had no idea how I had got home. I barely made it out of my bed before the floor was covered in vomit. Now I know how my father felt sometimes when he went to the bar, coming home drunk as a bat, and even talking to the animals. In that state, he swore that they were replying to him.

I attended Chelsea's classes and took notes for her even though I wasn't doing that course. The University experience was life changing for me. I saw everything there, some were shocking, and others weren't. I watched girls from nice Christian backgrounds, who came dressed in long skirts to their ankles, and who in a short time were sporting minis, competing to see whose was sexier. I had also seen others who appeared to be so gentle, turn into monsters. I remember a young man who was training to be a doctor drop out of university in his second year. He grew his hair, started smoking weed and saying he "burns" government institutions. He met some Rastafarian guys from Warwicka Hills where he joined what they claimed to be the *Back to Africa Movement*.

Chapter 3

In my second year I met a guy named David. He was not like the other guys I knew; he was intelligent, kind and good looking. David was studying law when we met. I stumbled upon David in the cafeteria; I spilled my juice on him and from that day his nickname for me was 'Clumsy'. After my degree I went on to do my Masters and eventually my Doctorate in Psychology. I received a post as Head of the Psychiatric Department at a clinic in Kingston named Human & Social Interventions. The clinic was designed to focus on undisciplined adolescents.

Chelsea went to America within that period and came back at the time David and I were engaged. I was very happy my best friend was home. With her by my side it was not just the two musketeers together, David made it three. We did a lot of things together. There were times when we would go to the North Coast for the weekend, or one weekend David surprised us and took us to the Blue Mountains where we rented a cabin. When it came to relationships, Chelsea was the opposite of me. She liked to date many guys. Sometimes she made comments such as "I can't believe that you'll really tie down yourself to one man for the rest of your life! You are still a young girl, I mean…life is too short and there are too many men in this world." So I never expected what happened to me to occur.

When David asked me to marry him, I brought him home to get my parents' blessing. My father smoked his tobacco pipe and muttered something under his breath, while my mother was trying to make David feel as welcome as possible. Daddy sat on the verandah by himself, so I went out and stood beside him. "Daddy, what do you think of David as my husband?"
"I know you would marry somebody like that. Him look like fi him hand nuh touch grung either. wey you

a do wid someone like dat, eeh? Is shame you shame a wi?"

"Daddy", I replied, "I am not ashamed of you. It's just who I am."

"So you tink say tru him drive a fancy car and wey yu say him do again?"

"He's a lawyer," I said.

"And being a lawyer, him betta dan any odda man in di area?" He spat on the ground and his face was contorted into an ugly scornful smirk.

"Daddy, I'm not saying that. What I am saying ..." I cautiously stepped backward away from him, "I'm just saying you cannot help who you love, when you and mommy were getting together, her parents used to curse saying she was taking up a worthless man. Now, look how long you and mom have been married for, forty years. You have eight kids and several grandchildren. Please be happy for me because I am very happy."

"Alright, wi will si. So when you t'ink you a get married?" he asked, "Furthermore remember is church you a get married inna because a deh so you born, christen and grow inna, and mi not comin inna town in no big church whe I don't know of."

To make him happy, I agreed to get married in our church.

"Good," he said, "Pastor Benson will be happy. So when u t'ink you a get married?"

"Well daddy, I've known David for seven years. So, we are not going to have a long engagement. We are getting married within six months."

"Alright then, mi hope him no shame fi bring him family inna di bush!"

I smiled. "Daddy, why do you always say those things? Why would David be ashamed? You are a good farmer, husband and a good provider. Now, let's go in to them."

Chapter 4

Chelsea, David and I spent a lot of time together. Sometimes I would be so busy writing reports and Chelsea would invite David out to have fun.

"Come David", she would say, "Let's go out and have some fun. Susan is burying her head in her work as usual."

The plans for our wedding went smoothly, never thinking six months would pass so quickly. We were getting married on the last Sunday in June, and the Friday night I had a bad feeling in my stomach. I only knew that I did not want to be alone. Normally if I called Chelsea she would come and stay with me, but this time for some strange reason I didn't call her, and decided to go to her apartment instead.

I jumped into my car and drove through the city. My eyes glanced at the clock. It was after eleven. I knew Chelsea would be home because although she was a party animal she told me she was not feeling well. Arriving at her apartment I went up to the third floor. Coincidentally, a pizza delivery man from Domino's was at her door about to ring the bell. My hands were sweating and my head was spinning. I wasn't sure if it was because if I had wedding jitter, or if I was catching the flu. Putting on a brave face I smiled at him as he rang the doorbell, acknowledging who he was as Chelsea asked.

I heard her saying "Good. You've come very quickly. I called only five minutes ago!" she said as she opened the door but when she saw me her face went pale, as if she had seen a ghost.

"What are you doing here?" she asked in shock. The pizza guy looked from one of us to the other in confusion.

"Is that anyway to greet a friend?" Reluctantly she reached out her hand and paid the pizza man. I stepped inside the room and sat on the couch before she had the chance to say anything else.

"I am not feeling well, so I decided to spend the night with you," I paused, looking at how she was dressed in a see-through night gown, "Do you have company?"

"Well I..."

She was interrupted by a voice saying "Honey, is the pizza guy here yet? Let's go a second round!"

As he walked out of her bedroom, my heart sank as I realized it was David.

"Susan!" he said in shock moving towards me but I jumped up and ran out the door, even forgetting there was an elevator and racing down the stairs. I think I reached the ground floor in ten seconds flat.

Before I knew it, I was in my car driving at high speed. I did not know where I was heading, just that I had to get away as quickly as possible. With tears streaming down my face and the pain in my heart, I could barely see where I was going. Hearing my phone ring, I saw his name on the screen and I could not imagine what I would say to him. Reaching over to shut it off, I was totally oblivious to the red light at the traffic stop and went straight through. The only thing I remembered later on was waking up in the hospital. My mother was over me crying, "Honey, you are back with us!"

"What happened" I asked blankly.

"You did inna one accident."

"A tell you say di girl can't drive. Mi no know how di hell dem give har licence!" That was my father standing by the door.

"Shut up Joshua," my mother snapped at him, "Did you not see mi daughter dead and come back?"

My father came over to me and gave me a peck on the cheek. "Welcome back pickney gal."

"How long was I asleep?"

"For two days but doctor says nothing seriously wrong with you and dem do all kind a test." My father said to me "I never know seh dem need so much machine just fi one body. Weh dem tink dem ago find inna you...gold?"

My mother said "David is here...as a matter of fact he's outside."

"I..."

My father interrupted her "Pastor Benson say that alright bout di wedding. Anytime you ready again he will give us di church."

"There won't be any wedding."

"How you mean there won't be any wedding?" my father asked.

There won't be any wedding," I reiterated.

"The bwoy outside a tell me how much him love you. A weh di bwoy do you? Tell me meck a limb him up from pillar to post!"

"Don't worry yourself."

"Tell me what him do you!"

"Nothing. He only let me see the light."

"Him turn Christian?" My mother asked.

"Not really, but he let me see what I was afraid to see."

"Do you want to see him?"

"Send him in but I want to see him alone."

"All right baby, we deh outside a wait pon you when you finish" said Daddy.

David came in looking as sharp as ever. I said "I heard that you were here for the two days I was unconscious."

"Yes he said, sitting beside my bed. "I'm sorry I arrived late today, I had to go to court, but I had to see you to explain what happened between me and Chelsea."

"There is nothing to explain," I said, "I wish you and her the best."

"But I don't love her!" he jumped up. "I love you and you alone. Listen babe, I just had what you call a one night fling before the wedding but it meant nothing to me, nothing."

"Well, it meant something to me," I replied. "Please go, I'm really tired."

"Listen Susan," he stood over me, "Give me a second chance and you won't regret it. I promise you it will be better for me and you. Clumsy, you know it's only you I love."

"Maybe" I said, "But my heart can never take again what I saw that night, and how would I know it will never be repeated?"

"Listen, it will never happen again, I swear to you" he said, "…and Chelsea is feeling bad also. She feels terrible and wants to make it right with you."

"I need some time to see where I stand with my feelings towards both of you."

"Please Clumsy" he said, "I want us to be a family. I love you from the first day I saw you. Remember when I was sitting at the cafeteria reading when you accidentally spilled your juice on me? That day when you tried to clean my shirt but instead messed it up more, I said to myself this is the girl I want."

"Well, I was a challenge and you conquered me. You got to know me. Now, leave me alone. Please go, I'm tired."

He was about to start speaking again when the nurse came in. "Time for your medication, Miss Daublin. Visiting time is over. You have to go sir."

A week later I was discharged, and during that time I refused to see David or Chelsea. After leaving the hospital I was depressed, feeling lonely, rejected and confused. My mother stayed with me for about three weeks and then I went back to work. I begged her to leave, not because I didn't love her, her constant hovering was driving me crazy. I appreciated that I was her baby, but I am twenty-seven years old and had to stand up for myself, so I could feel I had a purpose in life. When I was younger I depended on my family, then Chelsea came into my life, and my dependency shifted to her, then to David and now it was time I became independent.

The last night my mother stayed with me, I took her to dinner at Gloria's in Port Royal, where we laughed about the times I was home in the country before leaving for University. The following morning I took her to the bus stop, kissed her and sent her home to dad, then went back to the office.

I knew then what I had to do. Writing emails to both David and Chelsea stating my decision to let them go physically and mentally in order to get my life back on track. I thanked them for the impact they made on my life over the years of our friendship. Despite my lingering pain and hurt, I will never forget them.

Chapter 5

The next day after going through my session with my client, I wanted to relax by detoxing. Taking a five, my office phone rang, jolting me back to the moment. It was a co-worker of mine, Johnathan. "Hi Susan, I'm so happy you are back, well and fine. Listen, I know that you normally deal with adolescents, but I have a gentleman here that needs some advice. I don't know if you can help him."

"Well, I...I... I'm not in the position to give advice to adults but you could consider assigning him to someone else."

"Everyone's client load is full right now, and this gentleman is in a bad way mentally. I spoke with your secretary and she told me your workload is kind of light, so please just help him out for me, even to talk with him once until you can assign him to someone more suitable."

He sounded desperate. "Alright", I said finally giving in, "I can schedule him for 3 o'clock today."

"Ok, I'll see to it that he will be here."

"No problem," I said and hung up.

The day went by like clockwork. I saw a little boy who bit other kids, a young girl who believed her dolls spoke to her, and the gentleman for the 3 o'clock appointment came on the dot.

"Hi, I'm Phillip. Phillip Johnson."

"Hi Phillip, what can I do to assist you?" I said, leaning back in my chair

"I have a problem", he said.

She said, "That is obvious, that is why you are here."

He smiled, "I am married for the past nine years, with two kids, and I'm no longer in love with my wife," he stated staring me in the eyes.

"Well sir, explain more", I suggested leaning towards him.

"I'm not into her like before."

"Give me an example," I suggested.

"Well," he leaned back, "When I met Patricia, we were hot, very very hot. She was so sexy! We met at a friend's party and afterwards we started dating. Not even one month passed before I was popping the question to her. I thought I had found the love of my life so I didn't hesitate. I thought, well maybe another man might take her up if I didn't do it myself. After nine months our daughter was born and within two years, our second daughter was born. I soon realized that we had little in common apart from the physical attraction. Her values and beliefs were markedly different from my own and I felt like I was living in the house with a stranger. Miss Daublin for my daughter's sake, I wanted the marriage to work. My family does not believe in divorce. My grandparents were married for sixty years before they died and my parents are now married for forty years. If I ever divorced her, I know that they would feel as if it is a shame and disgrace, and you know Jamaican society. As far as they see it uptown people are perfect. They should have a perfect life, with a perfect wife and a perfect home and perfect children, even a perfect dog! I don't know what to do."

"Have you ever thought of going on a second honeymoon?"

"I do not think a second honeymoon can help me. I am telling you the truth, if something doesn't happen soon, I am going to crack. I'm honestly going to crack."

I noticed that as he spoke he was nervously biting his nails. I found myself staring at his face but saw David. I listened to his voice but could only hear David's voice.

"Can we meet some other time?" I asked, afraid that I might not be able to control myself. An hour was already gone.

"No", he muttered.

"I have an appointment that I have to make. It's very important. I'm so sorry. I will instruct my secretary to refund half the money for this session, ok?"

"When can I see you again?"

I stumbled to my feet and grabbed my appointment book.

"Ok, what about Monday? No, make it Tuesday at 4 o'clock."

"No problem" he said, "If I survive that long."

"Don't worry Mr. Johnson, you'll survive."

I went home that evening and took out a frozen pizza, after microwaving it, I then reached for a slice of cake, then to complete my "balanced meal" I washed it all down with a bottle of coke. I could hear my father's voice saying "Dem deh tings will kill you off before time. You fi eat di ground food dem and you live till you a 115 years old! Look pon you great grandma Mazie. Mazie live til dem hav fi sun har! A golden age of one hundred and fifteen! And she no eat nothing from a fridge. Strictly ground food. Not even pipe water. She drink only the tank one."

I gulped down the last slice of pizza, finished my glass of Coke and burped. *Good fi Grandma Mazie.*

I brushed my teeth and crawled into bed, checking my messages. There were six. Four were from Chelsea telling me she'd got my email and how sorry she was, and she wanted a second chance because I was her best friend and sister, and she didn't want to lose me. One was from David telling me he had also received my email and how much he still loved me. The last one was from a co-worker of mine.

I cleared my messages, turned off the light and pulled the cover over my head. My poodle dog Whisper climbed into bed with me sensing my distress. I started to think where did I go wrong in my life? Where did I go wrong in choosing my friends? I am not seeing the signs? I was so blind that I did not even pick up certain signals. Images started flashing through my mind and I finally admitted I was partially to blame for what happened. The signs were there but I'd refused to think they were significant. I remembered the time when Chelsea was touched by David on the bottom. She came into the room wearing really tight jeans with her birthmark printed out on her bottom. David spanked her. I remember the time she was laying on the couch and David bent over her claiming he was massaging her. That was a sign. Or even when we went to the beach and I was too tired to continue swimming and they were out in the water all alone swimming and playing around. That was a sign also. I was trying to remember something else but I fell asleep.

For the next few days, things were much better. I was getting back into my routine and I felt happy, but I could not take my mind off Phillip Johnson. Why did he have such an effect on me? Was it because he looked like David, or even sounded like him? I shook my head. No, it must have been my imagination.

Tuesday at 4:00 p.m. he was back at my office, walking in more confident than he sounded. We talked and he started telling me about himself. He was a chartered accountant. He had followed his father's and grandfather's profession. They started an accounting firm called Johnson and Johnson. He was the third generation in his family to continue in that profession. He also spoke of his childhood. He was born and raised in St Andrew, went to Campion High School. After leaving, he went to Barry University in Florida. I found myself attracted to him. I tried to fight it but I failed. We went to lunch the Friday afternoon and by the Sunday he was visiting my apartment. We made love that night and a few hours later while he was asleep beside me, I knew deep down inside this was wrong, but I tried to justify my actions by saying he was no longer my client. I assigned him to Mrs. Baker after our last session. Something was telling me I cannot base a new relationship if I'm not completely over the previous one. I got up and went to the bathroom, splashing cold water over my face. Shaking my head, "You are doing too much thinking," I told myself, "It is time you stopped thinking and act instead." All my life I planned and configured my life, yet it got nowhere. It is time for me to take a chance as I told David and Chelsea, "It is time for me to really live in the present." Filling a glass with water, barely able to swallow its contents, I returned to bed.

For the next two months I found myself contented. I stopped thinking about David and Chelsea and what they did to me. I was on top of the world and I wasn't coming down soon. Philip took me to places I had never been before. One weekend he surprised me with a trip to Miami. I could not tell my parents about him because I know they would be ashamed and I could not convince myself that it was wrong, because I felt so good doing it. Phillip was very loving and attentive, but the nights were lonely for me because I knew that he was home with his family, while I was in bed with only Whisper, my poodle for company. I soon bought my first home and Philip started to help me pay the mortgage. He was not there emotionally, but financially I have his absolute support.

Chapter 6

My sister Michelle sent me a text message asking permission to come and visit for a few days. I told her it was okay since I hadn't seen her for seven months. Picking her up at the bus stop and driving home, I started to enquiry about the family. Well, she said "Joanne is not doing well with her husband because she found out he had an affair with another woman; and congratulations," she said to me, "You will soon be a grand aunt, Keysha, their first daughter who was only fifteen years old is now pregnant.

"What?!" I exclaimed. "Pregnant?!" I asked in shock.

"Yes, she is. I should not have told you so suddenly. I know how much you love her. Keysha is your favourite," Michelle said.

"I know. I guess I don't keep in touch with home that often."

"Yeah", said Michelle, "but I know you are busy. We understand."

"So, how is Jack?" I asked her. Immediately I could see the change in her demeanor. It took her a few seconds to reply.

"He's there. We've been married for three years now."

"Three years! That's long? It seems as if it was just yesterday."

"Yeah."

"So is everything going your way?"

"We get on and he loves me and we spend a lot of time together."

"Do you still spend time with Janet?"

"Yeah! She said with an exciting look on her face then suddenly she got serious. "What am I going to do Susan?" She asked turning to me. He now wants a family. Sleeping with him is one thing but having a child is another. I mean I respect and admire him. He has a lot of ambition and goals but its Janet who I love. What am I going to do? Help me Susan, please give me some advice."

The mid-day heat was taking a toll on me, and I began to feel nauseous around the steering wheel, gripping it tightly in my hand, taking in deep breathes I decided to tell her the truth. Turning to her and I said "You are my sister and I love you very much. I do not care who you want to spend your life with. It is time for you to think of yourself, not what society dictates who you are. This double life of yours is driving you crazy. Don't you think it's time for you to get out of the closet?"

"Yes, I guess, "she said, "But it's not that easy. You know about Jamaican society and how they think about gay people. Do you remember Mr. Earl? That lived down the road from us?"

"Yes," I replied.

"You were about eight years old when he died, but what you don't know is that he liked men."

"What?"

"But he never touched a little boy. He treated the children in the community very well. Anyway, when the people found out he was gay they started to stone him and disgraced him. One night when he had a little too much to drink and fell asleep, someone went to his house, and set fire to it. He had no chance of surviving. He was burnt alive. Instead of mourning for such a nice man, everyone cursed him, making comments like '*that homosexual should be dead long time*', '*dat man shouldn't have been born in the first place, much less fi go dead!*' I could count on one hand the number of people who attended his funeral."

"Another thing you should consider Susan," she continued, "What would happen if our parents found out about my sexual preference? It would kill them! I could never get over it if they go to an early grave because of me. Our mother is now a Deaconess in our Church, and despite our father's ignorant behavior, he has started to attend services with her." Wiping tears from her eyes she whispered, "I mean, I love them. Do you understand Susan?"

Smiling reassuringly, I responded, "Yes, I do. Don't worry about it, we can figure something out while you are here. Sometimes a new environment and new people can give you different perspectives at life."

"Yes," she agreed, and we continued home without talking.

I made it my point of duty not to let Phillip visit me while Michelle was staying there. It was enough that my family had so much to worry about to also put my love life on the list. On the fourth day of Michelle's visit I got an idea, so I turned to her and said, "Hey, you were a good Art student. Why don't you apply for a scholarship to go to Edna Manley School for Visual Arts here in St. Andrew and see if you can get the opportunity to study? This would give you a break, to sort out your life. Holding her hand we walked to the couch I said to her, "The reality is Michelle, you will have to tell him the truth. Despite it all, Jack is a good guy." She closed her eyes and fell back in the couch. Finally, she said, "I know."

"If things work out," I said reassuringly, "You will have a break from Jack for a year or two. Hopefully your marriage can be ended as quietly as possible. I'm sure Jack's family wouldn't want the disgrace also."

"How long since I've sat in a classroom?!" Michelle exclaimed, "I don't know if I am brave enough to concentrate on studies."

"Well, anything is possible. You can do it, and you never know, Janet might can come live with you in Kingston."

"You know what? She said. I'll think about it. Even though I know Jack would be heart-broken because I have no doubt he love me but for his sake and mine he would have to let me go. And another thing, the baby will not happen for me." She added sitting up on the couch.

Michelle turned to face me.

"Most people in our community are now concerned that after three years of marriage we have no children. Some of the girls are beginning to whisper that that I'm a mule, or barren as town people would say."

"Well, that's their problem, isn't it?" I replied.

"Yeah, I guess."

"Listen, if you want something good out of life you have to take chances. You know I will support you in any decision you make." Hugging her, I said once more, "You are my sister, and I love you." The flood gates now burst open and she cried openly in my arms.

After some time she said, "It feels so good to have someone in my corner no matter what. I will think about it."

I smiled in acknowledgement.

On the Saturday, we both went clothes shopping. Afterwards, we visited the supermarket to get some groceries. I was so busy talking to her that I was not paying any attention to where I was going and my trolley collided with someone else's.

"I'm sorry" I said quickly, looking up at the person. I was shocked to see David.

"Hi Susan," he said.

I had not seen or heard from him for eight months. I felt guilty because I knew deep down inside I still loved him. He was not far from my thought but after a while I found out how to control those feelings. I loved him from the first day we met at the University, and seeing him brought back a tsunami of memories and emotions. I was feeling things I didn't know I still had inside of me.

"How are you?" I managed to utter.

"I'm fine", he said, "And you?'

"I'm ok….are you still doing Law?" I asked.

"That's what I was trained for, Susan," he said.

"Foolish question," I muttered to myself, "…well, nice seeing you David."

I was walking away when he said "Listen, I tried calling you a couple of times but it seems as if that number is no longer in service."

"Yeah," I answered.

"Don't worry about it," he interrupted, "I understand." Then he turned and walked away.

Michelle turned to me and said "Oh child, he looks damn good."

"Yeah, he's ok."

"What do you mean? This guy is a ten!"

"Hey! I thought you only liked girls."

"Well, I like David. By the way, you never told me what he did to you…"

"It is a long story."

"I have time," she said smiling.

"I didn't know you have time to listen to my love life."

She held my hand and said "I do now."

Looking at her I opened my mouth," "Don't be shocked Susan," she said, "I guess I wasn't all that good of a sister to you."

"That's ok," I said.

"No, it's not. I should have listened to you more Susan. I'm so sorry. I normally put my burdens on you and I never one day sat and listened to your problems."

"Don't apologize," I said.

"No, but I should, she said. "Especially when you recognize your fault, and accept it then you can work on it."

"Oh Hell! Stop being a psychologist on me and be a sister!"

We both laughed. When we got home I sat her down and told her everything the whole story of David and Chelsea. When I was finally finished she said, "Damn!" She sighed, "I thought David was conservative, you know... full of values. I never thought he would cheat on you."

"Yeah, me neither. It's a good thing I found out before we got married."

"For real. But don't you think you should give him a second chance. I mean..."

"You mean what?" I said sharply, "Not only did he cheat on me but with my best friend. My best friend. Do you understand that Michelle?"

"Yes I understand."

Not wanting her to feel bad, I said "Listen Michelle, forgiveness is one thing, but you should understand I need time."

"I know what you are saying but you grew up in a Christian home with Christian family members and values. You remember what Mom always says? We must learn to forgive and forget in order to see the Pearly gates."

"Guess what! That's Mom, not me. Besides, I'm moving on with my life. I have met..."

Before I could continue, she said smiling "Mmm...you have met....? Who? I want to know who, how, when and where!"

I smiled at her, "Life is too short to live in the past, don't you think?"

"Stop changing the subject!" teased Michelle smiling. "You have met who?"

"Well, I am seeing someone to be honest. We're just taking it step by step."

"Really? Tell me more."

"Oh my! Look at the time!" I got up. "I have to go now. I have an appointment."

"You don't."

"I do, really. I swear I do."

"Ok, no problem. I'm here night and day, and you have to come home. Then, I'll get the opportunity to drill you."

Walking towards the door I jokingly said "You must be a dentist, wanting to drill me. See ya later babes." She threw a cushion at me but I was already through the door.

Chapter 7

What I did not tell Michelle was who I had the appointment with. I convinced myself that I didn't lie to her. I met Phillip at the Wyndham Hotel, we had lunch and talked then we went upstairs and made love for the rest of the evening. I turned to him as we cuddled together, and I tried to look him in the eyes. "We can't go on like this," I said.

"What do you mean?" he asked.

"I mean …we have been together for a few months and I think it's time to make a decision. Do we want to continue this or go our separate ways? "

He was visibly pondering what I said, and there was a pause before he finally replied "I told you from the beginning, from the day we met that my family does not believe in divorce. So, you know where I stand with that."

"Yes I know where you stand and I know where I stand. I respect your principles so you have to respect mine as well."

"What are you saying?"

"I mean I think it's time to let go. I was not brought up this way and I lost my way for a while but it's now time for me to turn back."

He rolled over on top of me and said "Listen, I love you. I really do." At that moment I realized I never once told him I loved him and it was the first time he ever told me he loved me. Well, what could I do? He would never be free and I would never accept being the second woman in his life. I told him, "Let's think about it." Reluctantly he agreed.

Over the next few days the bond between Michelle and I deepened. I got to understand her better, and to accept her decision in choosing her sexual partner. Michelle didn't go out much, so I tried to entertain her as much as possible by taking her to places I knew she would never visit on her own. I immersed myself in my work. I stayed busy and tried not to think about Phillip. I knew I had to forget about him or die trying. It wasn't easy. Emotionally I was still a mess and I didn't know what to do about it.

One morning I got to work very early. Before I could sort out my day's schedule, I received a text message from Patricia, Phillip's wife. She found out about us through Phillip. I guess he could not keep it in so he told her we were involved and he was refusing to let me go. I called her and told her that I had no intention of continuing the relationship with her husband anymore. I thought that she would curse me and lashed out at me angrily, but surprisingly she listened calmly, and I respected her for that. Sensing that there was something else, I asked in a conceding voice, "I am not the first, am I?"

"No," she admitted, "But you are the first one he's ever told me about, so I guess you are special," she said wryly.

I felt like someone punched me in the stomach and I began grasping for breath. Throughout the process Patricia was patiently waiting for me to regain my equanimity. "I am not that special, even if he won't let go I will, because I know I am better than this." I said to myself not her. After our conversation I shook my head and my mind was racing. What did I get myself into? How did I go from one relationship to another without giving myself time to heal? Did I get involved with Phillip on the rebound? Did David hurt me so bad that I had to turn to someone else for comfort? I realized that I had no answers to these questions. I could not justify my behavior. I now realized that I had acted selfishly, only wanting to satisfy my immediate desires. This acknowledgement hit me dreadfully. I put my head in my hands and cried. I am not sure how long for, but finally I stood up, walked slowly to my window. Pulling away the shades I looked out on the city of Kingston. In the city, I saw people walking, talking and getting on with their lives. "Oh Lord," I said to myself, "Why can't I? Why am I such an emotional wreck?" David had hurt me but I was still in love with him, and as far as I can admit it now, I am no better than him, as I just did a similar thing. Maybe we'll never stand a chance of being together again, but I am now willing to look towards the future with the same values that my parents instilled in me.

After Michelle returned home, I felt lonelier than ever, because normally I would have Phillip as company. That Friday I decided to go to the Carib Cinema, something I had not done in a while. I chose to watch a horror movie. During the intermission I heard a voice behind me saying "Excuse me." To my surprise it was Chelsea. I thought I would feel hatred towards her, but the feeling was contrary. I missed her, our friendship, her company. I missed having her in my life.

"Susan?!" She said, astonished to see me.

Putting on a brave face I said "Hello Chelsea, how are you?"

She replied, "I am ok."

She was with a guy, and from the first glance I saw that he was very cute. I thought to myself - *another of her conquests*.

Maintaining eye contact with me, she said frankly "Susan, I miss our friendship."

"Same here," I responded.

She asked if we could meet for lunch.

"Yeah, I guess."

We made plans to meet on Monday. During our lunch date we tried to keep the conversation light. She asked how I was doing, how was work and family. I did the same, then she took the conversation to another level. I felt increasingly uncomfortable because the topic was about David.

"I didn't mean it," she apologized, "It happened on impulse."

"Tell me Chelsea, you slept with my boyfriend on impulse?" I said angrily.

"Calm down Susan," she replied quietly, "I didn't mean it like that. David is a nice guy and we spent a lot of time together. I guess it was something I wanted to do."

"You mean wreck my life!"

"No, I mean I don't know. I just don't know."

"Tell me something, what do you know?"

"I know I love you as a sister and a friend. I know it broke my heart every day to see how our friendship ended, and I know I miss you. I'm willing to do anything to make it right. That's what I know."

Before I could respond to her my phone rang. It was Phillip. I got up and walked away from the table to speak to him in private.

"What's going on?" he blurted out.

"What do you mean?" I asked somewhat taken aback.

"My wife told me you said it is over between us. Why did you talk to my wife?"

"Why did I talk to your wife? She was the one who contacted me, not the other way around. You were the one who brought everything out in the open."

"Yes," he admitted, "Listen Susan, I thought we had a good thing going on. I thought we could…"

"No!" I interrupted, "It's over! Forget about it and forget about me." I ended the call abruptly, and returned to the table.

"Something wrong?" Chelsea enquired.

"No, just something I forgot to do. I have to go."

"Can we see each other again Susan?" She pleaded.

"Yeah sure, why not?"

As I turned to leave she asked for my number and address. I gave her the details.

"See ya," I said.

"See you soon," she replied.

Trying to fill the void in my life, I began going to the gym regularly and started yoga classes, which gave me a great feeling of contentment and peace. A week later, Chelsea called me to ask if she could come over. I said no problem. She arrived at my door two hours later wearing blue jeans, white t-shirt, blue sneakers and sporting backpack.

"Are you coming from the gym?"

"No, I was just playing tennis," she replied, "I'm into sports, you know."

"Since when?" This was totally new to me.

"Since my boyfriend introduced me to it."

We sat down to watch a movie. We had some Coke and popcorn which reminded me so much of old times. During our conversation I realized how much I had missed her as a friend. She turned to face me and asked "Susan, is it possible we could be friends again and our relationship could get another chance?"

"If you had asked me this a month ago," I answered, "I would have said hell no! But knowing what I know now, anything is possible."

"I really appreciate that, Susan. I promise you this time I will be the kind of friend you deserve!"

I was becoming overwhelmed with emotions and had no intention of showing it at this moment. I jumped up and said to Chelsea "Listen, I have an early start tomorrow and its getting late..."

"No problem! I'll call you."

After she left I went to feed Whisper, and as usual he left his package in the bath tub. After cleaning that up, I went straight to my bedroom. That night I had a dream. I saw David. He came up to me, we were old and married with not only kids but grandchildren. We sat on a lovely verandah with one of our grandchild in my arms. I was rocking him to sleep. Chelsea was there also. She too was married. I was awakened by the alarm clock.

Chapter 8

When I woke up it was after five in the morning and I had an eight o' clock appointment with my supervisor. I put on my sweat suit and went for a jog. At that time of the morning, the air was fresh, the grass seemed greener and the scent of the plants was refreshing. The flowers were blooming in all their glory. I returned to my apartment, took a shower and headed out to work. When I arrived at eight o' clock on the dot, Mr. Gordon my supervisor came through the door.

"Hi Susan," he said sitting down in front of my desk. A middle aged man, about sixty-five, but took great pride in his appearance. Short and stocky with a round face yet trim body, he smiled broadly and said, "I have a proposal for you."

"Yeess," I answered reluctantly, in fear of what his proposal might mean.

"There is an orphanage called Hope Valley, and I'm trying to get some volunteers to go over there, to start a mentorship programme, as there are a lot of troubled kids who need not only counseling but also some role models in their lives. They need some big sister and big brother figures to look up to."

"When should I go?" I asked without hesitation.

"Saturday, if possible."

"Sure, sign me up", I said, thinking that this was the perfect opportunity to focus on someone other than myself for a change.

The next Saturday, I arrived at Hope Valley. The first thing I noticed was the wall fence all around with a large iron gate blocking out all view of the outside. I thought to myself, this seems more like a prison than a children's home. The security at the gate assured me the fencing was more to protect the safety of the children, but I knew this was separating them from society. Without interaction with the wider society they could not expand their knowledge. There were eight two-storey buildings in front of me which I assumed were boys and girls dormitories painted white, but what drew my eyes were the burglar bars covering every window. Some of these had broken glass with board covering the openings. The yard was paved concrete with a small play area containing some swings, a seesaw and jungle gym. There was no grass, so it must be very dusty when the wind blows making it difficult for the children to enjoy their play time. At the entrance door a few plants were struggling to survive.

Entering the main building, Mrs. Thomas, the social worker welcomed me warmly and offered to take me to tour the facility. The ground floor was the dorm for the younger girls ranging from newborn to five years old. It was also painted white, each dorm holding between fourteen to twenty children. The walls were bare, no pictures or mirrors. One side of the dorm held cribs, and I noticed some of them held two babies. The other side had single beds, and Mrs. Thomas explained that often two children shared a bed and sometime three. The bathroom had two toilets, and two shower stalls, one of which held a plastic tub, which she said the babies were bathed in. There was a broken crib in a corner, which was used to store toys such a stuffed animals and a few dolls which the children were allowed to play with when they behaved well. One House Mother was on duty when we walked through, Mrs. Veronica Whyte. Speaking to her, she explained how difficult it was with sometime twenty-two children demanding attention at the same time. She said, "When I started working here two years ago it was very difficult to have a crying child in your arms, and several others screaming for attention, and the one being held needed a bottle, so could not be put down." I tried to console myself by thinking that crying never hurt anyone, we all did it. She continued, "When my shift is over and I return to my family, my mind keeps returning to the kids left behind."

Heading upstairs, this dorm was painted pink. The difference being, this dorm only had eight beds on either side, with boxes beneath each to hold the children's clothes. Unlike downstairs, this dorm had a table with ten chairs, at which the girls used to colour, read, and play board games. It was dark in this dorm, as I realized many of the window had board where the glass was broken. It also made the room hot and stuffy as air could not circulate well. There was a bit of colour in the dark, as some of the girls had painted the wall around their bed in their own style. The bathroom was nailed shut, due to damaged plumbing, so the girls had to use the babies' bathroom downstairs. Returning to the front yard, Mrs. Thomas told me they tried to make the best with the limited funding available and most of the staff worked long hours with little pay, out of their love for the kids.

The rest of the facility was the same, except the boys areas were painted blue and green. I enquired about a round building in the centre of the facility. Mrs. Thomas explained this was the refectory where all the children had their meals, and where devotions for children and staff were held every morning. During my talk with Mrs. Thomas, children swarmed around me, every one grabbing my shirt, trying to take my hand. Mrs. Thomas told the children not to harass me, but I laughingly told her it was fine.

The children there, boys and girls ranging from newborn to fifteen, had no one to call family, no one to count on, except the caregivers who looked after them daily. While interacting with the children, I noticed a little boy who I assumed was six years old standing by himself. I learned that his name was Pete, and he was in fact ten years old. He was very shy. I went over to him and offered him some cookies I had baked and brought with me for the kids. I was not a great cook but I tried. By his reaction I noticed I had not made a great impression with my baking but he tried his best to continue eating. I had also brought some Pepsi to accompany the cookies. I met girls whom they had taken off the street who were prostituting themselves and boys who were involved in petty crimes such as stealing and shop lifting, among other things. I felt I had to do something not only to improve their lives but also mine, so I decided then and there to dedicate a few hours each Saturday to spend time with the children.

Mrs. Thomas assigned two girls, Shanna Kay, a fifteen year-old orphan who was found prostituting herself in the street. The judge warned her the next time she was caught, she would be placed in a remand centre. The other girl, Kay Anne, was thirteen years old. On every occasion that she was sent home to her mother, she was summarily returned to the home because her mother found her uncontrollable. Kay Anne had a record of shoplifting and stealing; which I experienced first-hand. After my first visit with her, I got home and realized my cell phone was missing. Fortunately for me someone saw her with it, called me and returned it. Even though I was assigned to mentor these two girls, I found I could not stop thinking about Pete, and wondering how to help him. I found out that his life was a struggle from the moment he came into this world. He only weighed two pounds, and was found in a dumpster behind a restaurant in New Kingston. No one knew the exact date of his birth, so they improvised as close to the date he was placed in custody. The Police that found him gave him the name Pete Brown. When he was medically examined, there were cocaine and alcohol in his system, which possibly impeded his birth weight and size. He was a loner from a tiny boy, but very intelligent, as he was always reading, and loved going to school.

Since I began volunteering at Hope Valley, I hardly had time to spend with Chelsea. After a few weeks of not hearing from me, she called out of the blue to reassure me that she had not given up on our friendship, but had to leave the Island for business, but reassured me that on her return she wants us to meet. I told her that the door was still open for us, and saying those words to her did not hurt, but made me feel better in myself. It is true the saying that time heals all wounds.

It was hard work getting the girls to trust me, but when they realized that I was coming faithfully every Saturday at ten, they began slowly to open up to me. All they wanted was someone to rely on who would not judge them, but treat them as equal, and not as "bad children". I started to bring books, and teach them to read.

Over the weeks, more volunteers started to spend time there and we proposed a treat for the last Saturday in August before they returned to school.

On that occasion, I walked into the room with some drinks, and bumped into one of the new volunteers, spilled juice on him. He turned around and smiled, "Hi Clumsy." My heart stopped. When I managed to speak I could barely whisper, "What are you doing here, David?"

"Same as you," he replied.

"Really, I never knew you were the type to volunteer."

"Yeah, I know. But I've been volunteering at different places for the past seven months now, but it's my first time here. How about you?"

"I've been here a few months," I replied, "Where have you volunteered to help out?" I asked curiously.

"Well, Boys Club, Lions Club, even the Police Youth Club. I'm just keeping myself busy. So, Clumsy...," he said still holding on to the tray and smiling, "Let's feed the kids before we have a riot in here."

Seeing him again for the second time within a few months, ignited the desire I felt for him. To my surprise, anger, hurt and disgust were no longer there. He was still handsome, dressed in blue jeans, and a white t-shirt. He seemed more muscular to me, as though he had been working out regularly at a gym, or perhaps running. Realizing my weakness, I tried not to be alone with him for the entire day. I supposed he noticed I was avoiding him because each time he walked towards me, I turned away and busied myself in the opposite direction, talking to anyone to distract myself. After two attempts, I appreciated the fact that he restrained himself and gave me space. After the function ended, I left the orphanage hurriedly. Not even for Pete did I stop to say goodbye. I didn't want to face David at this time. When I got home there was a message on the answering machine. My niece, Keysha had a baby girl and they called her Susan after me. *I don't know what they were thinking*, I muttered, trying to cheer myself up. As I was about to enter the shower, my phone started ringing. I answered it. It was David.

"Why did you run?" he asked.

"I didn't."

"Well you left without saying goodbye."

"I did not feel obligated to say goodbye to you." Realizing I must have sounded rude, I said, "I'm sorry."

"No need to be" he said.

"How did you get my number? From Chelsea?"

"No, I have not seen Chelsea for a long while."

"Then how did you get it?" I demanded.

"From your boyfriend."

"My boyfriend?"

"Yes, a little guy about four feet tall."

I realized instantly that it was Pete.

"How did you bribe him for my number?"

"I didn't bribe him."

"Oh really! The poor little guy didn't stand a chance," I said.

He laughed.

"So what did you do to get it? Was it blackmail? The truth..."

"The truth…the truth is that I love you and wanted your number. He gave it to me voluntarily, so I guess he likes me."

"Yeah right," I said, picturing him squeezing poor Pete to death.

"So, are you coming next Saturday?" he asked.

"No, I have plans."

"Really? Pete is going to miss you and so will I."

Without thinking I replied "Really?" Then I caught myself and said "Pete would miss me."

"Yes," he agreed.

"Listen David, I have something on the stove and I have to go now," I said, crossing my fingers.

"Running again?" he asked.

"No, I have something to do."

"So can I call you?"

"Can I stop you?"

"No," he said mockingly.

I hung up the phone.

After that conversation I went to take a cold shower. Hearing his voice over the phone made my heart race, my hands sweaty, and my whole body was shivering. What is this guy doing to me?

The next morning when I went to get the paper, I noticed there was a note in my letterbox from David. I was caught between deciding whether to read it or tear it up. If I tear it up, maybe there would be something I would never know, I reasoned to myself. So I decided to open it and put my doubts to rest.

Sitting on my sofa, I discovered it was a poem, and started to read:

My heart melts, my hands shake
Without you I feel I would break
I never stop loving you I do not know what I can do
To give me a second chance is like giving me a new life
I wish one day you would be my wife
Miss you each moment, each second,
Staring into space, I wish I could see your face
To kiss your lips and hold you in my embrace
To make love to you like I'm in a race
To give you all my attention, all that is in my heart
I wish to God you were still my sweetheart.
Give me a second chance and I will do good to serve you for the rest of my life.

I smiled at the corny rhyme, but appreciated the effort he had expended on my behalf. I knew I still loved David. I had no doubt, even though I was trying to fight it. I put the note in the middle of my book then laid back and put my hands over my face. For the first time in my life I felt I loved unconditionally. I mean, I know my parents love me, and I know they always will, but I never felt this way about anyone, not even Phillip, who showered me with gifts and cash, which felt so darn good.

I opened my window to inhale the fresh morning air. I enjoyed living in Mavis Bank. It is not far from Kingston but it's also not near enough to be disturbed by cosmopolitan life. I get to enjoy both worlds, I said to myself, both the country and the city. I see the trees around me, I hear the birds singing, and the river rushing by. It is a wonderful life. I love to walk in the early morning with Whisper, especially down by the river which bordered my home, my own private oasis. I reminisced about my past and looked towards my future. I knew I made some mistakes. Phillip was one. I entered that relationship without thinking twice. I now realize that I was trying to get over David and it didn't work. I was determined to take things one step at a time and see where it would lead. I retrieved the note from the book and took David's number and called him.

"I got your note," I said.

"Did you like it?"

"Maybe."

"It was from my heart Clumsy. I am really, really in love with you. I never stopped loving you and I don't think I can."

Without hesitating, I said, "I know."

"Susan, I know you don't trust me and maybe you never will, but I would love to take you out…even as a social friend. How about dinner tomorrow night? Also, there's a pantomime on, and I'd love for you to be my date."

"Sure," I replied, "I would enjoy that."

At the end of the call, I felt relieved to give in to my emotions, and not fight my feelings for David. Life is too short to hold back.

At work I was smiling with everyone. All the girls in the office were happy for me when a dozen roses were delivered to my desk. They all started questioning me about who the flowers were from. The office buzzed with the refrain "Susan has found a new guy!" Well, I just kept them guessing. I didn't want to think of my future at that stage, and where it would end up. For my sake, and the sake of those who love me, I hoped it would end happily. Sitting in my office and pondering certain things. Did I react hastily that night when I caught David and Chelsea together? Did I react foolishly by going into another relationship so quickly with Phillip? Did I criticize my parents, especially my father? I didn't know what to do, but I knew I had to change my attitude with regards to certain values. Forgiveness was something my parents taught me. I mean, I was going to church from I was a baby, so it shouldn't be so difficult for me to forgive, even if I cannot forget. Everyone needs a second chance. If I were in that position of needing forgiveness, I would have liked to be given a second chance. I remembered a passage from the Bible that states "Do not judge and you shall not be judged, do not condemn and you shall not be condemned." I picked up the phone and rang my mother. She informed me that my father was sick. I asked her what the problem was. She said that for the past two weeks he had a bad pain in his stomach and it seemed to be getting worse. He was refusing to go to the doctor. He said he would take care of himself by using his herbal medicine. While she was talking I heard my dad in the background saying, "Dem ya doctor de here fi suck money out a mi. Them is like some vampire, but dem not goin' to get fi mi money. You go to them wit' one sickness, and by dem done wit' you they find bout fifteen different tings wrong wit' you. Dem nah get fi mi money!"

"Susan, are you still there?" It was my mother.

"Yes mom, I'm still here. Tell dad to come and visit me."

"Your father in Kingston?" There was a distinct note of incredulity in her voice.

"Mom, tell him I need him. Please Mom, tell him I need him to come, ok?"

"Ok baby, but I can't promise you anything because you know him and the city don't 'gree."

"Tell him I have something to tell him."

"What do you have to tell him?"

"Nothing."

"Nothing? So why you tell me to tell him that you have something to tell him?"

"Please mother, tell him I need him to do something for me."

"Ok," she answered, sighing.

Hanging up the phone, I was determined to have a better relationship with my father. I knew we didn't see each other much but I loved and respected him and there was nothing I wouldn't do for him.

Chapter 9

The following evening, David and I went to dinner at Jade Garden, afterwards we attended the Pantomime at the Ward Theatre located in the heart of the city of Kingston. I laughed so much that even when he held my hand and squeezed it gently, I did not mind. Everyone who saw us laughing together smiled at us. It was so obvious we were enjoying ourselves. I observed that habits David portrayed in the past like: looking at other girls while we were out, or walking away to answer his phone while we are in a conversation, he refrained from doing. We had a wonderful time. He took me home later that night and surprisingly he kissed me good night and began to walk away. Amazingly I asked him to come in. He replied, "Are you sure?" I whispered "Yes".

After entering the house, we sat on the sofa in the living room. I could see that he was nervous as he began fidgeting with the TV remote. I turned to him and took the remote from his hand, "David, before we go any further I should tell you something." I began telling him about Phillip. He looked at me with a blank expression on his face. After I was through telling him about Phillip, I asked, "What are you thinking, David?" For a long moment he said nothing. "Please tell me what you think of me," I continued. I began to feel despair inside but finally he said, "I don't think more or less of you than I did before. I love you and I want us to work things out. I feel bad about you being with another man but it would be hypocritical of me judge you, knowing that I not only slept with another woman, but she was your best friend."

"Thank you for being honest with me. I really appreciate it."

We started kissing me, then he took me to the bedroom.

The next morning, the telephone awakened me. Rolling over David, I answered it. It was my mother.

"Your father said that he will be coming this Thursday, so meet him at the bus stop at 3:00 p.m."

"Ok, no prob," I responded, rolling back over David.

"Hmmm, I like this," he murmured in my ear.

"This?"

"Yes. I like waking up next to you…"

"David, please remember we are taking this slowly."

"No pressure."

After David left, I took a shower then headed towards the computer. I had a lot of files to work on but I took a minute to check my email. There was an email from Chelsea informing me that she was returning to Jamaica next week and that she wanted to see me. I paused for a second to think how it would be with both David and Chelsea back in my life and seeing each other. Could I handle it? I was determined not to let it bother me too much. *What's done is done. I'm going to leave it in God's hands.*

For the next few days, David and I spent a lot of time together but I deliberately didn't allow him to sleep over. That Thursday, at 3:00 p.m., I was at the bus stop in Half Way Tree in St. Andrew waiting for my father and saw him getting off the bus with two big boxes. I helped him with one as he placed the other in the back of the car.

"Dad, what are you doing with so much clothes?"

"Clothes? Pickney, is food I bring for you," he replied, coughing.

"Daddy, I'm going to take you to the doctor."

"Pickney, mi a deal wit it mi self."

On our way home, we argued the whole time.

"Daddy, you are going to the doctor. It's not gonna be your money spending, it's mine."

"You have money fi dash weh, don't? That job you have is payin' you good, don't it?" he said, grumbling.

"No matter what you say, I have passed twenty-one years old," I said.

"Whether yu are twenty-one or a hundred, yu still mi baby and a yu haffi lissen to mi, not mi fi lissen to yu."

I smiled. "Ok daddy, but you still going to the doctor."

We visited the doctor the next day and he confirmed that Dad had an ulcer. The doctor recommended a strict diet and plenty of fluids, along with some antibiotics. On the way home he started grumbling again.

"Si wat a tell yuh? Look how much money dat goin' cost yuh and a bet you nothing like dat doan wrong wit' mi."

"Daddy, I'm gonna listen to the doctor and do what he said."

"So yuh rather hear the doctor dan listen to mi?"

"No Dad. But I think I will listen to the doctor this time. Next time, I'll listen to you. How about that?'

"Yuh tink yuh smart, don't?" he replied.

At home, my father and Whisper did not get along at all. According to my father, only someone like me would get a dog like that. "That dog look like him can't even kill a fly. What kind of dog is that?"

"It's a pet dog" I replied.

"A pet dog? Yuh need a dog dat can protect yuh. What yu want pet dog fi do? Fi hug and kiss and rub up?"

"Don't worry daddy, I have an alarm system in my home so we are safe."

"So yuh sey," he responded, doubtingly, "By the way, yuh did know dat Michelle get into a Art school somewhere? Wha she a do bout she a go study again? She have har husband, a time fi dem start a family now."

"Daddy, maybe she wants to improve her skills."

"To do wha? Mek babies?

"No, she likes teaching and that is what she wants to do. You think is only your son can be a teacher?"

"I neva sey dat ennuh pickney..."

"Well, she wants to teach and that way, she can give back to the community."

"So what yuh giving back to di community?"

Feeling embarrassed I said "Daddy, I don't have time to come to the country. I do a lot of work here and I also volunteer at Hope Valley Orphanage."

"Yu wuk at a orphanage?" he asked amazed.

"I do. I forgot to mention it."

"Yeah," he said.

"I do it every Saturday. Actually I'm addicted to this little boy there. His name is Pete."

"Really? I mus meet him den."

That Saturday, my Dad accompaned me to Hope valley. I introduced him to Pete. Somehow my father and Pete got on really well. They liked each other. My father taught Pete how to build things with his hands and Pete was fascinated. Since that visit my father's opinion of Kingston became "Pete is the best ting in Kingston. Nothin else good, well , apart from yu, Susan, is not so bad."

"What do you mean?"

"Yuh shouldn't born in di bush and Pete shouldn't born in di city. It should be di odder way 'round."

"So Daddy, why don't you take him home?"

"Yuh t'ink I could?" he asked with a joyful look on his face.

"I don't know but I could do some investigation and find out. Most people don't like to adopt older kids, but perhaps you could be his foster father. They tend to prefer children under five years old. Pete is ten.

Also, he is physically disabled in the sense that he is really small for his age. He's very smart but they don't look at that as a requirement for him to be fostered. So, he is a perfect candidate for you and mom. It would not be a rigmarole to get him in our family."

Chapter 10

The following evening, I got a call from Michelle to help her find a room to rent. She was coming to Kingston to attend Edna Manley School for Arts and also to work.

"So Jack has finally decided to let you go?!"

"Yes but it was not easy for him when I finally told him about Janet and he took it very hard and for a moment, I thought he was going to kill me. Spent two days locked up in our guest bedroom before I decided to face him again. Surprisingly he was not angry and bitter. We spoke about it for hours and he decided that if I left the community to study as I said I would then he could find someone else to love him, we would get a divorce and no one would know the truth. He's a good man."

"You are right," I said.

"I'm so sorry I hurt him but I couldn't take it any longer, and I didn't want to use him anymore."

"It will be ok. Come into town and stay with me until you find somewhere to live."

She told me it wouldn't be too long, as Janet was going to join her.

While speaking to Michelle, Chelsea sent me a text message asking me to meet her for lunch. When I arrived at Cuddy's Sports Bar, she was there smiling.
"How are you Susan?"
"I'm fine. You?"
"You are looking happy, girl."
I pulled a chair and sat in front of her and told her bluntly "Chelsea, David and I are together again."
"Really?" she asked.
"Yes, and I want you to know that if it's going to be a problem for you, we should end it right now. I mean our friendship."
"Why should it be a problem? I already told you it didn't mean anything to me, and I assure you, it meant nothing to David either. I know he loves you. You are the one he wants."
Chelsea stretched out her hand across the table towards me. I was shocked to see a wedding band on her finger. She smiled.
"I got married last month in America."
"What? You got married?"
"That's right," she laughed, "You remember that night you saw me at the movie with a guy? He's the one. His name is Christopher Challenger.'
"So you are Mrs. Challenger?"
"Chelsea Challenger."
I sat back in my chair and laughed.
"Why are you laughing?" she asked.

"I guess he challenged you and you lost."

She laughed too. "He's an engineer and he got a contract to work in the US for a while. That's why I went up to be with him. He's gonna be gone for three years."

"And you are going to wait?"

"That's why we got married." She replied, "I will be joining him shortly."

I shook my head and looked at her.

"Of all the surprises in this world, this is one that I really liked. I never thought you would get married before me. You, with all the men in this world and your 'I'm so young' attitude, got married before me!"

We both started laughing again, and promised each other to stay in touch often.

For the next two weeks, to my surprise, I enjoyed my father's company. He took his medication, and followed his diet strictly, especially when the pains subsided, though he insisted it was his herbs that were curing him. While my father was visiting, David and I decided to keep our relationship quiet, not wanting to upset him. I felt like I was a teenager again, stealing moments here and there to see him before going home, but this excited David. I began working on the documents needed for my parents to foster Pete, and with the help of Mrs. Thomas, the process was going rapidly.

Approval was granted shortly after for my parents to foster Pete, and on the weekend when I was taking him to the country with the social worker, it was my twenty-ninth birthday. It was a long time since I had been back to my community and surprisingly, I missed everyone, including Bobo, who by the way, seemed to have lost a lot of weight. He came up and hugged me.

"Girl, is not the same since yu gone. No one can cook like yu."

To my astonishment the community had built up considerably over the years. A paved road now replaced the dirt track I used to know. Street light, cable and phone lines had been installed. The stand pipe which had been a gathering place, was no longer used, as water had been connected to each home. Our nearest neighbor was no longer a mile away. Every hundred yards or so there was a house now, ranging from board structures to concrete houses, some two stories, with balconies each of them painted in different colours, which enlivened the area. Some persons had even built large homes in the hills which overlooked the valley, giving them a wonderful view of the area past the river and down to the sea on a clear day. With the development of the road, many vendors had set up stalls selling fry fish, jerk chicken, pork, yam and corn to passing motorists. Some members who went abroad, invested in the area on their return. It was no longer a typical farming area.

Apart from the tiny shops, there was a mini supermarket, a Postal agency had been established, and a health clinic with a pharmacy. More trees seemed evident, as people were no longer cooking on wood fires, as a depot to purchase cooking gas was there. The HEART Trust of Jamaica had established a skills training school. Entrepreneurship was on the rise in the community. Kids I went to school with had established businesses; like Jason Baker who had a barbershop, and was training younger boys in the skill. Christine opened a restaurant and did catering for weddings and other church functions. Jack, in collaboration with HEART trust started a garage, and helped train boys interested in mechanics. Peter Wilson, who had a crush on me from I was in third form opened a carpentry shop and supplied furniture to several large stores in the western part of the island. When I saw the development that had taken place, I felt guilty that I had done nothing to help with this, and resolved to contact the Health Centre to offer my services in the Mental Health Department.

My father killed a goat and chickens and had a feast for Pete's home coming. There was even a sound system blasting out music. All the members of the community were there. Everyone was having a good time, eating and enjoying themselves, when I heard someone saying over the microphone "Susan, someone wants to say something to you."
I spun around. To my shock, it was David, on his knees, in the dirt proposing. Unbeknownst to me, he had been down here for the past two weeks getting

my parents blessing and sorting out the necessary documents for this moment.

"Susan, will you marry me?"

Tears welled up in my eyes. I looked at him and at the crowd that had gathered around us, and felt so nervous.

"Yes, yes I'll marry you!" I cried.

Everyone was elated. They started crowding around me until I felt like I was being crushed.

I heard my father calling, "Pastor Benson! Pastor Benson! Marry dem now before she change har mind again!"

It was not the wedding I had in mind, but both David and I were so happy that we got married right there. The homecoming feast turned into a wedding celebration. My only regret was not having Chelsea there. David looked at me and smiled. "Clumsy, turn around." I did and to my surprise, there was Chelsea. She walked up to me and kissed me. "Congratulations, Susan," she said.

"I'm so sorry you weren't here for the wedding," I said.

"Actually, I was," she replied, smiling, "But I didn't want to interrupt, so I just stayed in the crowd."

"But I wanted you to be involved."

"Don't worry about it. Everything worked out for the best. I'm still here and I'm still your friend.

Nine months later we had a beautiful daughter, we named her Zanya. We continued to help out at the orphanage when we could. Chelsea and Chris seemed as if they would never get over their honeymoon phase. Often they would go from one country to the other. My parents still don't know about Michelle, and as far as I know, they will never know that she and Janet are together in Kingston. I thought that my trust in David had been restored, but lately I am not so sure. I ignored the signs the first time, and refused to face it. Chelsea told me the other day not to be paranoid but I know that sometimes love is not enough. I know that deep inside David loves me, but there is also a saying that a leopard will never change his spots. I refuse to live in denial. After receiving several anonymous text messages and hang-ups on the phone, David frequently working late nights and not wanting to take Zanya and I out with him, and spending less time at home with his family - I am beginning to wonder if I can survive another *betrayal*.

~The End~

Generation

Joe Lee was born in the late 1930's in Spanish Town, Jamaica, the first and only son of a second generation immigrant from China, Wang Lee. His father worked as a conductor at the National Railway Station in the parish of St. Catherine. Against his grandparent's wishes for an arranged marriage, Wang Lee met and fell in love with a dressmaker called Dorothy Johnson. She had dark chocolate-coloured skin with the body of a model and ropy-long waist length hair. Her smile would light up her face so much that it would make your day when you came into contact with her. Two years into their union, Joe Wang Lee was born. Wanting the best for their son, they tried to give him every opportunity that was available. They believed this was only possible through education and exposing him to the wider world.

In 1953 Joe got a scholarship to study engineering at the International University of Technology in Pennsylvania, United States. That spring he arrived with great expectations. For the first year he excelled and got on with everyone in his class but by the second year he was having financial problems and unable to meet his expenses. With the recommendation of his Professor, he got a job as a tutor in Calculus tutoring first year university students (freshmen), one of whom was Jessica Liteburn. She had supple milky skin with stringy red hair and seductive dark blue eyes which enhanced the size of the mole above her lips. Things were going well for a few weeks until one Friday night he had to tutor her in her dorm room instead of the usual library. In those days there was a lot of segregation between races, and several groups like KKK, skinheads and other informal white power organisations were very active throughout the state. At the end of that session he was on his way back to his dorm from Jessica's, and was confronted by five white guys in masks with hoodies over their heads. They surrounded him with sticks and batons shouting racist remarks at him. Realising that he couldn't avoid them he began to defend himself but they were too much for him to handle, he was beaten unconscious. Although there were witnesses, no one came to his assistance. After the assault he woke up in the hospital with a broken hand and two broken ribs. Three days later he was discharged. He obtained a lawyer in the hope of getting redress from the university, since it was on its grounds that the incident took place. From his own investigation, he found out that his attackers all attended the university, he was amazed however, that no one was willing to testify. The Faculty Director called him to his office one afternoon and told him it would be in his own best interest not to go to the media with his story of an assault on campus. He was so shocked that he did not know how to respond, especially when the Director continued to say it would not hold up in court because Jessica was willing to testify that he was trying to rape her, and the guys (his attackers) had come to her defence. He said, "Mr. Lee you are here to study, and study you should. Do not get involved in things that do not concern you."

"What do you mean?" Joe asked angrily. "Don't be sassy boy!" he said, sitting back in his chair and lighting a cigar. "You are a black man from a third world country," he began, "…you came here, you saw a girl you liked and you tried to get personally involved with her by force."

"I did not!" Joe cried, stomping his feet, "I

was tutoring her."

"Really?" the Director inquired. "These boys' fathers are very powerful. One of them donated our library. "Now…" he paused, leaning forward, "…you have a year and a half left. Be a good boy, study hard and get your degree, then go back to your jungle because if you make things difficult for us, we'll make it difficult for you."

Joe's blood rushed from his feet to his head, the room began to spin, so he held his head in his hands. The Director got up and patted him on the shoulder, "I will give you a few minutes to think about it," he said as he left the room.

Fighting back his tears, he remembered all the sacrifices his parents had made for him. It was wrong, but if he tried to fight he could lose his scholarship. At that moment he realised that this is a white man's country, and he had to live and play by their rules. The Director returned. "So?" he asked, "What are you going to do... persist, or not, Joe?"

Swallowing the tears that were threatening to spill, he stood up. "I will study, Sir, and go home."

When Joe arrived back in Jamaica, his parents were so excited, as he was the first one in their family to graduate from a university. They told everyone in the community, and the small dinner they planned soon turned out to be a party. Joe made up his mind not to tell them what happened to him in the States. He was still hurting, but he felt time would heal all wounds. In no time he got a job as a supervisor at the railway station. His grandfather wanted him to have an arranged marriage in China, but with his father's blessing he refused. He wanted to fall in love before marrying someone. In 1960 he was invited to a party in Barbican, St. Andrew. There he glimpsed a girl that caught his attention. She was across the room talking and drinking with friends. Realising that his glass was half empty, he grabbed a bottle of wine and walked over. "Can I give you a refill?" he asked, smiling. Looking at him from head to toe she replied, "No thank you," and walked away. But Joe being persistent decided that he would not give up. Half an hour later, he noticed that she was outside by herself. Quietly he walked up behind her and softly touched her on her neck. When she spun around to hit him, he grabbed her hand. "Calm down and allow me to introduce myself. I am Joe. What's your name?"

"None of your business!" she snapped at him. "It's nice to meet you," he continued. She walked away and he followed. "Come on," he said. "I hear the accent, so I know you're not a Jamaican."

"And why would you assume that?" she asked as she turned to face him. "I was born in England, but my parents are Jamaican. So what does that make me?"

Folding his arms, Joe smiled. "That makes you a British-born Jamaican, so can you tell me your name now?"

"I thought you got that already." Joe smiled. "You mean to tell me that *none of your business* is your real name?"

"You figure it out," she said.

"Is that a challenge?" he asked. "Maybe," she replied, smiling for the first time. Joe realised her smile was so beautiful he wondered what it would be like to kiss her. She broke the silence that came between them. "Tell you what," she said. "I'll give you a minute to find out my name."

He approached a couple, and having no luck,

he turned to the door to check the Guest List. By the time he turned back, she was gone. Two weeks later, when purchasing some items at a grocery store, he went up to the counter and saw to his surprise that she was the cashier. "Well Kadie," he began. She smiled. "Don't smile at me", he said, "you tricked me."

"I did not say I was going to wait on you." She laughed. "So, Kadie McDonald, now that I know your name, what's next?"

"I did not know that there was going to be a 'next'." She said. "There has to be", Joe replied. "Can I take you out to dinner, dancing, marriage and some kids?"

"Wow, slow down," she said, laughing. "Typical Jamaican man, see something they want and have to get it, not thinking about the woman." Joe picked up the bag and said, "Does next Friday night sound ok?" At that moment, a well-built man came out from the back with some boxes in his hand. "Honey where should I put these?" he asked. "...By the second shelf where the tinned juices are." Joe's heart dropped. He could not believe she was already *married*. Not wanting to seem embarrassed or create a fuss, he turned and began to walk towards the door. "Hey!" she called after him, "How would you know where to pick me up if you do not know my address?" When he turned around, she saw the confusion on his face and laughed out loud. "See what I mean? Typical Jamaican man has to assume." "Dad…," she said to the man across from her, "This is the guy I was telling you about." Joe nimbly walked towards him and shook his hand. At that moment Joe convinced himself that he must work out because his grip was so strong. Joe and the McDonalds became extremely close after that day. They loved him like a son. It was no surprise when a year later Joe and Kadie got married, and within the next nine months, their first child, Andrew was born.

Joe went into business with his father-in-law, Frank by investing in his wholesale business. When Chris, their second son was born, the family had four wholesales in the parish of St. Andrew. Their third child, a girl, called Diamond, was born in the seventh year of their marriage. Joe tried to teach his children to love and respect everyone in the world but he also instilled in them that there is good and bad in man. As he would often say, "You have to know your place and let them know theirs. Socialising is one thing, but getting personally involved is another." Chris who was curious from birth would always question him. "Love is blind and once you love each other, nothing else matters." Joe sat him down, "Listen son," he said, "I love my parents very much, but the reality is that I am half-Chinese and half-Black. In Jamaica this is not a problem, race is not a factor in achieving your success but if I was living in Europe or the States, I would never be accepted by either race, too black for the Chinese and too Chinese to be black. This would affect where I live, the type of job I could get, and even those that I associate with. Do you get it son? The world is not ready for human beings to become one."

"It's just not right." Chris replied. "It's what is inside of a man that counts." Joe hugged his son. "The world is not fair, and we just have to live by the rules." "Whose rules…?" Chris asked. "…white man, black or 'chiny' man?" Joe looked in his face and said, "It's the rule of humanity."

Financially the family was stable. Every two years they would take a vacation to Manchester, England where Kadie's family came from. In 1977 when Chris was 14 years old, his Grand Aunt Mazie offered to keep him with her so he could attend school there in England. After much family meeting and consideration, his parents agreed. Chris was so excited, it was the first summer he wanted to come and go so fast. He and Andrew were very close and he knew he would miss his bigger brother. They spent the holiday fishing, bird shooting and go-cart racing. The beginning of his school year in England, Chris found it so confusing to find his classes that he had to draw a map to find his way. His Grand Aunt and Uncle Joshua treated him like a son. On Saturdays he would go to the race horse track to watch and bet on the races with his grand uncle. This often caused an argument since his Aunt Mazie was a Christian. Chris tried to please both of them, being with his uncle on a Saturday and his aunt on a Sunday. He knew it was wrong, but he couldn't help it. He loved horses, but to please his aunt and also god, he stopped betting, only watched the races.

A few weeks later he was rushing to his English class not taking notice of where he was going. He collided with a young woman and both of their books fell to the floor. They leaned down to pick them up and their heads bumped into each other. When Chris looked up, it was a slim blond white girl with the most beautiful blue eyes he had ever seen.

"Sorry," he said, "let me help you." "I think you have done enough." she replied. "What were you trying to do, kill me?" she asked. Standing up he replied, "No. I was not paying attention to where I was going. I apologise again." Then he turned and walked away. He was just in time to hear his name called for his assignment. Going through the folder in his hand he realised it was the wrong one. "Mr. Lee…" his teacher said, "I am waiting, I don't have all day." "I am sorry sir but it got mixed up." "Really?" he asked doubtfully, "don't you know that its 10% of your grade?" "Yes Sir," Chris said, "I did it." The teacher stood up and walked towards him. "I guess this is a zero for you." At that moment the same girl walked into his class and asked permission to speak to him.

At lunch Chris ordered his favourite food, Fish and Chips and went to his usual table in the corner where he knew he wouldn't be disturbed. Looking through his comic book he was so engaged in it he didn't realise for a few seconds that someone was sitting in front of him. His eyes came slowly up from the book to see her sitting there. "By the way," she said, "I am Zoe." "I am Chris," he replied. "Thank you for saving my butt this morning." "It's ok," she said, "It's my good deed for the day, although you do not deserve it." "Why?" Chris asked surprised. "All because of you I got a detention." "Because of me?" he asked. "Yes, I am late three times now, and this is automatic detention." "It was not my fault," he said defensively. "Maybe, maybe not," she said laughing. "I can see that you love horses." "How did you know?" he asked. "Your folder this morning, there were some horses drawn in it. You're a good artist. My family owns a ranch." "Really?" he asked, surprised. She continued "…and if you want I can arrange for you to have a job there on the weekends. You would have the opportunity to interact with the horses, and you'll have some extra Pounds in your pocket. Are you interested?" "Don't ask twice," he said, smiling at her.

By the following week he was working on the ranch. It was a new adventure for him. Although he had to clean the barn, the horse mess, and feed them, he found the experience self-satisfying and rewarding. He and Zoe got on well. She would often sit in the barn and speak with him while he did his work. He found himself getting nervous yet excited when she was around. His body was going through some hormonal changes that made him confused and frustrated. He wished his dad was near for him to talk to. He realised he felt a lot better by swimming in the pool. Zoe had three older brothers, Matthew, Mark and Johnston. They hardly spoke to him apart from giving him orders, but this suited him because he did not talk a lot especially to people he didn't know. One afternoon Zoe came by to see him. His Aunt and Uncle were not there. "My father gave me your pay to give to you. I looked for you all day at school, what happened?" "I got the day off," he replied. "Is something wrong?" she asked concernedly. "I have tonsillitis, they have to be removed. I am going to get it done next week." "Oh," she said, "Can I do anything for you?" "Yes," he replied, "I was hoping that you would ask your father for two weeks off for me. I really like my job here but if he has to let me go I'll understand." "I will see what I can do," she replied. At that moment she realised that he had a can of soup in his hand. "I am sorry to take you away from your meal," she said. "It's ok, would you like to come in for a second?" The second turned out to be two hours. They ate and talked and got to know each other better. He found out that they had a lot in common from the type of music they listened to; to the sports they watched. He was so tired he fell asleep; when he awoke she was gone.

Over time, she taught him to ride his first horse and in return he would tell her about Jamaica and his life there. He was settling down so well getting less and less. Chris realised his feelings towards Zoe were changing from friendship, but he tried to fight it because of what his father told him about one's social status in life. A few weeks before his 16th birthday they went riding together. Stopping to rest under a tree they started talking. Suddenly he took her hand and gave her a kiss. To his amazement she did not resist but she began kissing him back. Softly she whispered in his ear, "I love you." "Can it work?" Chris asked in a hoarse voice. "It has to…," Zoe replied, "It has to." They vowed not to tell anyone of their feelings for each other because of fear of the repercussions to Chris. It was the hardest thing he ever had to do not to touch her in public. He wanted to shout from the roof tops of his love for her. The night of his birthday, they met secretly and made love for the first time. He was her first and she was his. It was so special. They did not want to let go of each other but they knew that they had to part and get back to reality. On Saturday morning Chris was in the barn getting some hay for the horses. She came in to talk with him. They began laughing and playing around. He grabbed her and they both fell on the ground and he went on top of her. The barn door opened and her brother Mark was standing over them. "What the hell's going on?" He shouted. Chris jumped up. "Nothing, we are just playing." "Playing my foot," he shouted, "tell me the truth!" "Nothing", Zoe kept telling him, but before Chris knew it, Mark was on top of him beating him. The other two brothers heard the commotion and came to investigate. Mark told them what he saw and they started also on Chris. He was so badly beaten he could hardly stand up.

The Police came to get a statement from him. He told them that Zoe was a witness to the incident but when they questioned her she denied her brothers had attacked him. Chris was heartbroken; he could not believe what he was hearing. He stayed home for two weeks and she came by several times to see him, but he refused to see or speak with her. The last time she came by, his grand aunt told her that he had gone back to Jamaica. She went home and went straight to her room and started to cry. Not only did Chris go out of her life but he left without knowing the truth about why she had lied or *what* he had left behind.

In 1985 Andrew turned 24 years old and he became a partner with his dad in his business. Joe was very proud of his success. Out of all his children, Andrew was the only one that showed interest in his family enterprise. Chris on the other hand was a music producer and refused to come into business with him, but Andrew learnt from scratch and now his first-born was working with him. Unfortunately he was not so proud of his social life, because he was a party goer, and every week he had a different girl. He would explain, "Dad, life is too short to settle down early with one woman, so I'm having my fun until it's over." Joe did not approve of that lifestyle for him, but there was nothing he could do. His wife would often say, "They are young people, and we cannot force our beliefs or lifestyles on them, only pray for them." This didn't stop Joe, as whenever they had their monthly family dinner, he would encourage Andrew to settle down and find himself a good girl. This would often turn into a big argument, with Andrew sometimes jumping in his car and speeding away, leaving his mother behind to cry to Joe, "You're going to make your son crash one of these days!" Andrew would feel bad afterwards. He loved his dad and hated arguing with him, but he wished for God's sake he would get out of his personal life regarding finding a wife. Some people are not meant to be married and he knew he was one of them. Three months later, he went to Taiwan on a business trip, and talking to one of his associates there, he came up with a brilliant plan. There are many girls there who need a foreign husband. He would get one, marry her and take her to Jamaica as a front up girl, and still have his fun with other girls in Jamaica. This way he would please his father by having a wife, but still enjoy his lifestyle the way he wanted. "After all," he said to himself, "If it does not work out, all I need to do is give her some money and send her back home."

The beauty about Taiwan is that money talks, and within 24-hours Andrew was choosing a bride from about fifteen girls. Walking past each of them he would ask them to tell him something about themselves and why they wanted to get married. They were all talking about finding a rich husband and the ability to travel all over the globe, but when he came in front of Mayling she said, "I am nineteen years old, and all I want is to find someone to love and care for me." There was longing in her voice, and when he looked in her eyes there was something there that he could not quite put his finger on. "So you don't want to travel?" he asked. "No," she replied. "And why not?" he demanded. "If I have everything at home I don't need to travel outside," she replied. He told them which one he wanted in the morning. Partying and going out with friends that night did not help his mood, and even taking two women to bed, he could not help thinking about Mayling. Lying in bed he was beginning to doubt himself, wondering if it was a good idea, but the phone rang and interrupted his thoughts. "Hi son," his mother said. "Hi Mum," he replied. "Are you ok?" She said, "Your dad has lined up two girls for you to meet when you return home. Both of them have studied in the States. One is returning to practice medicine out here, and the other to do business." "I do not need Dad to find women for me!" Andrew snapped. "Honey", his mother said softly, "…your dad will never give up on this." With this realisation, Andrew made up his mind, and by 4:00 p.m. that evening, he and Mayling got married. They spent two more days in Taiwan, but he never made love to her because he felt that he didn't want to get emotionally involved in this marriage. As far as he was concerned, this was just a front, a false marriage for convenience and nothing more. When he returned to Jamaica, he put her in a separate bedroom, and was thinking of the best opportunity to introduce her to his family. Mayling was confused. "Why is it that he did not consummate our marriage or make me sleep with him?" She was beginning to wonder if it was a different culture. She was hoping that they would be together from the first time she met him. Her heart leapt and she knew he would be the one for her.

A week later the opportunity arrived for Andrew. By questioning his mother, he found out that his father had invited the two girls for dinner. He deliberately came late. As soon as he entered the dining room his father looked up and his mouth dropped open. "Hi everyone," Andrew said proudly. "This is my wife, Mayling." His mother's fork dropped to the floor. Chris was staring at him and Diamond was clearing her throat every five seconds. You could hear a pin drop in the room by the time he pulled out Mayling's chair and she sat at the dining table. Regaining his composure, Joe said, "Can I see you outside, son?" "Sure Dad." Andrew got up and went out with his father ready for a battle. "What hell is going on?" "What do you mean?" Andrew asked, with a smirk on his face. "A couple of weeks ago, I was fighting with you to have someone steady in your life, and now you present yourself with a wife. Are you trying to pull something over on me son?" "No Dad, we really got married two weeks ago in Taiwan." "How long did you two know each other?" "A few months," Andrew said with a lying tongue. "And how did you communicate?" "It's 80's technology," Andrew said, proudly. "So you deprive your mum and me of a wedding?" "Dad, I am not Diamond, you do not have to give me away." "That's not what I mean son," Joe snapped back. "I want to be at my children's wedding. Is that hard to understand?" "No Dad."

"How old is she?"

"Nineteen years old."

"Where is her family?"

"Taiwan".

"What do they do for a living?"

"Farming."

"What's her profession?"

"I am going to send her back to school."

"Son," Joe said softly, "…you had the opportunity to marry a lawyer, doctor, accountant and a business woman. Anyone you wanted, and you choose someone that you have to send back to school?" "It's how I live, dad and as you said, it is time for me to settle down." "We'll see," Joe said, "we'll see."

For the next few days, each evening when Andrew came home, Mayling had dinner prepared for him. "She is a beautiful girl," he thought to himself, "...and very attractive." He found himself getting aroused by her. So he deliberately came home later than usual, but this plan crashed within a few days when his father called him, stating that he wanted to spend a night at his home because he did not feel to drive to St. Catherine that night to his house. Hanging up the phone, Andrew rocked back in his chair. He was living on his own for six years now, and never yet did his father want to spend the night. Why now? Is it just to check up on him to see if things are as exactly as he says? "Damn it!" he said to himself, he would have to let her sleep with him tonight. That's all he needs in his life.

When Andrew came from work that evening and started to move her things into his room, Mayling was sitting in the chair watching him and wondering what was going on. Did he finally want a wife? Was she going to stop being his live-in helper and become part of his life? That night after everyone said goodnight and retired to bed, Andrew told her goodnight and turned his back to her. There was a thunderstorm and each time the lightning flashed and she heard the thunder roll, she scrunched up beside him. It was more than Andrew could bear; he turned around and started to kiss her. She started to kiss him back and by the time he was on top of her, his passion was boiling like a volcano. The thunder drowned out her screams as he entered her. In the morning when they got up he realised that she was hiding her face with the pillow. "What's wrong?" he asked, softly. "Nothing," she replied. "Why are you hiding from me?" "Nothing," she answered. But he knew she was lying. When he tried to draw her closer to him, he jumped up and looked at the sheet, and realised when he saw the blood. He knelt down beside the bed. "Why didn't you tell me?" "Would that make a difference?" she asked softly. "Yes it would," Andrew said. "I would have been more gentle. I've never been so, you know, wild." "It's ok," she said. "You are my husband; it is your duty." Andrew tried to speak again, but she placed her hand over his mouth. "Don't worry," she whispered. He got up, went to the bathroom and made a hot bath for her. He felt so bad; he did not know what to say. He had been with so many women, more experienced than her, and yet he was gentler with them. He had to make it up to her, one way or another. When Mayling went into the bath, Andrew went out to the kitchen. His dad was already there drinking coffee. "How was your night son?" "Fine," Andrew stuttered. "Is something wrong?" "No." He thought that his dad would press more, but he just said, "I am off to the office, see you later, son," and stepped out of the house. Joe whistled all the way to work. He had gotten what he wanted. Knowing Andrew thought he was pulling a fast one on him, but he was outside his room and heard everything. They really are a couple!

By the time Mayling came out of the bath, Andrew had her breakfast ready. "Would you like to come to work with me?" She opened her eyes wide in surprise. "Can I?" "Yes," he said smiling at her. "But I don't understand business," she confessed. "Don't worry, I won't give you anything hard, just showing you the basics. We can start from there."

At work that day, Andrew found himself checking on her every five minutes to see how she was getting on. He was thinking about her to the point that he could not concentrate on his own work. "What the hell is going on with me?" he wondered. "Am I falling for her?" It was not meant to be this way, it was just for convenience, but now the thoughts of his life without her scared him. "What the hell am I going to do?" he thought. He returned to his office to call the one person in his life that would understand, Chris. They had lunch that afternoon, and Andrew told him everything. As usual Chris would listen, giving his brother all his attention until he was finished. "Look Andrew," Chris said, "you went in as the player and now you have fallen for her. It is as simple as that." "What should I do Chris?" Andrew asked desperately. "I am not the best person to advise you on that," Chris said. "But you are," Andrew said. "I am not in love," Chris said, "…but you are." "I am not in love, Chris but you were once," Andrew said. Chris leaned towards his brother, "But look what that got me? Maybe I should have been a player like you, I would never have felt hurt like that." "Do you regret it?" Andrew asked. "I will for the rest of my life," Chris said. There were a few minutes silence between them, then Chris said, "Look Andrew, just take it easy and see where it leads you. Maybe this is the woman for you."

"I am a player," Andrew said, "and always will be, but I don't want to hurt her. Is this wrong Chris…should I change my lifestyle to suit her?" "No", Chris said, "…do not change your lifestyle to suit any woman, you will just get hurt in the long run."

It is 1986 in London. Zoe opened the front door to her flat and went inside. It had been a hard day at work, and she was really tired. She studied for years as a designer, sending herself back to school and finally completing college two years ago. It wasn't easy. Since most of her study took place in the night, she had to work in the day to make up for lost time. Entering her bedroom, she lifted up the cover then held the most precious thing she had in her life, her baby girl, kissing her. She opened her eyes. "Hi Mummy." "Hi sweetheart," Zoe replied. "How was your day?" "Better since seeing you…have you eaten supper?" Zoe asked. "Yes Mummy." She sat on the bed, and Chrystal climbed into her lap. "I saw your teacher today…we had a meeting, remember?" At this Chrystal held her head down. "I do not like French," she said softly, "why do I have to learn it, mum? Are we going to live in France?" "Honey it's a good language," Zoe said stroking her cheek. "Go back to bed, we will talk more about this in the morning." Putting the cover over her, she kissed her and turned off the light.

Zoe went into the living room, turned on the computer and put her hand to her face. She looks more and more like him every day, she thought. Not only that, she is beginning to ask questions Zoe knows she can't answer. It's been eight years, but she will never forget it, the hurt in his eyes or the disappointment in his face, but she had to do it because they were going to charge him for rape. She was not yet sixteen years old when they made love. It was either lying, or him going to prison. After he left, she tried to hide her pregnancy from her parents for five months. When she could not hide it any more, they tried to get her to destroy the child, but she fought tooth and nail for that not to happen. She even threatened them that she would disgrace the family. Forging her mother's signature, she got some money, packed her bag, she walked out of the house one night, and never looked back. She ran away to London, where she got a job in a restaurant. She told them she was eighteen years old and they believed her. Changing her name, and with a new appearance she got away with it for over two years, until her mother finally caught up with her. Her daughter Chrystal, was already one and a half years old, but instead of wanting her to come back home to be with her family with her child, they wanted her to come alone, giving up her daughter this time for adoption. She would not agree to it, telling them she would rather die than part with her child. It's either both of us or none. When her mother would not back down, she moved again, and this time she made sure they wouldn't find her.

It was hard, working her way through school. Since completing college two years ago this was her first real break of making something with her life. Six months ago she got a job at International Design as a junior in the advertising department. She was trying to save to buy a bigger flat, one with two bedrooms. She liked sharing with her daughter, but she wanted to give her a real home with a room for herself with toys and everything a little girl would want. Dating over the years had been a disaster. She never found someone whom she was compatible with. There was one or maybe two that showed promise, but unfortunately she had to punch one of them who suggested that her daughter call her aunt instead of mum, because her skin was much darker than hers.

After the incident the guy ran for his life, saying that she needed to be incarcerated in a psychiatric clinic and the key thrown away. Since then she decided that only she and her child will make it.

It all started a month ago. Chrystal was alone and found a key by going through her stuff. She found a picture of Chris and started asking questions. "Who is this guy mummy?" She asked. "How come I have not seen him before, where is he? Is he my father? Can we go see him? How come other kids have fathers and I don't? Doesn't he want to see me? How comes he has never visited? Can we go see him please?" Zoe thought to herself, "I do not want to hurt or lie to her, but how can I tell her that he doesn't even know she exists? He might be married and have his own family." Being a ghost of the past she cannot come to haunt him now. Each time she thought of it, just the thought of seeing him again puts her body in ..... But she knew in her heart that he and Chrystal have a right to know each other, to have a father and daughter relationship. She went to the Jamaican Consulate yesterday and got a copy of their telephone directory. There she saw several names with the same name Lee. "Tonight," she said, "I'll begin making the calls." As she picked up the phone she heard her daughter scream for her. Rushing back to the bedroom she turns on the light and saw her. "I had a nightmare Mummy," her daughter said, trembling. "It's ok baby, I am here now." She climbed into bed with her and started stroking her hand through her hair and there they fell asleep in each other's arms. Zoe ignored the problem for a week until one afternoon she came home from work early and saw Chrystal holding the picture of her father again. This time she knew she had to do it.

November 1986 Chris returned from Sweden. He had just promoted two new artists, and one of their singles was doing well on the World Top 20 Chart. He was on top of his game. Everyone knows him in the island, as one of the best and youngest producers. He was in high demand, and to top it off, Alicia called, wanting to spend the night with him. She is a doctor that he sees on and off. Although he is not a player like Andrew, he tried to keep the ladies far and few. As soon as it is getting serious, he will let them go. He was smiling from ear to ear, as he just launched his new company Lee's Entertainment Enterprise, and knew he would have a beautiful woman in his bed tonight. "What more," he asked himself, "could a man want?" That night they went from club to club, anywhere the excitement was, there they were; and like clockwork, by 3:00 a.m. they were in bed making love.

Chris was in his deep sleep when the phone woke him. Shuffling his hand around in the dark, he managed to pick it up. "Hello?" he said, in a sleepy voice. "Is this Chris?" the voice over the phone asked. "Yes." "Chris Henry Lee?" "Yes," he replied. "Hi, I am Zoe." He thought he was not hearing correctly. "Excuse me?" he asked. "I am Zoe Shepherd, do you remember me?" His whole body went tense, and his heart began to beat rapidly. "Are you still there?" she asked. Finally he managed to say, "It's been a long time Zoe, how are you?" "I am fine, you?" "I am ok," he said. "The reason I am calling, Chris is, oh God…," she said, "I don't know how to tell you this, but I have been trying for two days to get in touch with you, you have a daughter." "What?!" he shouted. "She's eight years old Chris", Zoe said softly, "…her name is Chrystal, and she is a beautiful girl." A silent pause between them and Chris could hear the beat of his heart all the way in his head. Then she spoke again, "I don't want to disrupt your life Chris, but please understand she needs to know about you. She keeps asking me questions and I don't know how to answer her. The reality is I need your help." "Give me your number Zoe," he said and taking it down, he promised to call her later that evening.

For the whole day it seemed like he was in a trance. Hearing from her again brought back so much emotion in him he never thought he had anymore, but the thought of having a child scared him. Chris had never pictured himself as a father and would go out of his way not to become one with his lovers over the years. But a daughter, he said to himself, I have to make it right with her. By the evening he was talking to Zoe again, who seemed less nervous now. For the first time he heard his daughter's voice. He fell head over heels in love with her, and they promised to exchange pictures. They also made arrangements to visit for Christmas. If it was up to Chrystal, it would have been the following day, but both of them work, so they tried to convince her that it cannot be any sooner. For a few days Chris was walking on cloud nine, not only about his daughter, but to see Zoe again. He did not have any expectations, but the thought of seeing her again put a smile on his face. Then it hit him...his father! How would he break the news to his father? For most of his and Andrew's adult life, their father kept giving them hints that it's time for him to become a grandfather. Now he's one, but Chris wondered how he felt. Would he accept this child as his grandchild, given that she is half white? He had to try for his daughter's sake before they come to Jamaica. He decided to break the news to everyone at the same time; "And further…," he thought aloud "…safety in numbers." His father would not react so badly if everyone was around him. The battlefield would be the family monthly dinner.

When Chris arrived, Andrew and Mayling were sitting, and not talking to each other but he didn't notice them. He saw his father looking out the window, smoking a cigar. "You're late Chris." "Yes dad, can we talk?" "Sure son, let's go outside." "No," Chris said, "I wish to stay right here with everyone including Mum." Joe called his wife from the kitchen, and she came out with a roast chicken and placed it in the middle of the table. "Your son wishes to speak to us. Go ahead," Joe said. "Do you love me dad?" Chris asked. "Of course," his father replied, "what kind of question is that?" "And would you love anything that comes from me?"

"What do you mean Chris?" Seeing that his father's smile turned into a frown, he stood back and said, "I have a daughter." Both Andrew, his sister and mother said at the same time, "What?!" "She's eight years old." His father put out his cigar. "And I am just finding out about her," he said. "It's a long story." "Where is she?" his father demanded. "England." "Is it from the time you were studying there?" "Yes dad," he replied. His dad turned his back and stared out the window, but Chris knew he was thinking. Finally he turned around and said, "She is family. We will buy her a ticket to come and meet us." "There is something else," Chris said, his dad was staring straight at him, "...it's about her mother." "What about her mother?" Joe asked. "She's white." Within a second, both Andrew and his mother stood in front of him before his father could grab a hold of him. The rage that came over his father's face, Chris knew if he had held him he would have hurt him. Not knowing what to say, he turned and ran out the door, got into his car and drove away. When Andrew got home that evening, he called him. "Is it Zoe?" he asked. "Yes," Chris replied. "Why did she not get in touch all these years?" "I don't know," Chris replied, "but I guess I'll find out. She is bringing her over for Christmas." "How is dad?" Chris asked. "He was still ranting and raving when I left," Andrew said, "…he disowns you…and Mum, she understands Chris but you know she loves him; she will do anything that he wants her to do, even disowning me too. Give him time," Andrew said, "…he'll come around."

Three days later Chris called Joe at his office. "What do you want?" he asked in a cold voice. "I want to talk dad." "Don't call me dad," Joe replied. "Please dad, give Chrystal a chance, get to know her before judging her… and Zoe also. She's a nice girl." "Is that her mother's name?" Joe demanded, "Yes." "Tell me something Chris, of all the black women in England, why did you have to lay down with a whitey?" Before he could finish, Chris shouted, "Dad don't go there! Of all the persons in this world, you should understand. Grandma loved grandpa, Andrew loves his wife." "That's different," he said, "they are Asian, not Caucasian. I do not want to see either her or her mother." "That means you don't want to see me," Chris said. The phone went blank and Chris finally said, "Goodbye Dad" and hung up. Chris never thought he would ever feel such hurt again in his life but he was wrong. It was one of the worse pains he had ever felt. For the next few weeks he tried to occupy his time by preparing for them, refurbishing the room in which they would stay, and even getting a helper. He had been a bachelor for so many years; he had to put some feminine touches in his home.

From the moment the plane landed, Zoe was so nervous. She was gripping her bag so tightly; she felt like she was drowning and it was the only thing that could save her all the way through the flight. She kept picturing him from his photograph. He was a very handsome man. Having gotten taller and more muscular but he was the same cute guy she fell in love with. She couldn't believe it when he told her he was not married. Although she knew that there would be no chance for her in his life, just Chrystal, she couldn't help hoping and wishing. Could it be again? "NO!" she said to herself, "the past is the past, and that's where it's going to stay. I am only doing this so my daughter can have a father."

He saw her before she saw him coming through the customs lounge. She was dressed in a tight mini black skirt with a red blouse and a well curved figure. She's now a full woman with the same sweet smile and blue eyes that took his breath away. "Hi Zoe." he said. She looked up, "Hi Chris." Both of them went into a world of their own just staring at each other. Chrystal brought them back to reality. Shaking her hands, "Hey, what about me?" she demanded. "I am sorry honey," Zoe said, "Chris, this is your daughter." He bent down and they went into each other's arms kissing and crying. "Let me look at you," Chris said with tears in his eyes. She was so beautiful, he couldn't believe it, a little bit lighter than him but a dead ringer. "You have my nose," he said. She smiled, "No you have my nose, and my eyes and mouth." Chris started to laugh so hard he almost fell back on the floor. By the time they were in the car driving home, Chris and his daughter were communicating so well it's like they knew each other all their lives. All Zoe could do was sit back and admire them.

Dinner went okay and Chrystal was so impressed that he owned his own music company. With this knowledge she started to show him her singing ability. After each one he would applaud her, and she was beginning another one even when she started getting sleepy. Her mum had to come pick her up and force her to her room. She insisted that

Chris should be the only to read her bedtime story. He felt so blessed, the emotions he felt inside of him that night, words could not explain. While he was reading to her, Zoe was busy watching him the whole time. As soon as they turned off the light in Chrystal's room, she volunteered to come and help him clear the table. "Chris," she said, "I have to explain...," "About what?" he asked, "...about everything," she replied. "The only thing I want to know, Zoe," he began, as she put the last set of dishes in the sink, "why did you deny me my child all these years?" "I didn't," she said. When she turned around she was between him and the sink, the tension that was flowing between them was unbearable for her, so she tried to walk past him but he grabbed her and put her in front of him. "Are you telling me that for eight years you cared for my child without my knowledge and didn't try to get in touch with me and now you're saying you didn't deny me her?" He made a step towards her using his body to brace her back on the sink. Holding her face up to his, he said, "Zoe I don't want to hear anything from you. You are a liar, and the only thing that matters now is Chrystal." He turned away and walked to his bedroom. She went to hers and slumped on the bed. "He hates me," she said to herself, and with that knowledge she started to cry.

Zoe did not know when she fell asleep, the only thing she remembered was Chrystal climbing on her and shaking her. "Mum, I am hungry." When she looked at the clock it was 5 in the morning. "So soon?" she asked drowsily. "Yes I am a big girl," Chrystal replied. She hugged her and gave her a kiss. "Big girls don't eat so soon," she said, smiling at her. "What time should we eat?" Chrystal demanded. "Nine, ten…?" Thinking for a second, Chrystal replied, "That's too long. I am going to ask dad." A few minutes later she heard when they were in the kitchen laughing and talking. "At least he loves her," Zoe said to herself, "that is enough."

Chris tried to make their stay as pleasant as possible, even giving up his working time to be with them, taking Chrystal around to show her the beauty of the island. By the third day, they had met everyone in his family except his dad. Zoe was enjoying herself. Katie, Chris' mother, was so in love with her newfound granddaughter. It was so funny to see her and Diamond fighting over who should take Chrystal shopping, but the tension between her and Chris was unbearable. He was in the shower when she pulled the screen back. He was so frightened he dropped the soap. Naked as the day he was born, she said, "You're going to have to listen to me now." He started to reach for the towel but she pulled it away. "Chris you're not leaving until you hear my side of the story." She told him everything, and when she was through she walked out of the bathroom. Ten minutes later he joined her in the living room. Sitting beside her on the couch he said, "I am sorry Zoe. I guess I never gave you a chance. You have suffered more than me; you lost everything, including your family. I didn't, I have mine, and for that I am sorry." "They did not deserve me," she said, "...they didn't deserve me." As the tears rolled down her cheeks he pulled her closer to him and held her in his arms. "Don't cry Zoe," he said, "...it will get better. I will make it better." Their lips met and they fell on the carpet in each other's arms.

The next day Chris' mother invited them for lunch, but when they arrived Joe was also there. When he realised what was happening, he started to get up but Kadie threatened him in such a way that he sat back down. "You are father and son," she said. "You have to make it right with each other, not just for your sake, but also for Chrystal." At that instant, Joe turned around and saw his granddaughter for the first time. She had a big smile on her face that took his breath away. "Hi Chrystal," Joe finally said. "Are you my grandfather?" she asked. "Yes," Joe admitted. With this word, she climbed into his lap and gave him a big hug and a kiss. For the first time Chris realised his father was speechless. The mighty Joe Lee was weakened by a child. Chris interrupted them, "Dad," he began, "Zoe and I are getting married next week. I asked her last night and she said yes." Joe slowly lifted his head from Chrystal's face and said, "Then son, you should give me and my granddaughter, along with my new daughter-in-law time to get to know each other." With this Chris and his mother got up and left the table.

The wedding took place a week later. As Chris admitted to Andrew, they had wasted enough time. Zoe went back to England to wrap up her business before returning. Andrew said that he was happy for Chris, but he did not know what to do with his life. Mayling had found out that he was having an affair, and she wanted to go back home to Taiwan. Chris asked, "Well isn't this what you wanted Andrew…to have the best of both worlds? You said you married her only for convenience, not love." Andrew paused for a second, then finally said, "I am in love with her Chris." Chris went over, placed his hand on his brother's shoulder and said, "Then save your marriage." "How…?" Andrew asked desperately. "By doing anything she wants."

After saying goodbye to Chris, Andrew went home. The journey that would take him two miles felt like it was two hundred to him. He was so nervous he did not know what to say or do. "I need her in my life," he said to himself. Admitting that out loud, he realised this was what he always wanted. When he opened the front door she was sitting in the living room with her hands folded in her lap. "Are you ready to buy my ticket home?" she asked. He went in front of her and knelt down. "Yes," he replied, "but before I do, I want to tell you something." "What is it?" she asked angrily. He took her hands, pulled them apart, and placed them in his. "Mayling," he said softly, "I am in love with you and always will be. I swear to you that I will never touch another woman if you give me another chance. I would understand if you want to go, as I only have myself to blame. I will never forgive myself or forget you." She was staring right at him without saying a word. Realising this he got up. "I'll go book your flight," he said dejectedly. He was on his way to the phone when she rushed over, spun him around and said, "I love you too, Andrew." He held her in his arms and they began to kiss. She whispered, "I have something to tell you." "What is it?" he asked. "You're going to be a dad."

October 1997 it was Joe's birthday and all the family gathered together at his home to celebrate. Andrew and Mayling were holding their newborn son in their arms, while Chrystal was busy rubbing down her mother's swollen belly as Chris sat watching them both and grinning from ear to ear. Zoe was five months pregnant with twins who Joe insisted that if one is a boy, he should be named after him. It was time for the family portrait. Everyone gathered around the table which had a big birthday cake on it. The camera was set and programmed to go off in 30-seconds. Fighting, grumbling and arguing seemed to be the order of the moment while Kadie tried to get everyone in place. By the time the flash went off, the dog was chasing the cat who took refuge in the birthday cake. Joe insisted on keeping that picture as the family portrait, as he said to his wife that night, when they were alone, "This is my family. Crazy as they are I love them."

~The End~

Glossary: Patois - English Translation

Word/Phrase	Meaning
a come up	is coming up
A dat mi used to	that's what I am used to
a dis mi nuh like	This is what I do not like
A fi ar family	Is it her family
A mi little dawta mi a wait pon. Shi a do extra lesson. As soon as she come mi a cut, because dem bwoy ya blood a boil hot	I am waiting on my little daughter, she is doing extra lessons at school. As soon as she arrives, I am bolting from here because these gunmen are cold-blooded killers
A nuff a unoo know di bwoy dem wey a do dis wickedness, but unoo nah talk	Many of you know the criminals who did this wickedness but no one is talking
A pon mi roof mi hear one a dem a come, yu nuh	It's on my roof that I heard them coming, you know
A we fi have sense fi nuh caught up inna it. Das why	We must be sensible and not be caught up in it. That is

yu fi educate yu pickney dem. When dem av dat, nobody caan fool dem	why you must educate your children. When they have an education, no one can fool them.
A wey yu a do roun yah?	What are you doing here?
A yer fault	It's your fault
Affisa	Officer
an	and
an mi neva	and I never
an wi nuh av no more time	and we have no more time
Anneda	another
Ar	her
Arite	Alright
Babylon	Police
Bag juice	Sweetened drink in a transparent plastic pouch
Brekfus	breakfast
Buss	burst
Bwoy	Boy
caan mine mi	cannot take care of/look after me
Chiny	Chinese

Dacta	Doctor
dat	that
De little buggas dem a try tek off mi roof, avoiding my Rottweiler in mi yard. Dem climb pon mi ackee tree next door an come pon mi roof	Those crooks tried to remove my roof, avoiding my Rottweiler (dog) in my yard. They climbed my ackee tree next door and came onto my roof
Dem	Them
Dem av dem owna family now an mi nah go ome go siddung, put up mi foot an watch soap opera. Mi use to mi workin, an a dat mi a go do till mi dead.	They have their own families now and I am not going to sit down, put up my feet and watch soap operas. I am used to working and that is what I will do until I die.
Dere	There
Di	The
Di mount a hole inna di roof	The number of holes in the roof
di odda one is a teacha	The other one is a teacher
dis	this
Doan	Don't
Dung a	Down at
Dung town	Downtown

dutty bwoy	Dirty boy
Eddication	education
Eida	Either
ere	hear
Fava	Looks like; resemble
Fi	For; should
Fine	Find
Flowas	Flowers
Fram	from
Gi	Give
Gwaan	going on
Gyal	Girl
haffi	have to
Har	Her
How mi fi just like im an mi nuh know im?	How can I be like him if I don't know him?
If yu nuh wa live, mi sure yu four pickney wan live	If you don't want to live, make sure your four children live
If yu nuh work, yu nuh eat	If you do not work, you do not eat

inna	In
It nuh matta wey it did deh	It does not matter where it is
Johncrow	vulture
Las	Last
Liad	Liar
likka	liquor
Likkle	Little
Madda	Mother
madda an fadda	mother and father
margue	morgue
Mawga	meagre
mawning	morning
mek	Make; made
Mi	Me; my
mi a beg dem fi cut di ackee limb, an now it almost cost wi wi life	I have been begging them to cut the ackee tree limb and now it almost cost us our lives
mi a go cut	I am leaving
Mi a go leave before yu sey nuttin more	I am going to leave before you say anything more

mi a go wash oonu back but not oonu belly (Jamaican proverb)	I am going to wash your backs not your bellies
mi a pray fi yu dawta come and unoo come off a di street, for tonight look like it a go be a bloody one	I am praying for your daughter to arrive and you both get off the streets because tonight appears as if it will be a bloody night
mi a sell	I am selling
Mi a try	I am trying
Mi caan live so	I can't live like this
Mi feel sey a ramp yu a ramp, eenuh pickney; but any day mi ever ketch yu, KPH (Kingston Public Hospital) nuh dey far fram ya so. Come, mi waan go home now	I believe you were playing, you know child; but the day I catch you (playing), the Kingston Public Hospital is not far from here. Come, I want to go home now
mi hear sey a tree dead dung dey. Nuh walk pon di road deh, tek di short cut tru di lane. Caw dem here bwoy nuh partial even though yu born an grow ya	I hear that there are three dead bodies (corpses) down there. Do not walk on the street, take the short cut through the lane because these gunmen will kill anyone even though you live in the community
Mi hear sey war a gwaan weh we live, an curfew inna di area. Yu don't know sey if it	I hear that there is a gun battle where we live and a curfew is in effect in the

get lata, wi caan go home tonight, because if Babylon nuh hole wi, di gun man dem will

area. Don't you know that if it gets any later, we will not be able to go home tonight because if the Police/armed forces do not catch us, the criminals will.

Mi jus waan dead

I just want to die

Mi know because yu walk an mek fren an idle chat

I know because you walk and make friends and chat idly

Mi nah kill out miself fi oonu, cause pickney ungrateful

I am not going to work myself to death for you all because children are ungrateful

Mi name

My name is

mi no badda nuhbaddy, an mi nuh waan nun a dem badda mi

I don't bother anyone and I don't want anyone to bother me

mi not styling yu, mi jus a sey wi can do betta as a family, an mi wouldna come roun here if mi neva love unoo

I am not being rude to you, I am just saying that we can do better as a family and I would not come here if I did not love you all

Mi nuh business inna nutten

I don't care about anything

Mi nuh know

I don't know

Mi nuh know wha wrong wid yu Madda. She nuh know she

I do not know what is wrong with your mother.

a destroy yu future? Mi a sell dung ere fi thirty years, but mi mek sure mi educate two dawtas.	Doesn't she know she is destroying your future? I have sold here for thirty years but I made sure that I educated my two daughters
Mi nuh si nuhbaddy. Yu sure smaddy live ya so	I don't see anyone, are you sure someone lives here
mi tell her dem tings dey, she cuss mi off. Ignorancy a go kill her	I tell her those things, she reprimands me. Ignorance will kill her
mi woulda live fi si	I would live to see
Mine mi run ova yu red dundus	Be careful, I don't run you over albino
Mongst	Around
Mumma	Mother
nah	Not
Neider	Neither
neva figet	Never forget
Nuh	No; not
Nuff	many; a lot
Nuh worry yuself, but yu shudda dey inna school	Don't worry yourself but you should be in school

nun of yu	None of your
nuttin	Nothing
Nyam	Eat
odda	Other
Oftin	Often
Ongl	Only
Onle	Only
Ooman	Woman
Ouse	House
Pantomime	a live play
Picher	Picture
Pickney	Little one; child
pickney gal	little girl
Pizen	Poison
Pon mi	on me
Puppa	Father
puss an dawg	cat and dog
Put imself inna trouble again wid di law, but if him tink mi a go bail him dis time, him	Put himself into trouble again with the law but if he thinks that I will bail him

run outa luck. Him a go stay dey an rotten.	(out of jail) this time, he has run out of luck. He is going to stay there and rot.
Seperet	Separate
Sey	Say
Shi	she
Si	See
Si wey mi business wid ya	This is what I care about
smaddy	person
So wey yu Madda dey?	Where is your mother?
Somebaddy a come	Someone is coming
Somebaddy inna di yard	Someone is in our yard
Streggy	Loose woman; prostitute
Sumpting	Something
Tek	Take
tek yu through di	take you through the
tilet	toilet
tink yu a go put mi inna	think you are going to put me in
tru	through
Undaneth	Underneath

undastan	understand
Unoo	You all; everyone
unoo arite?	Are you all/ Is everyone alright?
waan	want
weh	away
wen mi nuh	when I don't
Wey	Where; what
Wey mi tell yu bout back answer	What did I tell you about talking back to me
Wey yu a go	Where are you going?
Wey yu a say	What are you saying
Wey yu a tan up a watch mi fa? Yu nah go school?	Why are you standing there looking at me? Aren't you going to school?
Wi	We
wi	will
wid	with
Worl	World
Wuk	work

Witless	worthless
ya	here
Yeh man, sumbaddy mus dey ere so	Yes man, somebody must be here
Yu	You
yu a go walk	You are going to walk
Yu an yu ooman dem always inna war, but mi a beg yu, nuh bring it a mi gate	You and your woman always fighting but I am begging you not to bring that (quarrelling) to my home
Yu av	You have
yu av ole eap a pickney, dat nuh mek yu a man	You have a lot of children that does not make you a man
yu doan know sey dem a go divide and conquor we	you don't know that they are going to divide and conquer us
Yu know wha mi like about yu, pickney? Yu 'av manners.	You know what I like about you little one, you have manners
Yu mout	Your mouth
Yu nuh a fi av education fi come outa dis, a jus common sense do it. Because mi nuh av it but nuhbody eva si mi	You don't need to have an education to emerge from this situation, just common sense. Because though I am

rob, shoot and tief dem	not educated, no one has ever seem me rob, shoot or steal from anyone.
yu nuh memba mi	You don't remember me
yu nuh see mi mean sey mi nuh care	You don't see me means that I do not care
Yu nuh see yu a get redder and redder inna di sun?	Don't you see you are getting redder and redder (getting sunburns) in the sun?
Yu nuh worry yuself	Don't worry yourself
yu waan dem kill wi off?	Do you want them to kill us all?
Yu waan somting fi eat?	Do you want something to eat?